THE MIRROR WORLD OF MELODY BLACK

Also by Gavin Extence

The Universe Versus Alex Woods

THE MIRROR WORLD OF MELODY BLACK

GAVIN EXTENCE

HODDER &
STOUGHTON

First published in Great Britain in 2015
by Hodder & Stoughton
An Hachette UK company

1

Copyright © Gavin Extence 2015

The right of Gavin Extence to be identified as the Author of the Work has
been asserted by him in accordance with the Copyright, Designs and Patents
Act 1988.

A CIP catalogue record for this title is available from the British Library

Hardback ISBN 978 1 444 76591 5
Trade Paperback ISBN 978 1 444 76462 8
eBook ISBN 978 1 444 76592 2

Typeset by Palimpsest Book Production Ltd, Falkirk, Stirlingshire
Printed and bound by Clays Ltd, St Ives plc

Hodder & Stoughton policy is to use papers that are natural, renewable and
recyclable products and made from wood grown in sustainable forests. The
logging and manufacturing processes are expected to conform to the
environmental regulations of the country of origin.

Hodder & Stoughton Ltd
338 Euston Road
London NW1 3BH

www.hodder.co.uk

For ACE and TOE, when you're old enough.

THROUGH THE LOOKING GLASS

Simon's flat was a mirror of ours. One bedroom, a shower room rather than a bathroom, and a kitchen-lounge-diner that a letting agent – in a couple of weeks' time – would generously describe as open-plan. The central hallway was narrow and windowless, lit by a solitary uplighter which cast concentric pools of light and shadow over unadorned paint.

The lack of decoration was something I noticed straight away, in the several seconds in which I paused on the threshold. Beck and I had gone the other way in our flat. On our main lights we had those tiny imitation-glass chandeliers that you can pick up for ten pounds in any homeware store; and we had prints or photos on every available surface – landscapes and holiday shots – along with half a dozen mirrors of various shapes and sizes, to give the illusion of space. I've always believed that the way a person chooses to embellish his or her surroundings speaks volumes. My décor, for example, would tell you that I have a weakness for kitsch, tend to accumulate clutter, and dream of bigger things.

But what did Simon's flat say about him? On the face of it, nothing at all. It just added to the mystery. Peering into that hallway, there was not a single totem of personality to be seen. Nothing to fill in the poorly drawn impression I had of the man. In all honesty, I'm not even sure you could call what I had an impression. It was probably more fantasy than reality, the sort of half-baked fiction we tell ourselves to flesh out the bit-players in our daily soap opera. As far as facts went, I could have written everything I knew about Simon on a Post-it note. He was forty-something, lived alone, was well groomed, impeccably polite (in an arm's-length sort of way), didn't pronounce his aitches, and had a job that required him to wear a shirt, and sometimes a suit jacket, but not a tie. I'd never been interested enough to find out what that job might be.

I don't know how long I hesitated in the doorway. In my memory, the moment seems to go on and on – an insect caught in amber – but I'm sure that's just an effect of hindsight, of knowing what was to follow. The door to the kitchen-living-dining room was ajar and the television was turned up loud. This, I reasoned, was why he hadn't responded to my knocks. I knocked louder, on the inside of the door, then called his name, but there was still no response. Just the ongoing babble of the television.

Go on or turn back? Curiosity and caution fought a short, bloody battle (more of a bludgeoning, truth be told) and then four and a half steps took me to the half-open interior door, where I stopped mid-stride, left arm aloft and knuckles poised.

Simon was dead. I didn't need to get any closer to satisfy myself of this fact. He was sitting in an armchair on the far side of the room (about eight feet away), his eyes wide and his back preternaturally straight. But really, it was nothing to do with his posture; it wasn't even the glazed, vacant stare as the television continued to flicker in his irises. More than this, it was just a feeling of absence, the certainty that I was the only person in that flat. I was a person, and Simon was a body.

My immediate thought was that I needed a smoke, which seemed to arrive simultaneously with the realizations that I'd left my cigarettes in my shoulder bag and there was a pack of twenty Marlboro on the coffee table. And, after all, why not? Beck hated me smoking in our flat, no matter how far I poked my head out of the window. But it wasn't as if Simon could have any such qualms. This was a completely reasonable response to the situation in which I found myself. I stepped into the room, removed a Marlboro from the pack – there were seven left – and looked around for a lighter. Since there wasn't one by the ashtray, the next logical place to check would be Simon's front trouser pockets. That, however, seemed a step too far. Instead, I lit the cigarette from the gas hob in the kitchen area, taking care to keep my hair away from the naked flame, and then leaned against the counter and started to think.

I'd been in the presence of a body once before, at my grand-mother's funeral, but that had been very different in terms of atmosphere. There was a sense of public display, of everyone – me, my mother, the vicar, the organist – playing a part, bound to follow the stage directions of an inflexible script. Here, I was alone with my thoughts, and my predominant feeling was of calm recognition. At the same time, there was something almost exhilarating about the circumstance I found myself in. Of course, smoking always makes me feel more alive – that's the wonderful paradox of smoking – but this was something beyond that. The sensations were clear and vivid, like drinking cold water on a hot day, and I could feel my pulse throbbing in my fingertips. I made a mental note to tell Dr Barbara about these feelings the next time we met. But she was the only person I'd tell. I didn't think my feelings were suitable for anyone else.

Cigarette smoked down to the filter, I extinguished the remnant under the cold tap, rinsed the sink, and then walked resolutely over to Simon's chair. My finger hovered for just a moment before I took the plunge and prodded him in the cheek. His flesh felt inorganic, like rubber or latex, but it wasn't as cold as I'd been expecting. Not that my expectations had been at all realistic. You assume death must feel like ice; what you get, instead, is cooled bathwater. Or that's what you get on a London evening in late spring.

There wasn't a phone book anywhere near the landline, and inevitably I'd left my mobile in my bag, in the same pocket as my cigarettes, but I had a vague recollection that there was a non-emergency police number for situations such as this. Something beginning with a one. Beck would have known in a second – numbers were more his thing than mine – but I still didn't feel like going back to our flat to explain. I thought it was important that I deal with things myself, as though it were a test of my competence as a responsible human being. There'd be time enough for explanations later.

So I picked up the phone and started dialling all the obvious three-digit combinations beginning with a one that I could think of. There really weren't that many, but it took four attempts, nevertheless: 111 was an automated NHS helpline, 100 put me through to the phone company, and 123 turned out to be the talking clock – which I realized I knew, after the fact. By the time I got to 101, I noticed that my fingers were drumming the wall impatiently, telling me that I should have taken the time to light another cigarette before embarking on this trial and error lunacy. Then the speaker clicked and the police operator came on the line.

'I need to report a dead body,' I told her. *A dead body*: I'd decided this was the most concise way of explaining myself, since the relevant context was already implicit. Or so I thought.

'A body?' the operator repeated.

'A dead body,' I confirmed. 'My neighbour's.'

'Okay. Can I take your name, please? Then you can talk me through what's happened.'

'My name's Abby. Abigail Williams.'

'Abby or Abigail?'

This seemed a strange question.

'Does it matter? Either; both. Abigail on my birth certificate, Abby if you want to save yourself a diphthong.'

Silence.

'Okay, Abby. Tell me what happened.'

'There's not a great deal to tell. I came over to his flat and he's dead. He's cold and stiff.'

'You're absolutely certain he's dead?'

'Excuse me?'

'You've checked for a pulse? I can talk you through it if you need me to.'

I looked across at Simon's taut neck, his slack wrist. They looked equally unappealing. 'He's cold and stiff,' I repeated. 'He's obviously been dead for a while.'

'You're certain?'

'Yes, of course!' The woman was an imbecile. 'He's dead. He hasn't had a pulse for many hours.'

'Okay. I can appreciate this must be distressing. But you're doing really well, Abby. I just need a few more details before I ꜱend ꜱomeone over. You ꜱay the deceased is your neighbour?'

'Yes. He's my neighbour – was my neighbour. He lived across the hall. I came over to borrow a tin of tomatoes. My boyfriend is making pasta sauce. But when I got here he was dead, deceased, as we've established.'

'Abby, you're talking very quickly' – this was all relative, of course – 'I need you to slow down a second. What's your neighbour's name?'

'Simon . . .' I fumbled for a few seconds, trying to picture his post. 'Simon . . .' The image wouldn't come. 'I can't remember his full name,' I admitted. 'I didn't really know him that well.'

'Do you know his age?'

'Forty-something. Early forties, I'd say.'

I heard keys clacking down the line. 'And can you confirm your address, please?'

'129 Askew Road, W12.'

'Okay. I'm sending a police car over now. It should be there within ten minutes.'

'Great. There's an intercom. If they buzz flat 12 I'll let them in.'

'Thank you, Abby.'

'No problem.'

'It's imp—'

I realized there was more in the same instant I jabbed the hang-up button, so I didn't get to hear what *it* was. Important?

6

Imperative? I smoked half of another cigarette, waiting to see if the phone would ring.

It did not.

When I got back to our flat, Beck was still sweating a lonely onion, which had reduced down to a caramel mulch at the bottom of the pan. I set the tomatoes down next to the hob.

'Simon's dead,' I told him. There wasn't any better way of saying it.

'Dead.' He looked at me as if waiting for the punchline. 'What, he wouldn't give up the tomatoes without a fight and it all got out of hand? I guess that explains why it took you so long.'

I pouted a little. 'No joke. He was dead when I got there. In his armchair.'

'*Dead?*'

'Dead.'

'Like . . . actually dead?'

'Jesus! As opposed to what? Virtually dead? He's dead! Just dead. Cold and stiff.' Why did no one trust my judgement on this?

'Wow, that's . . .' A long pause, then he glanced left and frowned. 'Huh.'

'What?'

'You still got the tomatoes?'

I shrugged. 'What's the difference? We still need to eat. You can't make pasta sauce without tomatoes.'

'Right . . . That makes sense, I suppose.' Another pause, heavily pregnant. 'Are you all right?'

This question irritated me for some reason. 'Of course I'm all right. Why wouldn't I be all right?'

'Well, you know.' He gestured vaguely at the kitchen wall – or, rather, through the wall, to Simon's flat, separated from ours by maybe eight inches of brick and bad tiling. It was funny to think of him being so close, still sitting in his chair.

'I'm fine,' I repeated.

Beck nodded, but he didn't look convinced. The expression he was wearing – too purposefully neutral – told me he was already rehearsing his next sentence.

'Listen, Abby. Maybe you should just sit down for a second. You seem—'

'What's the non-emergency police number?' I asked.

'101,' he replied, no hesitation.

'Right.'

'I can call them if you prefer?'

'Already done – they should be here any minute.'

'Oh. So why did—'

'I just wanted to know if you knew. I thought you probably would. I think the onion's catching.'

Like most men, Beck had no ability to multitask. He turned to attend to the frying pan, and I took the opportunity to slip back out into the hallway. A minute or so later, the intercom buzzed.

I pressed my nose against the glass so I could see what was happening in the street below. My reflection dissolved. Blue light, flashing like a strobe. A police car and an ambulance. I wondered why an ambulance and not . . . something else – a van, cold storage. Maybe my diagnosis was still in doubt? You'd think there'd be some sort of competency test for police phone operators. Or maybe there was: if you passed, you got to answer 999 calls; if not, it was straight to 101.

It was another ten minutes before they took his body away, on a trolley, in a bag. Shortly after that, the police were knocking on our door. By then, it was almost dark outside, and I'd poured myself a glass of red wine. Beck made tea for everyone else – for himself and the two policemen – which made me the odd one out. One girl, one glass of wine. The irony, of course, is that it's completely fucking crazy to be drinking strong, sugary tea at nine forty-five on a Wednesday evening; I was the only one with an appropriate drink.

One of the policemen told us their names, but I forgot them instantly. PC Something and PC Somethingelse. I was distracted before the introductions were even half complete, thinking about the fundamental imbalance of power implicit in any interaction with the police, starting, specifically, with the exchange of names. They had our first names, we had their ranks and surnames. I remembered having a conversation with Dr Barbara about the moment in the early noughties when GPs seemed to decide collectively that surnames should be jettisoned in favour of Christian names, though Dr Barbara maintained she'd been bucking the trend for the best part of two decades (in part because she wasn't a GP). She realized early in her career that patients appreciated the fact that she was a human being, as well as a doctor, and they were more likely to engage with Dr Barbara than Dr Middlebrook. But, then, I supposed an equivalent rebranding was out of the question with the police. You couldn't have PC Peter or Inspector Timothy – the very idea caused an involuntary giggle to spasm in my stomach. It emerged a few seconds later, cloaked in a hiccup, but neither of the PCs seemed to notice.

They made me go through what had happened once more,

and then homed in on all the bits I'd left out for the sake of brevity, starting with the unexplained smell of cigarette smoke. Had I noticed that?

'No, that was me,' I clarified. 'I smoked a cigarette – one and a half cigarettes – after I found him.'

'You shouldn't have done that,' PC Something admonished. 'It's a potential crime scene.'

'Oh. Well, I kind of needed it. And Beck doesn't like me smoking in the flat.' I thought I saw the policemen exchange a sidelong glance, so I added, 'Not in a weird, controlling sense. It's just, you know, one of those issues you learn to compromise over. I mean, in general our domestic situation is a good one.' I rested my hand on Beck's leg and smiled at him for back-up. He was giving me a *what-the-fuck* look, which I suppose, in hindsight, may have been warranted. I'm not sure where the verbal diarrhoea had come from, but it was possibly connected to the general lack of space and air in the room. Needless to say, our flat had not been designed with four occupants in mind; it had not been *well* designed with a single occupant in mind. Beck and I were sitting on the two-seater, and the policemen had pulled chairs across from the dining table – such as it was. If you imagine each of us sitting at one corner of a washing machine, that was the approximate space we occupied. Is it any wonder that our dialogue felt more like an interrogation?

'Can we go back to the very beginning?' PC Somethingelse asked. 'What *exactly* were you doing in his flat?'

'Tomatoes,' I said. 'I wanted to borrow a tin of tomatoes.' I felt I'd been quite clear on this point.

The policeman nodded slowly. 'Yes, I understand why you went over in the first place. But then what? Why did you go into the flat? Did you have any reason to think something was wrong?'

'No, of course not.'

'So why enter? You said the door was closed.'

'Yes, it was.'

'He wasn't expecting you.'

'No.'

'And you weren't in the habit of dropping in unannounced?'

'No.' I decided not to mention that this was the first time I'd *ever* been in Simon's flat, that I hardly knew the guy. This was quite hard to explain already. 'I tried the door on an impulse,' I said. 'I wasn't really expecting it to open. I presumed it would be locked.'

'But it wasn't, so you entered.'

'Yes.'

'Another impulse?'

'Right. More or less. I mean, the TV was very loud, so I thought maybe he hadn't heard me at the door.'

'Quite a coincidence,' PC Something pointed out. 'That you happened to go over today.'

'Yes, that occurred to me too.'

What else could I say?

I sipped my wine and waited to see if there was more.

'Jesus, Abby! "Our domestic situation is a good one"?'

'Did it sound insane?'

'Yes – entirely!'

'Oh.'

'Are you drunk?'

'No.' After two glasses of wine, I was a little light-headed, but Beck didn't need to know this. It wasn't relevant. 'It was just the way they kept looking at each other. You must've seen. It put me on edge.'

'They were looking at each other because you'd just revealed you sat and had a cigarette – sorry, one and a half cigarettes – with a corpse. That's not the most normal thing to do.'

I shrugged. What part of this evening had been normal?

'I wonder what happened,' I said later on, not for the first time. We were back on the two-seater, having emptied one bottle of wine and started on another.

'God knows,' Beck replied. 'How old was he, anyway? Forty, forty-five?'

'Yeah, about that. No age to be dead.'

This was a fairly ridiculous thing to say, but Beck didn't seem to notice. He was stroking the nape of my neck with two fingers.

'Presumably it couldn't have been a natural death,' I said. 'I mean, it didn't look like a crime scene, but still . . .'

'Hmm.'

'Healthy people don't just drop dead in their early forties, do they? There must be more to it – suicide or something. Although . . . well, you do hear about these sudden, unexpected deaths sometimes: blood clots, haemorrhages, aneurysms – things like that.'

Beck's fingers were now massaging my left shoulder below the bra strap, and seemed to be migrating south with each passing second. What was it about men's brains? If there was a topic of conversation that could divert their attention away from sex, I had yet to discover it. I shifted my position and leaned back to reorientate his hand, a manoeuvre that was somehow misinterpreted.

'You know, I'm not feeling in a particularly sexy mood right now,' I told him.

'Oh.' The look on his face was confusion tinged with disappointment and a hint of resentment, as if I'd been making come-to-bed eyes for the past hour. 'Because of Simon?'

'Well, yes, that might be part of it,' I lied.

'I thought you were fine?'

I hesitated, for just a moment.

'No, of course you're not fine. You're—'

'I am fine,' I reaffirmed. 'That's not the point.'

What was the point? I didn't know. It wasn't as if sex was such an outlandish suggestion. We'd both been drinking, after all, and it was a Wednesday. Not that we'd got to the stage where sex needed to be timetabled, or anything like that. But nor was it purely spontaneous any more. It was just that Wednesday tended to provide the most convenient mid-week option. I think we both agreed, tacitly, that we didn't want to have all our sex at the weekend.

'I'm a little lost here,' Beck admitted. 'Simon's dead and that's . . . put you off sex? It didn't put you off his tomatoes.'

I didn't say anything.

Beck looked at me very earnestly for a few seconds, then took my hand and said, 'Look: if it makes you feel any better, we can have a two-minute silence before we start.'

I was smiling, despite myself – which I suppose was his intention. He was trying to help me deal with this on my own terms, however baffling those terms might have been.

'Or after. Or during. Take your pick.'

I rolled my eyes. 'Well, of course we'd be silent *during*. We're English.'

13

'I'll let you smoke a cigarette afterwards. In bed. Suppress all my weird, controlling instincts.'

I hate to admit it, but that was definitely the clincher.

Sex turned out to be surprisingly good, if a little strange. Not that the sex itself was strange – that was entirely regular: fifteen minutes of foreplay followed by five of missionary. It was more my reaction to the sex that was strange. At first, my head was all over the place. I was thinking about the outfit I'd picked out for tomorrow, for the Miranda Frost interview, checking the impression I made in my mental mirror. Cool, calm, incisive. Then I was thinking about Simon, about how his flesh had felt – tepid and spongy – under my forefinger. And it was at this point that something shifted. I started to feel curiously detached from reality. I was disembodied, floating somewhere above myself, as if watching some artily shot, though otherwise rather matter-of-fact, pornographic film.

When I returned, everything had changed, though I've little idea why. It might have been that I'd somehow managed to ingest the optimum amount of alcohol – enough to relax, but not enough to numb. It might have been that my libido was finally enjoying a renaissance, after so many months in free-fall. It might even have been thinking about Simon; there was something, I felt in that instant, quite pleasant about being alive and warm and motile. Whatever the case, I came very quickly, and after such a long period of so-so sex, it felt like an overdue release.

'I'm glad you talked me into that,' I told Beck afterwards, as I lay with my head on his chest. He ran his hand over my lower back and bottom, but made no other reply; and when I tried to speak to him again, he had inevitably fallen asleep.

But I felt wide, wide awake.

I rolled onto my back and smoked a cigarette, then another. Then I simply lay in the dark waiting for my mind to shut down, wishing, more and more, that I'd not switched off the bedside light. At least, then, I'd be able to read.

Our bedroom, I found, was a rather in-between sort of room. The curtains weren't quite thick enough to block out the light from the streetlamps, and the double glazing wasn't well sealed enough to cut out the London traffic. It got pretty stuffy in the summer, too. If I were ever to design a bedroom, I decided, it would be as cool and dark and quiet as the bottom of the sea.

It was 1.37 when I finally admitted defeat and got up. I eased the bedroom door open and closed with a burglar's stealth, and then put on the reception room light and got myself a glass of water. I felt like a coffee, but was, at this point, still nurturing the small hope that I'd start to feel sleepy some time before dawn.

Despite everything, despite the fact that I had to be in a rested, presentable state to interview Miranda Frost in not much more than seven hours, there was something oddly interesting about being up in the middle of the night, alone and for no particular reason. The flat felt unfamiliar – the way home feels after you take down the Christmas decorations, or return from a long holiday. It didn't feel at all like the flat I'd left earlier, when I'd gone to get the tomatoes. It was as if Simon's death had opened a portal on a subtly altered reality. I realized that what I wanted, more than anything, was to be next door again, just to sit quietly in that empty flat. But when I crept out and tried the door, it was locked.

So, instead, I opened the window in our reception room,

leaned out as far as I could, and smoked. There was the odd taxi passing in the street below, but nothing else. None of the house lights opposite was on. It was a solid mass of anonymous brick, each building melting into the next. I drew the warm smoke and cool night air into my lungs and wondered how many lonely deaths occurred in London on the average Wednesday night. And how many of those deaths were sudden and unexplained? Several, I was sure. Certainly enough to make Simon's death a mere statistic. Not the sort of thing that would warrant even a paragraph in the *Evening Standard*. Things would be different, of course, if I didn't live in London. In other parts of the country, where people weren't crammed one on top of the other like battery hens, it would be easier to grieve when a neighbour died. In other parts of the world, the simple action of going next door to borrow food would not be met with raised eyebrows and sidelong glances. But here, in a city of eight million, I couldn't escape the feeling that it was this action that had *caused* Simon's unlikely death. It was as if I'd broken one of the cardinal rules of modern urban living, and had to suffer the consequences. Maybe that was what I should have told PC Something: that there was nothing coincidental about my going over to Simon's flat today. It was just cause and effect.

My thoughts were spinning, so I left the window and tried to read for a bit. Then, when I couldn't concentrate on that, I flipped open my laptop and checked my emails. There was only one new message, from my sister. She wanted to make sure I wasn't planning to pull out of the 'family meal' at the end of the month. I sent a reply saying that I was still shortlisting excuses. After that I read my Google homepage for a while. Quote of the day was from Einstein: 'The difference between stupidity and genius is that genius has its limits.' Tomorrow's weather was grey, grey, grey. On a whim, I typed *lack of emotion death* into the search bar, and spent the next fifteen minutes completing a psychopath test, then started reading a forum post about a man who had felt no emotion when his mother died in a car crash. I clicked on link after link, following an erratic trail through cyberspace, with no destination in mind.

And this was how I first stumbled on the Monkeysphere.

THE TEMPEST

I awoke slumped across one arm of the two-seater, my spine twisted like a corkscrew. I couldn't have been asleep for more than two hours, but the muscles in my lower back felt taut as piano strings, and my head was full of thick, numbing fog – through which dim figures paraded like sarcastic wraiths: Simon, laid flat on a trolley; the policemen, casting conspiratorial glances; Miranda Frost, awaiting me in a faceless house in Highbury.

Shit.

I lurched into a sitting position, my eyes darting for the clock: 7.48. Why hadn't Beck woken me? The impulse to cast blame was hamstrung, a heartbeat later, by the inconvenient and obvious truth. Beck always slept like a corpse, and due to the ridiculously short amount of time it took him to get ready in the mornings, his alarm wouldn't be going off until eight. Mine should have gone off at six forty-five. I fumbled for my mobile. It *had* gone off at six forty-five; and my phone was set to silent.

How long would it take to traverse central London? Ten minutes speed-walking to Shepherd's Bush Market, twenty-five to King's Cross, then another five to Highbury and Islington. Add on fifteen, at least, to battle through the tunnels and wait for trains. Plus ten to find the house. Numbers tumbled through my mind like drunken acrobats, until I realized it was much too early for maths. Call it an hour, flat-out. That left less than twelve minutes to be washed, dressed and out the front door.

A shower was out, obviously, as was breakfast, as was coffee – despite the fact I'd never needed it more. There was a little bit of speed at the bottom of the freezer, but I was loath to take it on an empty stomach because of the ulcer I'd developed last year. Nevertheless, I was halfway to the kitchen before I'd talked myself out of it. Speed for breakfast; Dr Barbara would have kittens! Twenty milligrams of fluoxetine and a cigarette on the way to the Tube station would have to suffice.

Clothes, hair, teeth, make-up, toilet: my priorities arranged themselves before me like a row of dominoes already in motion. Fortunately, my clothes had been pre-selected days ago. The only thing I had to change was the footwear, replacing heels with ballet flats. Of course, I could have done with the extra inches – I can always do with the extra inches – but at this time of day, with so little sleep, heels were a visit to A&E waiting to happen.

After my own rude awakening, I had no thought of allowing Beck to wake gracefully. I flung the bedroom door open – he shot bolt upright – grabbed an armful of clothing from the wardrobe, and was back out and heading for the shower room in a matter of moments. Once I'd managed to wriggle into my tights, the rest of the outfit proved less of a challenge. Half a can of Batiste Dry Shampoo and a headband gave my hair the illusion of order and cleanliness, and then I gargled mouthwash while I peed to save myself thirty valuable seconds. I applied eyeliner and volumizing mascara with the deftness of a cartoonist creating features, then flirted with the idea of contacts before deciding that my big, black-framed glasses were a far better choice. Mack always said they made me look sexy and studious – and I hoped that Miranda Frost would appreciate at least half of this duality.

I sprang from the shower room in a cloud of body spray, with Beck saying something long-winded and, so far as I could tell, pointless through the open bedroom door. I couldn't wait for the end; I had to cut him off with a swift synopsis of the facts.

'Darling, I'm horribly late. I overslept, on the sofa – don't ask! I'm leaving in the next minute. Please don't get up or try to talk to me. You'll only slow me down.'

'Oh. Right. Okay. I hope it . . .'

The rest was lost as I gathered up my bag and phone and cigarettes. A fleeting glance out of the window confirmed that it was drizzling, but there was no time to be messing about with an umbrella. I descended the stairs three at a time and stepped out into the rush-hour rain.

By the time I reached the bottleneck of Shepherd's Bush Market, I was wet right down to my underwear. It was that damn stealth rain that feels like nothing more than a morning mist but saturates by attrition. Smoking was a logistical nightmare, and the Tube itself, needless to say, was Dante's Fifth Circle of Hell – the one reserved for the wrathful and sullen. My carriage was full when I got on, and got progressively fuller over the next eleven stops. For half an hour I steamed in my own tights.

Then, when I changed at King's Cross, Marie Martin was every-where – on the platforms and in the tunnels, occupying every third space on the escalators. She looked amazing, of course, shot in soft-focus black and white, with hair as dark as death and a pout to make men melt. More specifically, she looked as if she *smelled* amazing, by some indefinable photographic alchemy. Maybe it was those tiny, glittering beads of moisture on her upper lip. Maybe it was just a negative association on my part. I was certain that I didn't smell particularly great at that moment. A mixture of cheap body spray and wet nylon.

Marie Martin: Séduction

Abigail Williams: Hot and Humid

My best hope was that I smelled inoffensively damp, like the Amazon rainforest.

I wanted to text my sister to vent my spleen. I wanted to text my father to tell him he was a superficial prick. I had time for neither.

I emerged from Highbury and Islington at 9.07 and ran the rest of the way to Miranda Frost's house, a cigarette in one hand and my phone, switched to Google Maps, in the other. When I arrived, at 9.14, the hollow throb of hunger in my stomach had been replaced by a stitch.

'Ah, Miss Williams.' Miranda Frost glanced theatrically at the watch she wasn't wearing. 'I'm so pleased you could make it. It is Miss Williams, isn't it?'

'Uh, yes. Abby. Hello. Sorry – I had some trouble getting here.' I waved vaguely at the sky, as if for corroboration. My mind was a sinking ship. 'I would have rung, but . . . well, I didn't have your number.'

'I didn't give you my number.'

'No.'

'So the fault lies with me?'

Never back down; not once you've committed to an excuse.

'Yes. Incontrovertibly.'

Miranda Frost did not smile. 'Well, you'd better come in. We haven't got all morning. I intend to be working by ten. Shoes off, please.'

It was technically a flat, I supposed, but bore nothing in common with the shoebox I called home. It was spread across the bottom two floors of a Georgian town house overlooking Highbury Fields. It had a private rear garden and windows larger than the floor space in our kitchen; Miranda Frost's kitchen, in turn, was larger than our entire flat. Indeed, the notion that our residences fell into the same broad category was patently absurd. Miranda Frost and I were both living in flats in the same sense that John Lennon and Ringo Starr were both respected song-writers.

'You have a lovely home,' I ventured.

'This isn't my home, Miss Williams. It belongs to a friend. I stay here whenever I'm in London, which is as seldom as possible. I couldn't afford a place like this. I'm a poet, not a barrister.'

'Oh.' There was a leaden silence. 'What about your friend? What does she do?'

'She's a barrister.'

'Right.'

I busied myself with my bag.

'Do you mind if I record this conversation? It will save time.'

'Whatever you find most efficient.'

I delved deeper into the side pocket, spilling half its contents – cigarettes, lipstick, a tampon – over the kitchen table. 'Shit! Sorry. I didn't get much sleep. My co-ordination isn't great this morning.'

'Evidently. Part of the trouble getting here, perhaps?'

'Yes.' With things going as they were, there seemed little point denying it. 'But it wasn't entirely my fault,' I added.

Miranda Frost shrugged. 'Far be it from me to question your professionalism. You're young. No doubt you lead a fascinating life. Would it help if I made some strong coffee?'

I decided to interpret this offer as sincere, despite abundant facial evidence to the contrary. 'Yes. Thank you. That would be very kind.'

She looked at me, without comment, for several seconds. Then there might have been the briefest flicker of a smile. But more likely it was a hallucination. 'Very well. I'd hate for this morning to be a *complete* waste of time.'

When she returned with the cafetière, I had already started drafting copy in my head.

We're sitting in the ~~high-ceilinged~~ airy kitchen of a Highbury town house. Miranda Frost, 52 [check detail], is dressed in a cashmere cardigan and pleated skirt. When she speaks, her voice carries the brisk precision for which her poetry is famous. She makes a lousy cup of coffee and is much more of a bitch than you'd imagine.

'Mmm, caffeine. Thank you, Miranda. May I call you Miranda?'

'You now have thirty-three minutes, Miss Williams. It's your time to spend as you will, but I suggest that we dispense with the pleasantries and press on.'

I smiled through clenched teeth. 'Yes, let's. Just bear with me a second.'

The rain had permeated the outer layer of my shoulder bag and soaked through to the back page of my notebook; where once had been questions, now dwelt an unnavigable sea of blue ink. I decided to stall first and improvise second. 'Forgive me. Do you mind if I start slightly off track?'

She sipped her coffee. 'I'd expect no less.'

'Okay . . . Well, you're a notoriously private person.'

'Is that a question or a statement?'

'It's a statement.'

'And an oxymoron.'

'Yes, perhaps. But they sometimes have their place.'

'In Shakespeare, Miss Williams. Not in competent journalism.'

'Right. Well, I suppose that's not a million miles away from the point I'm trying to make. You rarely give interviews. Your last, I believe, was in 2010, for *The Culture Show*.'

'Correct.'

'So, er, I guess the question I'm asking – just for personal curiosity, really – is why now? Actually, scrap that. Not why now. Why me? I mean, I'm not exactly *The Culture Show*.'

Bumbling and disjointed as this was, it was nevertheless the first thing I'd said that seemed in any way to please Miranda Frost. That flicker of a smile was back.

'It was your name, Abigail. Nothing more. Your name amused me, so I chose not to delete your email. I assume you must be aware of your literary forebear? Salem? *The Crucible*'s central harlot?'

'Oh, right. Yes. Ever since I was about fifteen. We read that play in school. You have a good memory for names.'

'Only in fiction, as a rule.'

'It passes most people by.'

'As it did your parents, presumably?'

'Yes. I mean, my mum reads a little, but not widely. And my dad despises culture in all its forms; he's in advertising. I can't imagine he ever took my mother to the theatre.'

'Ah, "took". Past tense. They're separated?'

'Divorced.' I was aware, of course, that Miranda Frost had somehow inverted the interview, that it was her asking the questions. But at least she was starting to warm up a little. I decided I had nothing to lose and ploughed ahead. 'My dad left us for his secretary. It was the most appalling cliché. Now he's hooked up with a French perfume model, four years older than me.'

'A perfume model? How does one model perfume?'

'A model who's in a perfume ad. Marie Martin. *Séduction*. She's all over the Tube, if you're interested.'

'I wouldn't take the Tube if you held a gun to my head. How old were you when he left?'

'Fourteen.'

'And your mother?'

'Forty-five.'

'Ah. A lethal age. My husband left me when I was forty-four. When I was thirty-four, he used to recite Yeats to me. You've read Yeats?'

'Yes, of course.'

'How many loved your moments of glad grace,
And loved your beauty with love false or true;
But one man loved the pilgrim soul in you,
And loved the sorrows of your changing face . . .'

'Lying fuck.'

25

'Yeats?'

'My ex-husband. But yes – Yeats too, I'm sure. You know how men are. Or if you don't, give it time. They all think with their willies, to a greater or lesser extent.'

'Right. Their willies   '

Miranda Frost shrugged. 'It's the word I prefer these days. Men can call them their cocks or pricks or schlongs or love muscles, or whatever ridiculous metaphor they choose, but we don't have to go along with it. Men hold their willies in far too high an esteem.'

I nodded. It was a difficult analysis to dispute.

'Thank God lesbianism isn't simply a lifestyle choice, as the fundamentalists would have us believe. It would be the end of the human race.'

'Do you mind if I ask you a few questions now? You know, about your poetry?'

'Yes, I suppose you ought to.'

'Great.' I took a sip of coffee, then cleared my throat. 'So, your latest collection has been released to huge critical acclaim. Do the reviews still matter to you, after so many years?'

'Yes.'

I waited.

Miranda Frost gave me a look that would wither a vase of sunflowers. 'What, you want more?'

'It would help.'

Miranda Frost's eyes continued to bore into me for what seemed like another minute. 'It feels good when people praise your work, bad when they don't. What more is there to say? You could ask a schoolchild a similar question and get the same response.'

'Right . . . So, er, does writing still give you the same thrill it did thirty years ago?'

'Tell me, Miss Williams: are all the questions going to be this conventional? I've answered their like a dozen times; it's all on the internet, I'm sure. Don't you think your readers might like something different?'

'Sorry. I did have some good questions but' – I showed her my notebook – 'they dissolved.'

'So I see. Still, you were doing well enough a few moments ago. We were having a reasonably stimulating conversation. I'm sure you can spin it into a couple of thousand words.'

'I'm selling it to the *Observer* as an exclusive interview,' I pointed out. 'Not an essay on men and their willies.'

'Very well. So ask me something interesting. Ask me something I'm not expecting.'

'Okay.' I glanced once more at my saturated notebook, then set it down on the table. I thought for a few moments. 'How well do you know your neighbours?' I asked. Miranda Frost exhaled with infinite disdain. 'Would you care, for example, if one of them died?'

'I don't have any neighbours, Miss Williams. I live in a cottage miles from anywhere. I find the isolation suits me.'

'My neighbour died last night,' I blurted. 'I found the body.'

'Excuse me?'

'My neighbour died. I found his body.'

There was no doubting the smile now. For the first time since I'd arrived, Miranda Frost looked unequivocally intrigued.

'Go on,' she said.

SOMETHING DIFFERENT

When I got home, I made myself a fresh pot of coffee and listened back to the calamity that was my exclusive interview with Miranda Frost. So far as I could tell there was nothing salvageable. Nothing. Should I email again, ask for a follow-up? Even if it were likely, there didn't seem much point. Who cared about the witch behind the words? It was the words that mattered. Still, I knew that I had to turn in something. By my standards, this was a lucrative piece of work. I couldn't afford to let it slip away.

I toiled on my laptop for three hours straight, trying to come up with a clever angle, something postmodern. *Deconstructing Miranda: a non-interview with the woman who hates interviews.* It was a terrible idea that grew more terrible with every unnecessary word I pumped in, like a blood-bloated mosquito ready to pop.

I changed tack. *Meander Frost: psychoanalysing what the poet won't tell us.*

This, of course, was even worse.

I emailed Jess at the *Observer* to tell her that the write-up was coming along, but might take a couple of days longer than anticipated – due to the death of someone close to me. Even as I was typing, I didn't know how to feel about this not-quite-a-lie. On the one hand, it was devious and emotionally manipulative; on the other, it was just the kind of creative thinking I'd need if I was to transform this Miranda Frost interview into something printable.

By then it was late afternoon, and it was my turn to make dinner, so I went to the shop and bought eggs, bread and a salad in a bag – destined to become an overcooked omelette and accompaniments. For my late lunch, I had two more cigarettes and a bar of chocolate, then returned to my laptop with renewed determination. The next thing I knew, I was being interviewed for a PR job in Canary Wharf. The interview took place on the 101st floor and, due to a lack of foresight with the laundry, I'd had to borrow an ill-fitting trouser suit from my sister; under this, for reasons less clear, I was naked as a new-born.

I awoke twenty minutes before Beck got home, feeling slow and stupid.

I served dinner with a strong bottle of Rioja and an abject apology, because it felt like a dinner that needed both. Beck put on a brave face, but I knew that if this meal lived long in the memory, it would be for all the wrong reasons. He deserved better, really, after a nine-hour office day bookended by two grimy Tube rides, even though he always insisted that he liked his job and found the underground much more bearable than I did.

Beck worked for a digital consultancy on the South Bank, a couple of stones' throws from Waterloo. It was the kind of cool tech company that modelled itself on Google. They posted job adverts that included phrases like *We work hard, we play hard.*

The office had a games room with pool and ping-pong tables, and beanbags and a beer fridge – and a tacit understanding that no one should open the beer fridge before 6 p.m. (unless it was a Friday or summer). And, so far as I could tell, the workspace was almost entirely devoid of interior walls. According to the company's mission statement, this was to nurture an atmosphere conducive to creativity, collaboration and cross-pollination. But if you wanted any privacy, then I supposed your options were limited to the toilets or the stationery cupboard. The toilets, to my knowledge, were not open-plan. Even so, thinking too much about life in an office – any office – filled me with a profound sense of dread. I'd temped all over central London between the ages of twenty-one and twenty-four and still felt like I was suffering post-traumatic stress disorder.

'So how was she?' Beck asked, as we continued to run through the edited highlights of our respective days. By this point, the uninspiring omelette had been eaten, the last of the salad was wilting in its bag, more wine had been poured, and the living area smelled strongly of cooking oil. Anything fried, in our flat, tended to linger.

I'd already told him about the hellish commute; now we were on to the woman at the end of the line, whom I conjured in a few sharp sentences. 'Imagine the lovechild of Miss Havisham and Hannibal Lecter,' I concluded, 'played by Bette Davis with a hangover.'

'Pithy. I like it. Except for the image of Hannibal Lecter having sex. No one needs that in their head.'

'I came up with it between Euston Square and Great Portland Street. It's one of the many ideas I'm not going to be able to use.'

'No – obviously not.'

'I'll have to make something up. Honestly, you should hear the recording. It's like picking through a train wreck.'

'Hmm. That actually sounds pretty interesting.'

'It *is* interesting. Probably more interesting than whatever bullshit I end up writing. But that's not the point. It's still unusable.'

'Maybe a second opinion would help?'

I thought about and quickly dismissed this suggestion. I didn't really want Beck to listen to the recording. Not all of it. I changed the subject.

'Listen: have you ever heard of something called the Monkeysphere?'

Beck looked at me like I'd started speaking in tongues.

'How about Caborn's number? They're essentially the same thing, but one has a catchier name. It's sciencey,' I added. 'I thought you might have heard of it.'

'I haven't,' Beck assured me.

'Right. Well, it's basically a theory of primate societies. Professor Caborn is an evolutionary psychologist. He spent a lot of time examining monkey brains and discovered a correlation between the size of the brain and the size of the monkey's social sphere. So baboons tend to form cliques of, say, thirty, and chimps fifty, and so on. Are you following so far?'

'Yes: the brainier the monkey, the more monkey friends it has. Is this going somewhere?'

'Yes. Be patient.' I took a deep glug from my wine glass. 'So Caborn's number is a theoretical limit. It's the number of social relationships a monkey can cope with, as determined by the size of its brain. Or, put differently, it's the maximum number of monkeys that can live together before their society becomes unstable and fragments.'

Beck looked at me for several seconds. 'I'm confused. What does this have to do with Miranda Frost?'

'Nothing. This is a new topic, or a tangent, at least. I should have made that clearer. Anyway, just let me finish. Caborn's number applies to humans too. Actually, I think it refers specifically to humans; the monkeys are just context. You see, Professor Caborn drew a graph with different primate brain sizes on one axis and the average size of their social groups on the other. And from this he was able to extrapolate the maximum size a human society should be – or *can* be – before it starts to break into pieces. Turns out it's about one hundred and fifty. Humans can maintain up to one hundred and fifty meaningful social relationships, but no more. After that . . . I don't know. Our brains overheat or something. They haven't evolved to cope with very large populations.'

'Our brains overheat?'

'Okay, I'm paraphrasing. Trust me, this is credible science, backed up by a mass of supporting evidence. So, for example, guess the average clan size in a traditional hunter-gatherer society?'

'Er, one hundred and fifty?'

'Bingo! Same story for pre-industrial villages. And guess what the Amish do if their communities grow to more than one hundred and fifty.'

'They start to strangle each other?'

'No need. Their communities split into two at this point – invariably. Because the Amish have figured out that below the one fifty threshold, society is essentially stable and self-regulating. Everyone knows and is emotionally connected to everyone else, so there's a natural drive towards cooperation, reciprocal generosity, trustworthiness – stuff like that. It's only when the population creeps past Caborn's number that things start to go wrong, people begin to feel a little more anonymous in the group, less mutually dependent. Morals take a small but noticeable dip. Basically, people lose their capacity to care about everyone else in the community, so the social glue starts to fail.'

'Okay, that's all very interesting . . . And where has this sudden interest in evolutionary psychology come from?'

I shrugged. 'I was reading about it last night, when I had the insomnia. I just kind of stumbled on it online and it seemed weirdly pertinent. You know, because of Simon.'

'Simon?' Beck let the name hang in the air a few moments. 'This is to do with Simon?'

'Right. Because we knew next to nothing about him. He wasn't really a person to us, not in any meaningful sense – just a face we passed on the stairs every so often. We lived yards apart but never interacted, and his death was just a weird blip in our day. It had no emotional significance whatsoever.'

Beck grimaced, the way people do when you say something true but unacceptable. And this made me smile a little.

'Not in our Monkeysphere,' I concluded.

I couldn't sleep again that night.

By twelve thirty, I was back at the computer, alone, banging my head against the brick wall that was the Miranda Frost recording. There was simply no point of entry. Anything vaguely relevant disintegrated within a couple of sentences; contrarily, anything that struck me as interesting – anything worth writing about – was irrelevant, had no place in a broadsheet interview.

I wondered if the problem was focus. I couldn't seem to grip anything in my mind for more than a few seconds. My thoughts kept jumping, like a scratched CD. And all the while, Miranda and I kept twittering in the background, our voices muted and tinny. There was a strange interior logic to what we were saying, a back-and-forth, tennis-match rhythm, but no wider sense of meaning or even reality.

I thought again about the speed in the freezer, and again decided not to. It might have helped me concentrate, but, just as easily, I could have found myself staring at the wall and grinding my jaw until sunrise. Instead, I drank a pint of water, opened the window as far as it would go, and lit another cigarette.

The wind was picking up. Its sound combined with that of the fizzling rain to create a sweeping curtain of white noise. I perched on the edge of the window sill, stuck my head out and let the dirty city air buffet my face. Then, without thinking too much about what I was doing, I returned to my laptop and started transcribing the interview.

I played the recording from the beginning and I wrote out each sentence in turn, one after another, changing or omitting not a single word; and the more I typed, the clearer everything seemed.

After a couple of hours, I'd almost reached my two thousand words, and all that was left was my account of discovering Simon's corpse. At this point, I went back through the dialogue and added some expositional gloss here and there. Then I returned to the top of the document and added a long but satisfying title: *Something Different: Miranda Frost interviews Abigail Williams, literary harlot (words Abigail Williams; invective Miranda Frost).*

Then, at approximately quarter to four in the morning, I started writing the companion piece.

'Simon's flat was a mirror of ours . . .'

My mind was as clear and keen as a shard of glass.

GONZO

To: jessica.pearle@observer.co.uk

From: abbywilliams1847@hotmail.co.uk

Date: Fri, 10 May 2013, 6:48 AM

Subject: MF Interview

Jess, hi

First, let me apologize. The death I spoke of was my neighbour's: he was close to me geographically, but not in any other sense. I'm afraid I misled you with a half-truth because I was in a bit of a flap about the Miranda Frost interview, which did not go at all as planned. You'll understand when you read the attached article.

Also attached is a companion piece, which I felt compelled to write. It follows on directly from the 'interview'; please read them in turn, as this is the only way they make sense.

I realize, of course, that I haven't delivered the piece I promised, and I'm sure these articles are a million miles away from what you were expecting. But I hope you can find a home for them, nevertheless.

What do you think? Are they printable?

Let me know; and, again, please forgive me for my small deception

Abby

....

To: j.b.caborn@ox.ac.uk
From: abbywilliams1847@hotmail.co.uk
Date: Fri, 10 May 2013, 7:01 AM
Subject: Lunch?

Dear Professor Caborn

My name is Abigail Williams and I'm a freelance journalist.

For reasons slightly strange – too strange to explain here – I recently stumbled on your work regarding socio-cognitive limitations in primates. I'd very much like to meet up to talk about 'Caborn's number', with a view to writing an article on the subject.

If you could spare an hour, I'd love to come to Oxford to ask you some questions. Perhaps I could buy you lunch?

Yours expectantly

Abby Williams

....

To: abbywilliams1847@hotmail.co.uk
From: jessica.pearle@observer.co.uk
Date: Fri, 10 May 2013, 12:03 PM
Subject: RE: MF Interview

Hi Abby

Yes, this is printable (my God is it printable; by the end of the first paragraph, I couldn't put it down!). But are you sure you *want* me to print it? I'm saying this as a friend, you understand, not as an editor. It's very provocative stuff.

A couple of questions to settle my mind:

1) Is it all true? It has the ring of truth, but I need to know for certain – especially with the Miranda Frost interview. It's not exactly flattering; I need to be sure there's nothing libellous there! You say it's a transcript: is this literally the case? (It's not some weird gonzo experiment?)

2) I don't want to sound like a broken record, but have you thought this through? Some of the details, in both pieces, are extremely intimate. Presumably this is going to upset a few people. (Your father? Your boyfriend? Will they be okay with this?) Uncompromising honesty makes great reading, but I doubt it's going to make you very popular. Are you sure there's nothing you want to change?

Think carefully about these things before you ask me to proceed.

Jess

....

To: jessica.pearle@observer.co.uk
From: abbywilliams1847@hotmail.co.uk
Date: Fri, 10 May 2013, 1:15 PM
Subject: RE: RE: MF Interview

Jess

1) Attached is the mp3. As you'll hear, I haven't changed a word. Everything else – 'she makes a lousy cup of coffee', etc. – is just my opinion/interpretation, obviously. There's nothing libellous there.

2) Thank you for your concern, but either it all goes in or none of it does. I've given a completely honest account of Miranda Frost, so I can't very well cut the bits that are unflattering to me. The intimacy is what makes the articles work, as I'm sure you'll agree. It has to be 100% candid. Beck will forgive me (there's nothing *that* terrible there), and my father doesn't even pretend to read my articles any more.

Please proceed!
Abby

....

To: abbywilliams1847@hotmail.co.uk
From: jessica.pearle@observer.co.uk
Date: Fri, 10 May 2013, 4:22 PM
Subject: RE: RE: RE: MF Interview

Abby

I can get you the £500 previously agreed for the MF interview, plus another £500 for the additional piece. We would print both in the magazine – MF next week and 'Simon' the following. You can probably see the reason for the time lapse: they're too long to print side by side, and the MF piece ends on such a natural cliff-hanger.

Let me know if this is all okay with you.

Jess

· ·

To: jessica.pearle@observer.co.uk
From: abbywilliams1847@hotmail.co.uk
Date: Fri, 10 May 2013, 4:42 PM
Subject: RE: RE: RE: RE: MF Interview

Brilliant – if all my work was this well remunerated, I'd finally be earning a wage that didn't fill my father with shame.

A

· ·

To: abbywilliams1847@hotmail.co.uk
From: j.b.caborn@ox.ac.uk
Date: Mon, 13 May 2013, 11:08 AM
Subject: RE: Lunch?

Dear Abigail

While I must admit to being intrigued by your 'slightly strange' story, I'm afraid I must decline. I'm exceptionally busy with my research at the moment, and will be for the foreseeable future. I gave several interviews about my work a few years back, and found that it rather ate away at my time.

I'm sorry that I'm unable to help you with this.

Yours (apologetically)

Joseph Caborn

· ·

Gavin Extence

To: j.b.caborn@ox.ac.uk
From: abbywilliams1847@hotmail.co.uk
Date: Mon, 13 May 2013, 11:59 AM
Subject: The offer includes pudding

Dear Professor Caborn

I can appreciate that you have a busy and demanding job. But scientists, surely, have to eat? One hour is all I'm asking for. Please consider it!

Yours beseechingly

Abby Williams

....

To: abbywilliams1847@hotmail.co.uk
From: j.b.caborn@ox.ac.uk
Date: Mon, 13 May 2013, 1:44 PM
Subject: There's no such thing as a free lunch

Dear Abby

I admire your persistence, but my answer remains the same. I may be doing you a terrible disservice, but in my experience, a journalist's 'hour' is rarely the same as a scientist's.

Yours intransigently

Joseph Caborn

DR BARBARA

'. . . and at that point I wake up. It's always at that point – when the interviewer asks me if I wouldn't be more comfortable without my jacket. I don't know if he realizes I'm naked underneath, and he's toying with me, or whether it's genuine concern, since it's such a hot day. But I guess that doesn't matter; I never have time to work it out. The dream always ends at that exact moment. I wake up and the bedroom's hot and stuffy, and I'm wide awake and need to pee. Generally that's around four in the morning, and I can't get back to sleep. I just get up and read. Although sometimes it happens the other way round: I can't fall asleep until the early hours, so I don't even try. I read or write until I'm exhausted, then manage maybe three or four hours' sleep – at a push . . . On the plus side, I'm getting through a lot of books. I managed to read *Bleak House* in two and a half nights.'

Dr Barbara nodded thoughtfully. 'The sleeplessness is definitely something we should keep an eye on.'

'Right. And what about the dream?'

'The dream tells me there's nothing wrong with your imagination.'

'Freud would say it's a classic anxiety dream.'

Dr Barbara smiled and shook her head in a small but resolute motion. As always, she had no interest in playing the dream interpretation game. She was happy enough to listen – to whatever I wanted to tell her – but she wouldn't indulge me past a certain point.

'There aren't any constraints on what we talk about,' she once told me, not long after our first session. 'We'll talk about anything you deem important – anything at all. But this is a dialogue, not a monologue. Sometimes we'll talk about what you want to talk about, and sometimes we'll talk about what I want to talk about. There has to be some give and take, as with any worthwhile conversation.'

Freud was one of the subjects Dr Barbara did not want to talk about. She told me that for most psychologists or psychiatrists, those with an ounce of common sense, he was a historical curiosity but little more. There was no point wasting time (her time) and money (my father's money) talking about Freud.

But today I was feeling stubborn. 'You haven't even read him,' I pointed out. 'You can't dismiss something you've never tried.'

'Of course you can!' Dr Barbara countered. 'Astrology, chakras, numerology. I know enough to know these subjects have no basis in reality, just as I know that Freud has no relevance in this room.'

'I think you're missing the point,' I said. 'I don't care if Freud is correct. He's interesting and he writes well. That's good enough for me. I'd rather read well-written bunkum than poorly written fact. Wouldn't you?'

Dr Barbara was still wearing the same narrow smile. 'Okay. Let me ask you a question. What do *you* think your dream means?'

'It's obvious,' I replied. 'It's painfully obvious. I'm worried that sooner or later I'll have to grow up and get a serious, secure job that I despise – like my sister. I mean things haven't been so bad recently, but most of the time I'm just treading water. Without Beck's salary, we'd have no security at all, and I hate feeling . . . dependent. But, then, I think I'd feel like a fraud if I did something I hated, just for the money. I'm not even sure there's any regular job I'd be competent in. That's why I don't have any clothes on beneath my sister's trouser suit.'

Dr Barbara waited patiently until I'd finished, then nodded again. 'Okay. And if you know all this anyway, then what's the point of analyzing the dream?'

'Yes, fair enough. There is no point. It's just a more interesting way of looking at the same problems.'

'It's a more opaque way of looking at the same problems. If you're feeling anxious, we should talk about that. But there's no need to muddy the waters by bringing in dreams and so forth. Why circle the issues when you can confront them head-on?'

I didn't know if this was an open question or something more pointed, with implications. Probably both. Whatever the case, Dr Barbara was right. There was no reason to complicate matters by introducing Freud into the picture.

My second therapist had been a card-carrying Freudian (literally; his card read: *Dr Bryce: Freudian Analyst*). I found him advertised at the back of the *London Review of Books*, and he had been an unmitigated disaster. He was patronizing and arrogant, and far less intelligent than he assumed he was. He reminded me of a medical student I went out with in the first year of university, a pompous idiot who read only the *Lancet* and genuinely believed that George Eliot was a man. That relationship had lasted three weeks; I walked out on my psychoanalyst after less than an hour.

The therapist before that, my first therapist, had not fared much better. She was an NHS counsellor, a woman in her early forties who worked three days a week in the local surgery. Her office was an awful pastel blue, and littered with the drawings her children had presented to her at the various stages of their artistic incompetence. For five weeks, I found her to be merely ineffectual. Then, on the sixth week, she started expounding with increasing insistence on the value of medication 'as well'. Not necessarily lithium, given how it had made me feel the first time round – fat, flat and stupid – but perhaps one of the newer line in mood stabilizers, which might present fewer side effects. At this point, I realized that she was in league with my GP and left.

Compared with these earlier experiences, Dr Barbara was a godsend. She was neither patronizing nor wishy-washy, and she had no hidden agendas. She might have agreed with my ineffectual counsellor when it came to medication; a mood stabilizer, she once said, probably *would* be of some benefit to me in the sense that it would do precisely what it was meant to do: it would stabilize my mood. But that was not the point. If I found the cure worse than the disease, she respected my right to refuse it. One day, the balance might change, but that was something I would have to evaluate.

Dr Barbara was a sharp-eyed, sharp-tongued woman a couple

of years younger than my mother. She had steel-grey hair and a tastefully bookish office in South Kensington. There were no children's pictures papering her wall; Dr Barbara had known from the age of fifteen that she didn't want to have children, and this, too, was something I respected. Her desk was a rich mahogany, and upon it sat a dragon tree and a Newton's cradle – its playfulness counterbalanced by the framed Ph.D. certificate affixed to the wall behind it. It was rare, however, to find Dr Barbara sitting at her desk. She preferred to conduct her sessions in the two leather armchairs, which faced each other against the backdrop of one of the several oak bookcases.

All in all, there was a pleasant weightiness to the furnishings in Dr Barbara's office. I liked being there. There was something comforting about the routine of it all: the armchairs, the unrushed journey through affluent central London, the black coffee from the Caffè Nero across the road. After seven months of fortnightly appointments, even the fact that I had to rely on my father to foot the bill had stopped rankling. Because, really, this was money he owed me. It didn't feel like the guilt money he had tried to throw at me in the past; this felt more like compensation I'd been awarded by a benign, sagacious judge in a small claims court. I felt I deserved it, and I knew that Freud would have agreed.

'I read your article,' Dr Barbara told me. 'The interview.' Only the interview had been printed at this point. Simon was due the following Sunday.

'What did you think?' I asked.

'It was very compelling. And well written, of course. But you don't need me to tell you that.'

'Thank you.'

'You found a body?'

'Yes. My neighbour's.'

'Do you want to tell me about it?'

It didn't take long to think about this. 'Actually, Barbara, I'd rather not. I'd rather you read about it next Sunday. Is that okay?'

'Yes. It's your choice, of course. But . . .' Dr Barbara laced her fingers and probed the top-left corner of her mouth with her tongue, the way she always did when taking some care over her next sentence. 'But I'd like you to tell me a couple of things, concerning both articles.'

'Fire away.'

Dr Barbara sipped her coffee. 'I'd like to know why you'd rather I read about what happened, instead of just talking. It seems a convoluted way of doing things.'

This first question was easy to answer. 'It's not about being convoluted,' I said. 'It's about being clear. What I've written expresses exactly what I wanted to say. It's as perfect as I could get it. Anything I told you now wouldn't be as accurate. It wouldn't be as truthful.'

'Okay. I think I can accept that argument. But it also leads on to my second point. I'm all for honesty – it's indispensable within these four walls – but you've chosen a very public forum to talk about some rather private issues.'

'My father?'

'Your father, your thoughts, your feelings. Is this the best outlet?'

'My father doesn't read what I write. And as for my thoughts and feelings, well, I didn't really plan to write about myself. It just turned out that way. With the interview, it was pretty much thrust upon me.'

'You have a choice about what you put into the public domain.'

'Yes, granted. But I suppose it felt like quite a liberating thing to do. It felt nice to tell the truth, and not have to dilute it. If I'd tried to write up the interview in any other way, it would have had no basis in reality. I don't see the point in writing something dishonest.'

'There's a difference between being honest and writing without self-censorship. Everyone self-censors, all the time.'

I shrugged. 'As I said, it felt liberating not to. Besides, I don't think Miranda Frost self-censors, or not very much. So the format of the interview made a certain amount of sense.'

'And what about the follow-up? Does it make sense to go on offering up your life for public scrutiny?'

'You sound like Beck. Except he said that I was *dramatizing* my life.'

'How do you feel about that?'

'I think he's being a bit unfair. I'm not dramatizing my life. I'm writing about something dramatic that occurred in my life. There's a difference.'

'A subtle difference, some would argue.'

'It's a big difference! I mean, with the Miranda Frost interview, it's mostly just transcription. It's objective journalism in its purest sense.'

'And the follow-up?'

'Well, no – that's a personal account. It has to be subjective; that's what makes it interesting. But that doesn't mean I'm dramatizing. I mean, yes, there may be a dramatic element to the language and structure, but that's because I wanted to capture the feeling of the experience. I wanted to be emotionally truthful.'

Dr Barbara weighed this argument in several seconds of silence.

I obviously hadn't made myself entirely clear, so I tried again. 'Put it this way. We all use one or two dramatic tricks when we're talking about our lives. Say you were late for work – you missed the bus or got stuck in traffic or something. It's very difficult to tell that story straight, without emphasizing certain details: the frustration, the watch-checking, the idiot in front of you who was on his mobile and didn't realize that the lights had changed. You want to convey the experience as it felt at the time. It's normal, and it's not dramatizing as such. It's just drawing out what's inherently dramatic in the situation.'

These were arguments I'd already rehearsed for when Beck read the follow-up; I was making him wait, too. Yet based on this trial run, I thought my explanation could do with some fine-tuning. Dr Barbara still looked sceptical.

'I'll reserve judgement until I've read the article,' she said.

Outside, the sky was starting to darken. There had been only a little high cloud when I'd entered Dr Barbara's office, fifty minutes ago, but now it was dim enough that she had to switch on both of the floor lamps. As she did, I thought idly about how the session had not quite met my expectations. True, I was used to Dr Barbara challenging my thinking, on most topics, but today there was something else. I'd been left feeling defensive and a little misunderstood, as if my words weren't having the effect I intended for them. It was in this mindset that I decided to mention that my libido seemed to be coming back. I wanted to give her some unequivocal good news, proof that despite everything – despite the arguments with Beck and the anxiety dream and Simon's corpse – I was feeling generally better. But even here, Dr Barbara's reaction was guarded.

'I think that's something else we need to keep an eye on,' she told me.

'It's a good thing,' I assured her. 'I mean, I actually want sex again. I'm enjoying it – really enjoying it – for the first time in months. I've had three orgasms in the past fortnight. I think it's a pretty clear sign that my mood's improving.'

Dr Barbara frowned a bit as she settled herself back in her chair, but she didn't blush. It was impossible to make Dr Barbara blush, as I'd discovered months ago. She knew, of course, that my sex drive was the first thing to go when I was getting depressed. I'd told her that before Christmas; it was as predictable as the tides. Her response was that I should focus less on the physical side of things and more on the emotional closeness that making love could bring. This almost made *me* blush; it certainly made me cringe, which caused Dr Barbara to posit that I might have 'intimacy issues'. (Paradoxically, she also thought I had an unhealthy dependency on romantic relationships, since I hadn't been out of one for more than a fortnight since I was about fifteen.) But the only issue for me was Dr Barbara's choice of vocabulary. I didn't think a doctor should be using a phrase like *making love*. In all honesty, I didn't think it was a phrase that had any place outside pre-1950s literature, where the meaning was different and less cloyingly euphemistic.

Contrarily, I assumed it was my diligent logging of orgasms, this focus on the physical, that was now causing Dr Barbara to frown like that; though, in truth, her frown was difficult to read. It was also possible that she had more general concerns about my sudden uplift in mood. This was understandable, of course, but that didn't make it any easier to deal with. It was frustrating to feel reined in like this, to have every emotion – even the positive ones – viewed as a potential symptom.

'Is there anything else you'd like to talk about before we finish?' Dr Barbara asked.

I was feeling slightly petulant at this juncture, but at the same time I still wanted to win back Dr Barbara's approval before we ended the session. This is why I started to tell her about the speed – how there'd been a couple of instances in the past fortnight when I'd wanted to take it, but both times I'd resisted. It was an achievement of sorts, though I realized, halfway through my story, that it was unlikely to be met with any great approbation. Dr Barbara's frown deepened, losing all traces of its previous ambiguity. In retrospect, it was stupid of me to expect anything else. When it came to drugs, Dr Barbara and I were never going to agree; we couldn't even agree on terminology. I talked about recreational use and blowing off some steam; she talked about ad hoc self-medication and comorbidity.

When I had finished my exposition, she sat for a moment in stony-faced silence, then said, 'Okay, that's something we *really* need to keep an eye on.'

So that was three eyes now: sex and drugs and insomnia. We were fast running out.

'I think you're missing the point,' I told her, after waiting calmly for a few seconds. 'I decided *not* to take it, despite being exhausted and stressed out of my mind. A few months back, I wouldn't have given it a second thought. But on this occasion, I decided that given the time of day and general circumstances it would be better – in the long run – not to. That's progress, don't you think?'

This last was said jokingly, to try to force a wobble in Dr Barbara's anxious pout. But it wasn't a joke. I wanted to make her see that things were getting better, for her to give some indication that she agreed with me, even in a very limited sense.

She didn't.

'Abby, this is lunacy. As I've told you again and again, I'm not going to be happy until you've stopped entirely. The amphetamines, the MDMA – all of it. It sets you back a long, long way every time you take it.'

'Which I didn't,' I noted, since this emphasis was getting rather lost.

'Wonderful. So why not go one step further and just get rid of it? Take away the temptation.'

'I've told you. It keeps me on an even keel. Sometimes it's the only thing that does. Besides, it's much better for me than too much drink. I know that from experience.' I pointed to the scar in the centre of my right palm, a perfectly circular white disc, about the size of an ibuprofen. 'I've never wanted to do anything like that on speed, and certainly not on ecstasy.'

Dr Barbara acknowledged this fact with a curt nod. But I don't think she was any closer to accepting the broader picture I was trying to paint.

I left feeling vaguely dissatisfied.

DADDY

I wanted to kill my sister.

She called me the day before the family meal – the day before! – to tell me that some work thing had come up. She was being flown out to New York that very evening. It was something she simply could not get out of.

'You bitch! You absolute bitch!'

There was a long unruffled silence down the line. 'Listen, Abby. I know it's a pain. I'll make it up to you, I promise.'

'You've spent the last fortnight haranguing me over this. How could you?'

'It's work. I don't have a choice. It's not as if I wanted to pull out. Daddy's gone to a lot of effort, booked a really nice restaurant. I was looking forward to it.'

'Great. So how about you go to dinner with Daddy and I'll fly out to New York and eat canapés and hobnob with a bunch of idiots and close whatever stupid fucking deal it is you have to close?'

My voice was getting increasingly shrill. I was very aware of this, but I couldn't do a thing about it. Francesca, in contrast, had started using her telephone voice – which was so enunciated you'd have thought she'd been taught it in finishing school. In actual fact, I think she'd been taught it on some moronic assertiveness course at work. It was the voice she slipped into whenever things got heated, and it always made me feel like I was eleven and she was fifteen again, and there was this unbreachable gulf that existed in our relative levels of maturity.

The more I thought about it, the more I was convinced that this four-year age gap had defined all the major differences between us. It had definitely defined our different attitudes to our father. Francesca had been eighteen when he left us; by that time she had gone up to Cambridge. She had more important things to worry about than the final death rattles of our family. I had been fourteen, and was left wondering, *Why now?* The answer, I could only assume, was that my sister had been the mysterious glue that kept my parents together. And her relationship with our father had emerged from the divorce pretty much unscathed. Twelve years later, she still called him 'Daddy' like she was a girl from Beverly Hills asking for a lift to the Prom. When I called him 'Daddy', I was being Sylvia Plath.

'Abby, you're being very unreasonable about this,' my sister continued.

'*I'm* being unreasonable? I'm not the one who's spent the past two weeks going on about how important these horrendous family get-togethers are. I'm not the one who drops every other commitment the second work calls.'

'Oh, come on. That's hardly fair. Our jobs are very different. Yours is much more . . .'

'More what? More frivolous? More dispensable? More of a hobby, really?'

'It's more flexible. You don't have things like this dropped on your plate at the last minute. You get to work to your own schedule. You should count yourself lucky.'

'Jesus! Do you know how patronizing you sound?' The weary sigh down the phone suggested she didn't. 'That's it – I'm not going either!'

'Don't be silly. You have to go. Daddy's already called the restaurant to change the booking. They were really good about it. And you must know how difficult it is to get a table there. They're always booked up months in advance.'

'Oh, yes. I'm sure it was nearly impossible for them to change a table for six to a table for five.'

'Four.'

'What?'

'A table for four.'

'Fucking hell! Adam's not coming either?'

'No, of course not. Why would he go without me? That would be weird. You wouldn't make Beck go to a family dinner if you had to pull out.'

'Yes I bloody would! I'd make him go and take notes and report back on the whole sorry affair.'

'Ha ha.'

'I'm not joking.'

I heard another deep breath down the line. 'Listen. When did you last see Daddy?'

'Don't guilt-trip me. You have no right.'

'When was it?'

'It was recent enough.'

'When?'

'Around Christmas.'

'That's not recent.'

'I didn't say recent. I said recent enough.'

'He's worried about you. He asks how you're getting on all the time, whenever we speak.'

I didn't say anything. It probably wasn't true. But there was a part of me that wanted it to be true. And I hated that part of me very deeply.

I felt hollow in the pit of my stomach, like I was going to cry.

I didn't cry. Instead, I told my sister that she wasn't getting a birthday present this year. 'You don't deserve one and I can't afford one.'

Then I hung up.

I was lying, of course. I wouldn't have made Beck go to the meal without me. I couldn't have, not at the moment. He still hadn't forgiven me for the second article.

So far as I could tell, his main grievances were as follows: 1) I *was* dramatizing my life – our life – no matter how I chose to dress it up. 2) I'd written about private conversations and given too much personal information. 3) I'd made a couple of passing references to our sex life – even though I hadn't said anything bad about our sex life. (Admittedly, this could have been included under the previous point, but I knew from his tone that it should stand as a complaint all by itself.) 4) I was being deliberately provocative. 5) Neither of us came off well.

But, really, it seemed to me that this was all just one mammoth, repetitive, mostly unreasonable grievance. Every point could be subsumed under the single theme that it was wrong for me to write about my life in a national newspaper.

'Who are you trying to be?' Beck asked me. 'Katie fucking Price?'

This was extremely unfair.

I wasn't trying to be anyone. I was just being myself, writing something open and honest. It wasn't as if I were standing on a table flashing my tits.

'That's *exactly* what you're doing,' Beck told me.

I was flashing my literary tits.

Six days after the article had been published, as we took a taxi through the narrow streets of Soho, we had argued ourselves to a frosty impasse. Tacitly, I think we'd agreed to stop talking about it for the time being. We'd stopped talking in general. It was getting us nowhere.

We had to take a taxi to the restaurant because walking, even to a bus or Tube station, was completely out of the question. I was wearing five-inch heels, which would go some way to narrowing the height difference between Marie Martin and me (assuming that she wasn't also wearing five-inch heels; I didn't think she would be because that would make her three inches taller than my father, and he was far too vain to feel comfortable with this arrangement). I'd spent at least a couple of hours getting ready for this ridiculous meal, and I knew most of my preparation was for her benefit.

This did not make me feel good about myself. And I felt myself sinking even lower as we pulled up outside the restaurant. I could tell straight away that I hated it. The façade was mostly glass. It was trendy. There was minimalist furniture and abstract art everywhere. One glance at the table of diners nearest the entrance confirmed that there wasn't a round plate to be seen. The crockery was all quadrilaterals – squares and rectangles mostly, but I could have sworn I also glimpsed a rhombus at one point.

My father and Marie Martin were waiting for us in the bar area. She looked incredible, needless to say. She was in a black halter neck that clung to the narrow curve of her hips like a second skin. Her make-up looked like it had been done by a professional and her hair was swept over one shoulder in a cascade of elaborate ringlets. She looked immaculate, airbrushed, as if she'd stepped straight out of one of her adverts. The only consolation I could find was that her breasts were no larger than mine; they were possibly a little smaller, depending on how much padding she was wearing. Definitely no more than a B-cup, though.

I don't know why this mattered to me, but it did.

My father and I hugged with the stiff, awkward hug we'd been perfecting over the past twelve years – the kind of hug you could imagine Angela Merkel and Silvio Berlusconi exchanging for the benefit of the assembled cameras before heading backstage to discuss fiscal austerity. Except I was nothing like Angela Merkel.

Marie moved in for the French double kiss, but I'd anticipated she would and was ready with my brusque British handshake. She stared at my extended left hand for several seconds, smiling an amused little smile, then countered with a flawless curtsy. This, of course, left me nowhere to go. I nodded in acknowledgement of her victory and withdrew my hand with all the good grace I could muster.

My father, meanwhile, was administering several overenthusiastic slaps to Beck's arm, allowing him to miss, or pretend to miss, all this embarrassing power play. Maybe I should have delivered a few friendly blows to Marie Martin's arm. That would have been a better rejoinder to that stupid curtsy. But the moment had long passed. She was now double kissing Beck, a manoeuvre that he made no attempt to forestall. It was hard to tell in the too-dim violet and turquoise lighting of the bar, but I thought he blushed a little, which I supposed was forgivable. At least I'd be able to ask him how she smelled later on.

I ordered a double vodka and Coke before we were taken across to our table.

Our table seemed to be in the exact centre of the room, which made me feel exposed and vulnerable. It didn't help, either, that Marie inevitably attracted a lot of staring. Some people were clearly trying to place her, to work out why she looked so familiar; others were just gazing at her, the way you might gaze at the roof of the Sistine Chapel, in awe that such a thing existed. And yet she seemed completely oblivious to the attention she was garnering. She was chatting to the sommelier in French; it sounded vaguely flirty, but then French usually does. I supposed she must be used to all this attention. She probably took it for granted. My father, however, was a different matter. I knew that he wasn't oblivious to the gawking. It would be like a dozen different fingers all massaging his ego. Though, surely, he must have felt just a tiny bit uncomfortable as well? A fair share of those onlookers must have been trying, unsuccessfully, to work out the peculiar dynamics of our table. The obvious assumption would be that this was a father taking his three similarly aged children to dinner – except no daughters would ever dress the way Marie and I had dressed for the benefit of their father. And there was zero chance the two of us shared a mother.

I glared at the pretentious menu while my father attempted small talk. How were things? What had we been up to? After less than five minutes of staccato chit-chat, he had moved on to work and money, the two themes that were never far from his mind.

'If you're struggling, Abigail, I can always find you some work writing copy. You only have to ask. We always need writers.'

'We're getting by.'

'Yes, I'm sure. But you could be doing so much more than just getting by. You know, you could earn twice as much writing for advertisers than you do with the papers. At least. It's worth thinking about.'

Beck nodded. It was a small, diplomatic nod, not very effusive, but it still annoyed the hell out of me.

'I've thought about it,' I said, 'and I'm not interested.'

My father cracked his knuckles, then sipped his wine. 'I just think it's a shame, that's all. You have a way with words – that's a marketable skill. Finding the right phrase, the right slogan to grab someone's attention, that's a talent worth having. You shouldn't waste it.'

'Waste it how? By writing about things that actually interest me? That I care about?'

'That's not what I meant. Of course you can do that too. This would just be a sideline, another source of income. What's wrong with that?'

'Daddy, I don't want to write pointless trash I don't believe in – to sell pointless trash I don't believe in.'

The look of incomprehension on my father's face was so pure it could have been miniaturized and used as an emoticon.

'I just want you to be a little more comfortable, a little happier,' he concluded.

This was a very simple and achievable condition in his mind: increase your income, increase your happiness. But I didn't feel like arguing the point. I downed the rest of my second vodka and told him I was going for a smoke.

'If you need to order while I'm gone' – I jabbed at the menu – 'get me the braised saddle of lamb with the carrot reduction.'

I had no idea what a carrot reduction was.

I'd miscalculated – badly, stupidly. I'd thought that I'd at least be able to achieve some respite from the torture with three or four tactically placed cigarette breaks, before and between courses. I'd been counting on it when I agreed to this meal; it was one of the few occasions when the indoor smoking ban seemed a blessing rather than a curse. Whatever tumult I had to endure inside, I'd still have this handful of moments, oases of calm in which to relax and regroup.

But Marie Martin was a model. She was French. *Of course* she smoked. I couldn't believe how dense I'd been not even to have considered this. But reality registered the moment I saw her stepping out of the doorway to join me in the street. She had a pack of Gitanes, the cigarette equivalent of a double espresso. Reluctantly, I handed her my lighter. She made a *thank you* smile, and I did my *don't mention it* shrug. Neither of us said anything for a while. A man in skinny jeans and a leather jacket passed between us, got about six paces down the road, glanced back at Marie, and walked into a bin.

I gestured with my cigarette. 'I suppose that sort of thing happens to you a lot.'

'Excuse me?'

'Causing men to walk into bins, or lampposts, or out into traffic. That sort of thing.'

She gave a modest nod. 'It happens sometimes.'

'One of the hazards of beauty.'

'It's something I try to ignore.' She took a deep drag on her cigarette and let the smoke trickle out of her nostrils. 'It's not nice to be judged always on your looks, you know.'

I snorted. 'You may have chosen the wrong profession.'

'Yes, perhaps. I was very young when I started. Sixteen. It was exciting at that age. But modelling is like being a football player. There is no career past thirty. Thirty-five if you're very lucky.'

She looked at me for a bit, as if studying one of the abstract paintings inside. 'I read your articles,' she told me. 'Both of them.'

'Oh.'

I was surprised, but I shouldn't have been. The articles were online. She probably had a Google alert set up on her name, or something like that.

'What did you think?' I asked.

'They were . . . interesting. I liked the Yeats very much. It was beautiful. It made me feel warm and sad at the same time.'

Fine. So she could appreciate Yeats. She obviously understood Yeats (even though she pronounced it 'yeets', to rhyme with teats and Keats). It didn't mean a damn thing. 'If you like Yeats, I doubt things are going to work out with my father,' I told her. 'He's not a sensitive man.'

Marie took another drag on her cigarette and didn't say anything. The silence felt vaguely accusatory, enough that I wanted it to stop.

'How did he take it?' I asked. 'My father?'

Marie shook her head. 'He hasn't read it.'

'What, he chose not to?'

'I didn't show it to him. I didn't think it would be kind.'

Terrific. A lecture on kindness from my father's thirty-year-old model girlfriend. I didn't know whether to scream, laugh or cry, but the second seemed the least of the three evils.

'You're pretty when you laugh,' Marie told me.

'Right. But not walk-into-a-bin pretty.'

'No,' she acknowledged. 'Just pretty.' She managed, somehow, to sound weirdly envious.

I thought it must be a front, some sort of mind game.

'I enjoyed our talk,' she told me. Then she crushed her Gitane under one of her two-inch heels and went back inside.

I lit another shaky Marlboro. Simon had given me a taste for them.

I was determined to get my five minutes of calm.

When I returned to our table, Beck and my father and Marie seemed to be sharing a joke. I thought it really would have been better if I wasn't there. Then everyone could go on having a good time.

'Well, you and Daddy certainly seemed to be getting on,' I said to Beck as we waited for a taxi to take us home. I didn't even try to keep the reprimand out of my voice.

'Oh, for God's sake, Abby!'

'What? It's good that *one* of us enjoyed dinner.'

'I can't believe you sometimes. Do you actually expect me to turn up to your family meal and spend the whole time being hostile to your family?'

He made it sound so unreasonable.

'I'm just asking for a bit of support. Is that so much to ask? I'm not saying that you have to be actively hostile to my father, but you don't have to nod and agree with every idiotic remark he makes. It undermines me.'

'I undermine *you*? Not the other way round – like when you told me to put my wallet away because I was "being ridiculous". You know, it's normal to offer to split the bill. It's the polite thing to do.'

'Oh, don't be such a man! It was ridiculous. How could we afford to split the bill? Anyway, Daddy had already made it clear that he was paying. You do understand that he earns four or five times our combined income?'

'Don't exaggerate. He doesn't earn anything like that amount, not after tax.'

I laughed, and it was a genuine laugh. 'Really, Beck! You're so naïve. Daddy doesn't pay tax. It's one of the few things he has a strong moral objection to. He pays his accountant instead. He has more money going offshore than either of us will earn in the rest of the decade.'

Beck scowled. 'Fine. Next time I won't bother coming at all. You can sit there and be miserable on your own.'

The awful thing, of course, was that I knew I was being ridiculous and unfair. I was being a complete bitch. But somehow I couldn't stop myself. Seeing my father brought out the absolute worst in me.

I knew I should apologize. I knew I should tell Beck that I did appreciate his being there, that it made such a difference to me, even if I acted completely to the contrary. But I thought that if I tried to say any of this, I'd just break down crying, and then we'd have to have yet another earnest conversation about my mood. I couldn't handle that at the moment. I'd had too much vodka; it was fogging my mind and making me depressed. And the thought of getting in a taxi and going home made me feel even worse. Our flat was not a good flat to argue in, and it was not a good place for tense silences. It was too much of a pressure cooker. There was nowhere to stomp off to, nowhere to cool down.

I needed to stay out for a bit. More specifically, what I *really* needed was that special clarity, that feeling of absolute tranquillity that only ecstasy can provide. This was the best solution I could see to our current situation. It would offer us a short cut to reconciliation, without the need for words or compromise or all those raw, dangerous emotions.

Beck, however, was resistant – even though he must have been as fed up of arguing as I was.

'I don't think it's a good idea,' he told me. 'Not at the moment.'

'It's a great idea. We need to have some fun, forget the past week. I can't face the thought of going home right now, not like this.'

'We'll still have to go home,' Beck pointed out. 'We'll have to go home to get the stuff.'

'No, I have the stuff in my bag,' I told him. We were calling it 'the stuff' because we were still in the street, and there was a certain amount of pedestrian traffic. Not that I thought anyone would care. Plus 'stuff' wasn't exactly the Enigma Code.

'It's in your bag?' Beck repeated, after a small, faintly pointed hesitation.

'Well, you know . . . dinner with Daddy. Hope for the best, prepare for the worst. I thought we might need it.'

He still looked far from convinced.

'Listen,' I said. 'How about we just go and find somewhere to have a drink? A soft drink – I realize I've had quite enough alcohol.'

This last was very true, but I also said it knowing it might placate him a bit. It was almost an apology.

'One drink?' Beck asked.

'Yes. One drink. If you still want to go home after that, we'll go home.' We weren't going home. 'Either way, I think it will do us some good.'

Beck weighed this proposition for a few moments. I could see the cogs turning. Going for a drink was obviously a more attractive proposition than going home in a huffy silence, but I still had to play this carefully, find the right balance of carrot and stick. I placed a hand on his arm and gave him a soft, tentative smile. Slightly manipulative, but never mind.

'Please? I just need to wind down. It's been a really difficult evening for me.'

A vacant taxi had finally emerged from around the corner. Beck looked at it for a moment, dropped his hand, and let it pass.

'One drink,' he said.

We found a club that was playing non-stop classic trance until 6 a.m. and stayed until it closed. When we got home, an hour later, we each had another pill, then had sex on the floor while listening to Blondie's *Greatest Hits*. It was languorous, and meltingly soft.

Halfway through, I started thinking about Marie Martin and began to giggle.

'What?' Beck asked.

'Marie Martin thinks I'm pretty when I laugh.'

'You *are* pretty.'

'Prettier than her?'

'Yes. Much, much prettier.'

'Thank you.'

'It's the truth.'

'I don't think many men would agree.'

'No, I'm sure they wouldn't. That doesn't matter. You're much more of a niche market – darker, quirkier.'

'Good. I want to be a niche market.'

'You are. They don't come any nicher.'

He ran his fingers through my hair. Debbie Harry was singing 'Sunday Girl'.

'What about Debbie Harry? 1977 Debbie Harry. Am I prettier than her?'

'Of course. No competition.'

I could feel tears starting to well in my eyes. I wrapped my legs tightly around Beck's waist and buried my face in his shoulder.

'I love you,' I said. 'I'm so fucking happy.'

LAUNDRY

The problem with drugs, of course, is that they work too well.

The comedown began on Monday morning. I awoke at nine to discover that Beck had left without disturbing me. I'd finally got to sleep around 3.30 a.m. At that point, I'd reached the hallucination stage of ecstasy sleep deprivation. My last memory was of lying in the darkness with my fingers almost paired, as if around an invisible Tesla Ball. Except I didn't need a Tesla Ball. Fine veins of electric-blue fire were sizzling between my splayed fingertips. I must have watched them for hours while Beck slept beside me. I listened to all of *The Orb's Adventures Beyond the Ultraworld* in my earphones, my finger-lightning dancing in time with the music.

The world I awoke to was a dull and washed-out version of what it should have been. I didn't feel much like getting up. I wanted to bury myself under the duvet and hide until it was dark again. But I knew this was probably the worst thing to do. Anyway, I had the vague notion that if I could get through the day on just my five-and-a-bit hours' sleep, it might finally reset my body clock, help me sleep through a whole night without waking.

I got up.

Beck had stuck a note to the coffee machine, It read: *You're a thousand times prettier than Marie Martin and 1977 Debbie Harry combined. Be kind to yourself today. X*

It was a sweet thing to do, but it didn't make me feel much better. I knew I didn't really deserve it. I folded the note to the size of a postage stamp and squirrelled it away in my purse.

In the living room, my dress and heels were posed in the middle of the floor like a still life. The shoes were standing side by side, as if in a shop window, and the dress was in a crumpled heap behind them. The effect was quite dramatic. It looked as if the occupant of those clothes had simply vanished, like Murakami's elephant, leaving the shoes in situ while the dress fell artlessly to the floor. I didn't move them yet. I sat on the sofa, smoked a cigarette, and tried to think about the things I should do to get through the day. It seemed a monumental task.

It sounds crazy, but in the end I had to imagine that my body was some kind of pet – a small, delicate animal that had been delivered into my care for the next ten hours. This allowed me to make a simple to-do list:

    1) Feed the animal.

    2) Give the animal a wash.

    3) Take her for a walk.

    4) Clean her cage.

    5) Give her some treats.

I knew that number three was especially important, since I wanted nothing more than to stay in the flat in my dressing gown all day. As for the others, well, I hadn't eaten a bite since the restaurant, and I hadn't showered either. I had no idea what the treats would be yet, but I thought that I ought to reward myself for the other achievements on the list. Beck had said I should be kind to myself.

Food had to come first, otherwise there was a reasonable chance I'd fall over in the shower. I needed sugar and protein and carbohydrate, so I fed myself a bowl of muesli with yoghurt and honey. Then I carried the laundry basket through to the shower room and dumped its contents in the washing machine.

Our washing machine lived in the shower room. This wasn't our innovation: it lived there when we moved in. There wasn't enough room for a bath because the room was an irregular L-shape, but the washing machine just about fitted in one corner; and since there was no place for it in the kitchen, this wasn't such a stupid arrangement, although it did make sitting on the toilet quite claustrophobic. The only real advantage to the washing machine's location was that you could strip in the shower room and throw your clothes directly into the cylinder. We only needed a very small laundry basket.

I like my showers scalding hot so that they seem to burn off the dirt like a chemical peel. But there seemed to be some sort of problem with the water pressure today. The weak trickle that dripped from the hose was barely lukewarm. I emerged from the shower feeing not much cleaner than when I'd stepped in.

Once I started tidying the flat, I couldn't stop. I cleaned manically, like a 1950s housewife. I had it in my head that if I managed to get everything spotless, it would be like resetting the clock, creating a blank canvas for the rest of the working week. And Beck would be pleased with me. He'd get home and see that I hadn't wasted my day crying on the sofa.

I needed music while I worked, to fill the empty space. A broad mixture of dance, rock and pop confronted me – two collections that had merged when Beck and I moved in together to create one sprawling entity with multiple personalities. Today, my eyes were inevitably drawn to the darker and more despondent of those personalities – Pink Floyd's *The Wall*, Radiohead's *Kid A*, the Cure, Morrissey, Nick Cave – but I resisted the temptation to wallow. At the same time, I couldn't cope with anything too positive or energetic, which would have felt like a bitter sham. Instead, I compromised, and picked out a handful of albums that straddled the upbeat/downbeat divide: PJ Harvey's *Stories from the City, Stories from the Sea*, Moby's *18*, Infected Mushroom's *Vicious Delicious*.

I mopped and hoovered, wiped the surfaces in the kitchen, cleaned the hob, emptied the bins and ashtray, hung out the laundry on the airer, scrubbed the shower, lit a couple of scented candles to make the place smell nice.

By lunchtime, I'd run out of obvious things to do, so I started on the less obvious. I polished the mirrors, descaled the kettle, cleaned the tops of the kitchen cabinets. Then I decided that I'd wash all our bedding – duvet, pillows, mattress protector, the works. This was perfect because I couldn't do it in the flat. I'd have to go to the launderette down the road, which would also get me out in the fresh air for a bit. I thought that I would take the bedding to the launderette, load it into the washer, walk to the Co-op to buy some cottage cheese – for the tryptophan –

return to the flat to get my laptop, go back to the launderette to transfer the washing to the dryer, go to the coffee shop for a double espresso and a piece of cake (my treat), then spend an hour people-watching and checking my emails until the dryer had finished its cycle. Then I'd only have to kill a couple more hours until Beck got home, and the day would almost be done.

Someone was following me. I knew it before I'd got fifty metres down the road. The sensation of being watched, of being *stalked*, was overwhelming. The problem was there was no way I could confirm what I knew, not with the sort of irrefutable evidence that would convince anyone else. Both my arms were bear-hugging the black bin bag that held our duvet and pillows. I had poor peripheral vision and couldn't turn round fast enough to catch my pursuer in the act. All I got was the occasional glimpse out of the corner of my eye, a figure in grey. I couldn't even work out what sex it was.

I thought my best bet would be to pretend I hadn't noticed anything, to act like nothing was wrong. Then when I got to the launderette, I could set the bin bag down on one of the machines, turn straight back out the door, and confront whoever it was in the safety of the busy street.

This I attempted to do.

When I stepped out of the door, there was no one there – or no one doing anything remotely out of the ordinary. A mother pushing a buggy, people at the bus stop, the usual shoppers and workers on their lunch breaks.

I felt ridiculous.

I went back inside and started loading my bedding into one of the machines.

Checking my emails turned out to be a surprisingly nervy exercise. Buried amid the usual junk – Viagra and phishing scams and penis extensions – was an email from Miranda Frost, and another from Jess at the *Observer*. I clicked on the former with some trepidation.

To: abbywilliams1847@hotmail.co.uk
From: miranda@mirandafrostpoetry.co.uk
Date: Sun, 2 Jun 2013, 11:03 AM
Subject: (No Subject)

Bravo, Miss Williams

My editor tells me that I'm currently number one on Amazon's poetry bestsellers list (another oxymoron I'm sure you'll appreciate). We're in danger of hitting five figures. I think I may have underestimated you. Turns out the cliché is true: any publicity *is* good publicity. Who'd have thought it?

I trust your career is likewise flourishing.

MF

P.S. Do you like cats?

I stared at the email for about ten minutes, as if it were a cryptic crossword clue, then hit reply.

To: miranda@mirandafrostpoetry.co.uk
From: abbywilliams1847@hotmail.co.uk
Date: Mon, 3 Jun 2013, 2:40 PM
Subject: RE: (No Subject)

I like cats very much. They're much easier than people.

AW

It took me a long time to write this because my mind felt like it was full of treacle. But after rereading the message three times, I was at least satisfied that I'd written two coherent sentences.

Jess's email was more complicated still.

To: abbywilliams1847@hotmail.co.uk
From: jessica.pearle@observer.co.uk
Date: Mon, 3 Jun 2013, 10:13 AM
Subject: More, please!

Abby

I'll get straight to the point. Have you been looking at the online responses to your articles? We've had several hundred, with more coming in all the time. If you haven't looked, just be warned: a fair proportion of them are hostile. But I'm sure you'll appreciate the bigger picture. A *lot* of people are reading you.

So how about a follow-up? Any ideas? Something on a related topic would be ideal, but don't feel constrained. We can give you a lot of freedom on the subject matter: life, death, sex, general cultural commentary – you name it. Very keen for you to write something else for us, though. There could even be a regular column in this.

Let me know.

Jess

I supposed this was good news. It was hard to tell because I didn't have any emotions at the moment. People talk about dark moods, black moods, all the time. But depression isn't a dark mood. It's an ash-grey mood, or possibly some type of beige.

There was too much information to process in Jess's email. I didn't reply at once. I opened a new tab, found the Simon article and started reading through some of the comments.

TheodoraEdison: Is this for real? It reads like fiction. Another frustrated wannabe writer?

EastofJava: Hate it. HATE it. What's the world coming to?

0100011101000101: @ EastofJava: Totally agree. I hate this so much I had to read it twice. Can't believe it.

JamesWoliphaunt: *This comment was removed by a moderator because it didn't abide by our community standards.*

Doctoroctopussy: Did anyone else find the part where she smoked the dead guy's cigarettes ever so slightly sexy?

ExistentialSam: What's the point of this?

I stopped reading. At least Doctoroctopussy found some merit in my work. He was clearly a pervert, but, right then, I was willing to take whatever praise I was given.

I reopened my email and concentrated very hard.

To: jessica.pearle@observer.co.uk
From: abbywilliams1847@hotmail.co.uk
Date: Mon, 3 June 2013, 2:58 PM
Subject: RE: More, please!

Hello Jess

I may have a follow-up. It's about monkeys. Actually, the monkeys are incidental. It's about how we're not designed to live in cities. Give me a few days.

Abby

It seemed a reasonable response.

I finished my cake without really tasting it, then went back to the Co-op to buy more cottage cheese.

I felt watched again, all the way home. I knew it was just para-noia, the fact that my brain was not working properly, but knowing this didn't change a thing. I still felt watched.

I plugged myself into my iPod, listened to some Tori Amos and tried to block out most of the external world.

It didn't work.

When I got back to our building, I was as tense as a tightrope. I hadn't been back to the launderette yet; I wanted to drop my laptop back home first so that I had less to carry.

I knew something was off as soon as I stepped in from the street. There was a draught carrying voices down the stairwell, but I couldn't make out what was being said. I removed my earphones, waited for a few indecisive moments, then crept up the stairs.

Simon's door was open. In the gloom of his hallway I could see two men and a woman.

'. . . you come this way, we have a modern, open-plan living area. Very low maintenance. Ideal for . . .'

The man stopped speaking and looked at me. I stood staring, just outside the door. He was wearing a suit, despite the fact it was a hot, muggy day. The other man and the woman were casually dressed, in a T-shirt and shorts and a skirt and a camisole respectively.

'Hello,' I said. It was only the second time I'd spoken that day. My voice was as flat as a pancake.

'Hello?' the suited man repeated. He said it like a question.

I looked at the woman. 'Are you moving in?'

'Er, just looking at the moment. Do you live here?'

'Yes, next door.'

'Oh, how nice. We might be neighbours.' She giggled nervously.

'We might be.' I couldn't think of any other response.

There was a silence.

The estate agent cleared his throat. 'Erm, was there something you wanted?'

'No. I just saw the door was open and . . .' I tried to think how to end this sentence. The estate agent stared at me. 'I guess I was a little creeped out. I was the one who found the body.'

'The . . . body?' This was the other man. I noticed the woman had taken hold of his hand.

I didn't really want to continue this conversation, but there wasn't much choice.

'Simon,' I explained. 'The guy who used to live here. He died.' I gestured at the interior doorway that the estate agent was standing in. 'Through there.'

'That's . . .' The man looked at his wife. I assumed it was his wife. She looked like a wife. 'Actually, I don't know what that is.'

'No, me neither.'

The estate agent shot me a look that I couldn't decipher.

'I'd better go,' I said. 'I have some laundry to collect.'

Back in my flat, I put my laptop down, then pressed my ear to the front door and waited for them to leave. I waited another five minutes after I'd heard their footsteps descending the stairs, just to be sure, then went back to the launderette.

When I returned to the flat for the final time, I saw that a note had been pushed under the door.

YOU NEED HELP

I reread it a couple of times, then folded it and put it in my purse, next to Beck's note from earlier.

After that, I lit a cigarette and sat down in the spotless living area. I listened to Johnny Cash's cover of 'Hurt' on loop while reading some more of my online hate mail. I must have listened to it six or seven times. I knew I was self-flagellating, but I couldn't help it. I wanted to stop and pick up the phone and call Dr Barbara. That would have been the sensible thing to do. But I couldn't face it. I couldn't face any more talking.

I smoked another cigarette and closed my eyes and waited for the evening to come.

SKYPE

Fran Skyped me that evening. If it had been left to me, I wouldn't have answered. I'd already switched my mobile to silent, as soon as Beck got home, and had no intention of talking to anyone else. It was hard enough as it was, trying to act normal. But I'd decided, earlier, that Beck didn't need to know how awful I was feeling. After all, it was mostly my own fault – I'd engineered this situation – and it wasn't as if either of us could do anything to make it better. This slump, I knew, was purely chemical in its origin, and if I ate enough cottage cheese it would pass. Of course, Beck realized that I wasn't one hundred per cent, but I'd managed to imply that this was largely a matter of overtiredness. If I seemed distant, that was the reason.

The water pressure had returned, so I'd had a long, burning-hot shower, thinking this might help me.

It hadn't.

I was drying my hair in the bedroom when Beck came in and told me that Fran wanted to talk to me. If I'd been more quick-witted, I'd have refused – said I was just about to go to sleep or something. But I was caught off guard, and instead found myself waiting dumbly while Beck brought the laptop through.

Francesca was in her kitchen. From what I could make out of the background, she might have been *standing* in her kitchen. But I didn't bother to ask if or why this was the case. Probably another trick she'd learned at work, projecting a strong self-image or some such bullshit. You could bet that Fran's work was full of people who habitually stood up for Skype calls.

'I was checking my email and I saw that you were online,' she told me.

'I wasn't online,' I replied. 'I forgot to turn my laptop off.' My voice was still devoid of emotion, but I think Fran interpreted this as hostility.

'You're busy?'

'No.' I couldn't lie. I didn't have the brainpower. 'I'm just not really up to this right now.'

'Up to what? Abby, it's a conversation with your sister, not armed combat.'

I shrugged in an attempt to show that I didn't see the distinction.

'Could you at least adjust your screen? I can only see half your face.'

I had no idea why this was important to Fran – it seemed a very trivial detail – but I wasn't going to make a fuss about it. I tilted the screen. 'Better?'

'Much. Now listen: I want to apologize.' Fran was the only person I knew who could make an apology sound like a rebuke. 'We need to clear the air.'

'Okay.'

'Okay? As in . . . ?'

'I accept your apology.'

I thought this would be the quickest way to end the conversation, but Fran kept staring at me in a way that told me things weren't going to be that easy.

'What?' I asked.

'I don't feel good about what happened, believe me.'

'I do believe you.'

'It was just terrible timing.'

'Yes. I know. It was terrible timing and it wasn't your fault.'

'Abby, don't.'

'Don't what?'

'The passive-aggressive routine. Let's just skip it.'

'I've accepted your apology. What else do you want from me?'

'I want you to talk to me. Shout at me. Anything. You can't just say you accept my apology. It doesn't mean anything.'

I thought this was pretty typical of Fran, wanting to dictate the terms by which I could accept her apology – the terms by which I was permitted to be upset with her.

'I don't need to shout,' I told her. 'I'm fine. I'm over it.'

'Oh, please! You're clearly not fine. You're still angry about what happened.'

'I'm not angry. I'm . . .'

'What?'

Hollow, depleted, empty.

'What are you?'

'Nothing. I'm nothing.'

'Abby, please. Can we at least try to sort this out like adults?'

I didn't know how to reply to this. Fran started to say something else but I wasn't really listening. A thought had occurred to me.

'Have you spoken to Daddy?' I asked.

There was a small hesitation, one that probably had nothing to do with the fact I'd cut her off mid-sentence.

'Daddy? No. I wanted to speak to you first.'

'You haven't spoken to him at all?'

'Well, we've messaged each other, but, no, we haven't actually *spoken* spoken.'

'Oh.'

'Oh, what?'

'Oh. Just oh.'

'Listen, I know what you're thinking, but Daddy and I have plenty of conversations that are not about—'

I realized there was no point going on with this any longer. But, equally, I had no idea what I could say to make Fran stop talking.

I hung up.

Then I shut down my laptop and put it on the floor next to the bed.

Several minutes passed. I lay perfectly still, with my eyes closed, waiting to see if the landline would ring and wondering what I should do if it did. But, thankfully, there was nothing. Just the ongoing groan and hiss of the traffic below, like someone's damning judgement on a piece of third-rate theatre.

I tried to work out if Fran was right, if I *was* still angry with her. I suppose there must have been some ember of resentment, buried deep, but, right now, it seemed a very small and insignificant thing, lacking any particular colour or shape. And it wasn't as if any of Fran's actions over the past few days had come as a surprise. The plain truth was that she had her own life – a busy, successful life – and I was not a major part of it. Little more than an afterthought, really. So why should I feel let down?

It seemed almost unthinkable now, as if I must be misremembering, but I knew for a fact that Fran and I were close once. When I was thirteen and she was seventeen, she was everything I wanted an older sister to be. She guided me through my first boyfriend drama. She showed me how to get my make-up right, at an age when all the other girls in my class looked as if theirs had been fired on with a cannon. She looked after me when I was at my gloomiest – always had time to listen.

Then when she was about to leave for university, in the summer just after the divorce, I remember her telling me that things really wouldn't be all that different. She'd only be a phone call away. And if necessary, she could hop on a train and be back in London within an hour.

I only took her up on the second offer once, aged fifteen, when I phoned her in floods of tears to tell her that I'd managed to lose my virginity at a friend's drunken house party. She turned up that afternoon with a morning-after pill, and to this day our parents haven't found out about it. Fran didn't even lecture me; she just took me for a long walk in Regent's Park and made me promise never ever to do anything that stupid again.

It was a promise I'd been struggling to keep ever since, and that was a big part of the problem, I supposed. In my late teens, my sister was more able to forgive my various failings: the recklessness, the irresponsibility, the lack of direction, the mood swings, my absolute refusal to speak to our father. And yes, I could be selfish and attention-seeking and narcissistic – but I was an adolescent; this wasn't exactly uncharted territory.

It was only a few years later, when I was in my early twenties and still 'acting up', that the rift between Fran and me had turned into a chasm. She no longer had the time to deal with the never-ending melodrama of my emotional life. She didn't understand why I still behaved more like a child than an adult half the time, why I could never hold down a job for more than a few months, was permanently in debt, went from bad relationship to bad relationship, acted in a way that was so patently self-destructive. Even after my diagnosis, she found it difficult to accept that there might be some element of this that was beyond my control. She thought I should just snap out of it; she even told me once that it wasn't *fair* of me to sabotage my own life in this way, not when there were so many people in the world living in poverty, all of whom would kill to have the opportunities I was born into. But, then, Fran was never someone who was likely to understand her little sister's mood disorder. In terms of her own mental health, she was the equivalent of the person who has never caught a cold. Actually, she was like that with her physical health, too. I was fairly sure that Fran had never in her life taken a sick day.

So I had no intention of trying to explain to her how I was feeling right now. It would be like trying to explain colour to someone born blind. About the best I could say for Fran was that now, unlike five years ago, she at least accepted that I experienced feelings she did not, that lay outside her emotional range. On occasion, she had even managed to identify such feelings in me, painstakingly, like someone trying to read music for the very first time. But not today, obviously. She assumed I was being passive-aggressive, and, right now, I had neither the energy nor the desire to tell her otherwise. It was just easier this way.

SLOUGH

By Thursday morning I had bounced back to normal. Actually, I had bounced back a little beyond normal, but I thought this was all relative. After two and a bit days of torpor, waking to find that my brain had apparently rebalanced its books was an enormous relief. By comparison alone, I felt tremendous.

I awoke at 3 a.m. that Thursday, my mind already racing with the beginnings of a plan.

Professor Caborn had stopped replying to my messages. Lunch, pudding, port, cheese, cigars – the man was unbribable. I now realized that there was zero chance of my convincing him to submit to an interview via email. Email was too easy to ignore. To get him on board, I'd have to talk to him face to face. I felt one hundred per cent confident that if I could see him – if he could see me – I'd be able to persuade him of the worthiness of my request. I could be extremely charming when I wanted to be.

The only problem was getting that face time.

Except it was no problem at all. This is what I realized that Thursday morning.

What was to stop me from simply turning up at his lab in Oxford and taking him to lunch? Why would he refuse? I could go that very day. It was only an hour or so on the train. Worst-case scenario: it would be a short, wasted journey. But I'd still get out of London for a few hours, which was worth the ticket price in itself. I could spend the day appreciating the amazing architecture and go for a drink in that pub where J.R.R. Tolkien and C.S. Lewis used to drink.

The idea of the day spread out before me like an astonishing picnic blanket. I felt bright and refreshed and ready to go. Except I couldn't go, of course; it was still technically the middle of the night – despite strong evidence to the contrary leaking through the curtains. This country was insane in June. How was anyone supposed to sleep through the night when the sun only set for a few hours? I guessed this must be yet another way in which modern life was at odds with the natural world, since our ancestors had evolved at the equator and wouldn't be equipped to deal with these ridiculous seasonal variations. I made a mental note to ask Professor Caborn about it later.

Beck was still sleeping like he'd been anaesthetized. I got up, went through to the living area and sat in my underwear checking the train times. The earliest was at 5.14, which would get me into Oxford at 6.20, but that was obviously crazy. I did like the idea of wandering around Oxford in the early hours: the old buildings would be that bit more impressive when they were deserted; I could imagine it was the 1500s – but then I'd have to wait six hours to take Professor Caborn to lunch. Unless I intercepted him on his way in to work and took him for breakfast instead? No, that seemed a riskier strategy; he probably breakfasted at home. Plus Beck would worry if he woke up and I'd disappeared, even if I left a note.

Having thought about this, I decided it would be better if I didn't mention any of my plan to Beck. I was aware – dimly aware – that he might not understand the logic of it. Much better to tell him after the fact, when things had already been brought to a satisfactory conclusion. This meant I'd have to leave the flat after he did, and the first train I could realistically make was the 10.22 out of Paddington. But this was perfect. It would get me into Oxford at 11.18. Then I'd have plenty of time to get my bearings, track down Professor Caborn, and take him to lunch.

I couldn't read, which was how I would usually have passed the dead hours of the morning. I couldn't concentrate on anything for very long. I was too eager to get the day under way.

I made coffee, showered, dressed myself in tracksuit bottoms and a hoodie, intending to change later – I didn't plan to meet Professor Caborn in my loungewear – then went downstairs for a cigarette. The morning was bright and already warming up. It would have been a good morning to walk a dog or go for a run – I felt a desperate need to be out and about – but I didn't trust my lungs to cope with anything more strenuous than a flight of stairs, and I didn't know anyone in west London with a dog that I could borrow. Instead, I decided to walk to the twenty-four-hour Nisa on Uxbridge Road, where I bought bacon, eggs and more cigarettes. I then zigzagged home down the empty back streets.

It wasn't yet six o'clock when I got back to the flat. I killed some time looking at maps of Oxford and researching the layout of the psychology department, then checked my emails, just to make sure Professor Caborn hadn't got back in touch in the past twelve hours. He hadn't. As always my inbox was mostly junk; someone out there was convinced that Abigail Williams was in fact a man – a man both pitiably endowed and with chronic erectile dysfunction. But buried in there was also another email from Miranda Frost.

To: abbywilliams1847@hotmail.co.uk
From: miranda@mirandafrostpoetry.co.uk
Date: Wed, Jun 5 2013, 9:00 PM
Subject: A modest proposal

Miss Williams,

I have a proposition. With some regret, I have agreed to spend the coming autumn 'teaching' poetry in the States. The decision, as I'm sure you'll appreciate, was purely a financial one.

To dispense with all irrelevant details, I am looking for someone to live in my house and feed my two cats. Perhaps you would like to be that someone?

Why you? Good question. The truth, I suppose, is that the idea amused me. But there is no reason this arrangement shouldn't be mutually beneficial.

My house is rather nice. It has a garden with a view and is a very peaceful place to write. If you would like a break from the horrors of modern urban living, I'm sure it would suit you. (You could have some uninterrupted time to work on that painfully honest, semi-autobiographical novel that is no doubt languishing in a drawer somewhere.)

The position would be for fifteen consecutive weeks and comes with no pay.

Think it over.

MF

I read this quickly, digested it, and sent my one-line reply: *I'll think about it.*

If I chose to interpret her latent, passive-aggressive sarcasm as a double-bluff – which I did – then it seemed Miranda Frost was suddenly taking an inordinate amount of interest in my writing; in my life in general. It was as if she were setting herself up as some kind of eccentric benefactress. Or maybe she just liked me? This was a slightly unsettling notion. Was it a compliment if a sociopath took a shine to you? Probably not, but I decided to shelve this thought and crack on with breakfast.

I was sort of on autopilot as I worked, my mind darting back and forth between several more important matters, like a skittish rabbit in a meadow, and consequently I didn't realize that I'd dispensed all twelve rashers of bacon onto the grillpan until it was too late and they were already cooking. In hindsight, I was impressed that I'd managed to get twelve rashers of bacon onto our grillpan; they were tessellated in a perfect rectangle, like a finished jigsaw. Yet when Beck came through from the hallway, he looked with a degree of suspicion at the generous plate I presented to him.

'Er, what's this?' He was still sleepy, so I was willing to forgive the pure idiocy of the question; in a way, it was quite endearing.

'It's breakfast,' I said. 'I couldn't sleep and it's a beautiful morning, so I went to the shops. Surprise!'

'Yes, it is . . .' He rubbed his eyes. 'You couldn't sleep so you decided to cook breakfast?'

'Yes: bacon and eggs.' I gestured to the plate with my spare hand. 'Mostly bacon, actually. It was buy one get one free. Do you think you can manage seven rashers? I don't think I can handle more than five.'

'Er, yeah, okay. I mean that's a lot of meat to digest on a Thursday morning, but I'll give it a go.'

'That's the spirit. I'm fairly sure the British Empire was built on bacon and eggs for breakfast.'

'Oh. I thought it was built on conquest and the ruthless exploitation of indigenous populations and their resources.'

I laughed. It was a very girlish laugh. 'Yes, that too. But you can't brutalize the world on an empty stomach. Captain Cook, Sir Francis Drake, Lord Nelson' – I was plucking names out of the air – 'they were all bacon-'n'-eggs men. Especially on a Thursday. Historical fact.'

'I'll take your word for it.' Beck pointed at the plate. 'But this is less breakfast and more food art.'

I shrugged. I had plated the food like a cartwheel, with a pool of scrambled egg at the hub and symmetrical spokes of bacon fanning out in an extravagant circle. There was a single leaf of parsley crowning the axle and seven blobs of ketchup marking the circumference, as if it were an unfinished dot-to-dot picture.

'I couldn't just heap up seven rashers of bacon in a tower,' I explained. 'It would have looked ridiculous. Do you want coffee, too? I've just made a fresh pot. It speeds up the metabolism, so it will help you digest your food.'

Beck gave me a quizzical look, but I'd been on enough crash diets to know what I was talking about here.

Paddington, 9.54. I bought a first-class return to Oxford because it was too hot a day to suffer second class; it was also too hot a day to be worrying about money. I was sick of watching every penny. Anyway, I reasoned this trip would pay for itself, several times over. Plus I'd probably need the free Wi-Fi and a table, and plenty of coffee to keep me sharp. You could never rely on the buffet trolley in standard, which always felt like a dreadful lottery. No, first class was justified on so many levels. And since this was a work trip, I could take the £65 out of my taxable income, so there was another incentive. My father would be proud.

Paddington, like so many of those grand old Victorian stations, was slightly shit in various ways. Peeling paint, blackened glass and brickwork, dirty, dusty, draughty, fumy. Nowhere to smoke. I hadn't been through the overground part of the station for several years, but it was just as I remembered it: basically, a vast glorified barn with one end offering up a tantalizing semi-circle of daylight and open space. Frankly, I don't know what Isambard Kingdom Brunel was thinking. I couldn't wait to be away, but since the train wasn't yet boarding, I went on a hunt for the bronze statue of Paddington Bear, which proved elusive. In the end, I gave up and went to the first-class lounge, where I availed myself of the first-class toilet, which was worth the ticket price all by itself. They had two types of hand lotion and theatre lights around the mirror. I touched up my lipstick, tucked away the few strands of hair that had blown loose in the Tube tunnels, pouted, and felt generally good about the girl who pouted back. She was wearing a fuchsia vest top with a sea-green A-line skirt – thin, floaty and falling just above her knees. It was a bold combination, but well judged, and clearly the most vivid colouring her skin tone would allow. The large pale pink flower on her hairclip sang of summer, while her glasses added just the right note of quirky bookishness. Her footwear wasn't quite visible in the mirror, but I suspected she was wearing turquoise sandals with heels large enough to lengthen her legs, but modest enough to suit the gaze of an ageing professor of evolutionary science. Her earrings and bracelets were also turquoise.

Satisfied that everything was just so, I picked up my laptop bag from beside the sink – black, unfortunately; white would have worked much better – and went to find my train.

It was all going very well for the first fifteen minutes. I drank one cup of coffee and got an immediate refill. I found and ordered two new laptop bags, one in white and one in taupe. I made small talk with the woman opposite as the semi-detacheds of Berkshire blurred across the window. She laughed when I told her she looked a bit like the Queen. I was having a perfectly harmonious journey until Slough, where three men entered our carriage and seated themselves at the table across the aisle.

I could tell straight away that they were dickheads. They were suited and sweating, and began talking loudly about the wholesale price of meat and last quarter's net profits and their BMWs and some fresh-out-of-school administrator that one of them was apparently banging like a drum at carnival time. I rolled my eyes and tutted quietly at the Queen, but she had her eyes fixed on the *Daily Telegraph* in a valiant attempt to ignore them. I decided to do the same, and set to typing a plan for a top ten train stations in film and/or literature. It was June, so a travel feature was certain to sell. MSN would probably snap my hand off.

1) Grand Central – *North by Northwest*. 2) King's Cross – *Harry Potter*. 3) What was the station in *Brief Encounter*? 4) I'm a big fan of Paddington Bear, but I can't really put Paddington Station in there, however wonderful the toilet. 5) Why can't they shut the fuck up and let me concentrate? It's a beautiful day for a

train journey and they're ruining it for every other person in this carriage. 6) Gare Montparnasse – *Hugo*.

Then the ticket inspector arrived, and my ears pricked up. For a moment, it seemed I was to be saved.

'What do you mean not valid?'

'I'm very sorry,' she repeated, 'but these are advance tickets. They're only valid on the stated train. This is the 10.36.'

'Yes, I realize this is the 10.36, love. We got to the station earlier than expected, which is why we're on the earlier train.' It was the largest and sweatiest of the meat men. He was speaking in the slow, patronizing voice usually reserved for the very young, the very old, or the very foreign. 'Anyway, the man behind the information desk at Slough told us these tickets were definitely valid for this train. If they aren't, it's his mistake not ours.'

The ticket inspector looked towards the door at the far end of the carriage, as if imploring for back-up. At the same time, the meat man winked smugly at his two sweaty colleagues. I tried to beam supportive thoughts into the ticket collector's head: *stand firm, tell him he's a lying bastard, call the transport police.*

'I'm sorry, but it's very unlikely that you were told that. Perhaps you misheard?' She was being far too gracious. 'The simple fact is that you don't have a valid ticket for this train. None of you do. You'll have to buy replacements.'

'*Buy* replacements? Because of someone else's incompetence? You've got to be joking!'

'If you wish to make a formal complaint you'll have to put it in writing to central office. They'll decide if the fare should be refunded.'

'Oh, what's the bloody point? Your man in Slough will just deny it.' He pulled out his wallet and slapped it on the table with the kind of indignation that only those feigning insult can manage. 'Well? How much?'

The ticket collector tapped at her machine. 'Three first-class singles to Hereford comes to two hundred and sixty-two pounds and fifty pence.'

'*How* much?'

'You can move to standard if you'd prefer. Then it's only one hundred and twelve pounds.'

'One hundred and twelve pounds! To sit in steerage? That's literally highway robbery!'

This jumble of metaphors, cliché and appalling English was the last straw.

'Oh, for God's sake!' Four sets of eyes swung in my direction. 'A highway is a road, steerage is a nautical term, this is a train, and you're being an absolute arsehole!'

I didn't say it in a hostile way, but just as a self-evident list of facts; I borrowed my sister's telephone voice. Nevertheless, the meat man's face went lobster pink. 'This has nothing to do with you, sweetheart.' He was trying to do alpha male, but sounded more like a sullen adolescent. 'Keep your opinions to yourself.'

'Ha!' My laugh was genuine, possibly borderline hysterical, but I couldn't help it. It was such a ridiculous thing for *him* to say. I turned to look at the ticket inspector, giving her my warmest smile. 'You know, I saw him wink at his buddies – just after that bullshit about being given inaccurate advice at the information desk. I can write you a statement if you like. How much is the fine for deliberate fare evasion?' She looked at the meat man and arched an eyebrow. He looked as if he'd just been kicked in the balls. 'Or maybe he'd prefer just to buy a valid ticket – for *steerage* – and keep his mouth shut for the rest of the journey?'

If life were a film, this would have been the moment when the rest of the carriage broke into spontaneous applause. If it were an American film, there would have been some whooping too, and maybe an involved 'You go, girl!' But this was reality and I was in Britain, the land that invented social awkwardness. I got nothing. Most of the other passengers had already averted their eyes from this unseemly public confrontation. The Queen looked mortified. The ticket inspector cleared her throat and returned the carriage to some semblance of normality. 'Er, yes. I think the young lady is probably right.'

The meat man shot me a look that said this wasn't over. I shot a look back that told him I was getting off at Oxford and had no intention of ever visiting Hereford, much less Slough, so it was. Anyway, his associates were already up and getting their briefcases from the luggage rack. I flashed him a catty smile and went back to my top ten stations.

PROFESSOR CABORN

I smoked a cigarette at Oxford Station and then looked up the number for the Department of Experimental Psychology. My plan was to phone reception to try to get a pinpoint on Professor Caborn's whereabouts. I would say I was an old colleague. But this was the full extent of my plan. I had absolute confidence that I'd be able to wing the conversation and everything would fall into place.

A couple of rings.

'Hello? Psychology – Sarah speaking.'

'Oh, hello, Sarah. My name is Julia. I'm trying to track down Joseph Caborn. I'm an old colleague of his. From Liverpool.' (God bless you, Wikipedia!)

'Joseph Caborn?'

'Yes.'

'I think he's in his office. Just a moment, I'll put you through.'

'No! No thank you, Sarah, but, well, I'd actually prefer it if he doesn't know I'm coming. We worked together a while back. Actually, I was one of his Ph.D. students four, no *five* years ago.

I haven't seen him since. I've just got back from Uganda and I'd really like to surprise him.'

'Oh.' A brief pause. 'What did you say your name was?'

'Julia. Dr Julia' – I searched for a likely surname – 'Walters.'

'Julia . . . Walters? Julie Walters?'

Shit. 'Oh, yes. Ha ha! No relation.' I found my feet. 'Sorry, I get this all the time. Phone calls are always a nightmare.'

'Yes, I can imagine.'

'I'm just thankful my surname isn't Roberts.'

Sarah laughed. Good: despite a shaky start, she was starting to relax. Charm and self-assurance – they can't teach you these things on a journalism degree.

'Sarah, I'm in Oxford, as you will have gathered, and I have a spare couple of hours. So I was planning to pop in to see if Joseph wants to grab a bite to eat. I'm going to come over now. Is that okay?'

'Um, well . . . If you're a friend I'm sure it will be fine.'

'Oh, yes. We used to be very good friends.' Too suggestive; I didn't want her to think there was anything funny going on. 'Actually, I suppose Joseph has always been more of a mentor to me. Almost everything I know about primatology came from him.' I was extremely proud of this line. Not only was it a good recovery, but it was also, technically, true. 'You won't tell him I'm coming, though? As I said, I'd really like to surprise him.'

'Er, no. My lips are sealed. He should be in his office until at least midday.'

'Thank you, Sarah. I'll see you very shortly.'

We said our goodbyes and I hung up.

*

I followed my GPS map through central Oxford, admired the dreaming spires, and thought a bit more about Dr Julia Walters. The telephone conversation had gone pretty well, but I knew I'd have to be even sharper in person. I needed to inhabit my character. I couldn't afford any blips.

So what did I know about her already? She'd done her Ph.D. under Professor Caborn five years ago. That made her thirtyish – easily within my range. She'd graduated from Liverpool, though she would have done her undergrad degree at Cambridge, I decided.

What else? She was a primatologist, apparently, and a snappy dresser, evidently – too snappy to make a convincing scientist, perhaps. Oh, well. Not much I could do about that now. She'd have to be one of those rare science babes they find to present documentaries on BBC Four. It wasn't difficult to imagine her dabbling in broadcasting. Maybe that's what she was doing in Uganda?

Hmm. Now that I thought about it, Uganda was another hole I'd dug for myself. On the one hand, the lie was exceptionally smart – lot of monkeys in Uganda – on the other, it was exceptionally problematic. Where the hell was Julia's suntan? I briefly considered nipping into a salon for a swift spray-on, but there wasn't the time. I'd told Sarah I was on my way. Much better if Dr Walters simply can't tan. She has to slap on the factor 50 or she burns like a vampire. Plus I never said how long she'd been in Uganda. Maybe it was just a couple of days. Maybe she was like Professor Brian Cox and just flew to exotic locations to film a thirty-second soundbite then hopped on the next plane home.

By the time I'd walked the mile or so to the psychology building, Julia Walters had a biography so intricate it could have been a Christmas bestseller. She was the second daughter of Paul and Annette Walters. Her father was a surgeon, her mother a human rights lawyer. She loved Thai food and was having a messy affair with her producer. And of course none of this was likely to come up in casual conversation. But it helped just to know it. It meant that when I walked up to reception, I *was* Julia Walters.

There was only one woman sitting behind the desk, so that removed the first potential obstacle straight away. I held out my hand and smiled. 'Sarah? Hello. Julia Walters. It's a pleasure to meet you. Awful day to be stuck behind a desk.'

It turned out that Julia was also quite a chatterbox.

Sarah smiled back and took my hand. If she was at all surprised by the young, fair, fuchsia-clad doctor of primatology she found herself greeting, she gave no sign. I think I introduced myself with so much aplomb she had no choice but to be swept along in the colossal fantasy I'd unleashed.

We chatted for a few minutes. I laughed and joked and gesticulated, made a couple of casual remarks about the job I'd just landed in Manchester. ('The north suits my complexion!')

Uganda, sadly, never came up.

Up the stairs, two lefts, a right, another left. The Department of Experimental Psychology turned out to be something of a maze. I never would have found Professor Caborn's office without Sarah's excellent directions. She would have shown me through herself, she said, were it not for the fact that she was the only person on reception and could not desert her post. This came as a relief. I felt that Sarah and I had bonded over the course of our two brief conversations, and the thought of her uncovering my deception was not a pleasant one.

I passed a few people in the corridors. I strode confidently and made eye contact, smiled a polite, professional smile. The reassuring click of my heels echoed off the bare walls and floor.

There was a toilet en route, where I took a couple of minutes to freshen up and reconfigure my mindset. I checked my appearance in the mirror – still fabulous – splashed cold water on my pulse points, urinated, and left Dr Walters in the cubicle like a forgotten umbrella. I was all Abigail again as I approached Professor Caborn's office – the first of six on an unremarkable corridor illuminated by two fluorescent strips. His name was on the door in simple black lettering, just above a narrow rectangular window. But I wouldn't have needed the sign; peering through the glass, I was able to extrapolate the back of his head from the photo I'd seen on his webpage. His hair was pearly white with just a touch of burned-charcoal grey at the temples. His shirtsleeves were rolled up to the elbows. He was in a swivel chair at his computer, the screen commanding his full attention. I watched him for several moments, then checked my watch: 11.58; perfect timing. I straightened my back and knocked briskly on his door.

'Come in.' He said this before he'd started to spin his chair, and by the time he'd finished the half-turn, I was already in the room, greeting him with my most disarming smile.

'Professor Caborn.' I extended my hand and walked the three paces to his chair so he didn't have to get up. 'How nice to see you. Please forgive the intrusion.'

'Er . . . no intrusion. I was just tidying up my inbox.' He glanced at our clasped hands through oval spectacles, his forehead wrinkling. His lips were slightly parted, framed by his small, tidy beard. 'Um, can I help you?'

'Yes, I very much hope so. I'm Abigail.'

'Oh, yes. Abigail . . .' Professor Caborn withdrew his hand. He had the look of a man who had walked into a film halfway through and was trying to get a handle on the plot. I kept smiling, reassuringly. He returned the smile, then cleared his throat, very delicately. 'I'm sorry: I feel like I should know who you are, but I don't. I'm afraid I'm not very good with faces.'

I laughed. 'That's quite all right. We haven't met. You recognize me from my profile picture. I've emailed you a few times. Abigail Williams. I've come to take you to lunch.'

'Oh. That's . . . odd.'

I shrugged. 'Are you hungry?'

'Um, maybe a little. I'm not quite sure. This is . . . Abigail, would you take a seat for a moment?' He gestured to the other chair in his office. It was against the wall, between an overfilled bookcase and a teetering stack of journals.

'Yes, thank you. That's very kind. I've just walked from the train station and I could do with taking the weight off my feet.'

'Where have you come from?'

'London.'

'Just to see me?'

'It's only an hour. Not very far.'

'Yes, but still. It's . . .' He trailed off.

'Odd?'

'Yes. Odd.'

This conversation was going nowhere fast. I decided to lay my cards on the table. 'Professor Caborn. I woke up at three o'clock this morning and decided to take a punt. I've come here hoping that you can spare just a small portion of your day to talk to me. But if you don't want to, that's fine too. I'm perfectly prepared to hop on the next train back to London, and I promise you'll never hear from me again. Just say the word.'

Professor Caborn didn't say a thing. He looked like a man

who'd been asked for his interpretation of an unyielding piece of modern art, all primary colours and abstruse geometry. I took his silence as leave to continue.

'Good. I can see you're at least interested.'

He put a hand to his chin and glanced away for a few seconds as if turning this statement over in his mind, assessing its validity.

I waited. A few more moments passed.

'Coffee,' he said eventually.

'Coffee?'

'I think I could manage a coffee.'

'Wonderful.' I rose from my chair. 'So let's go get a coffee. And maybe some cake?'

Professor Caborn nodded, slowly, as if in a trance.

I gestured to the door with my open palm. 'Are you ready?'

'Er, yes. I suppose I am.' He switched off his monitor, stood up, and parked the swivel chair neatly under his computer desk.

'Oh. Just one more thing,' I said. 'Will we be going out via reception?'

'Yes.'

'Can I ask you a small favour? Sarah, the receptionist: well, I'm not especially proud of this, but I wasn't sure she'd let just anyone in to see you. So I told her we were old colleagues, from Liverpool.'

Professor Caborn digested this information. 'I suppose that should seem odd too, but given everything else . . .' He shrugged. 'Fine. So we're old colleagues. Anything else I should know?'

'Yes: I also told her my name was Dr Julia Walters.'

'Dr Julia Walters?'

'Yes. I'm a primatologist. You supervised my Ph.D. That's how we know each other. Please don't contradict this. She seemed nice and I'd hate to embarrass her.'

Professor Caborn sighed at length. 'Tell me, Abigail. Is this a normal day for you? Because it isn't for me. I just wanted you to know that.'

I could see where he was coming from, of course; on reflection, some of my actions that morning had been slightly eccentric. But what choice had he left me? I'd tried to arrange a meeting by conventional means. That had failed, so I'd decided to get a bit creative. Standard journalistic practice.

'This isn't an entirely *ab*normal day for me,' I told him.

Then we went for coffee.

'I suppose you must need that?' Professor Caborn twitched a nervous forefinger at my double espresso. 'You mentioned you've been up since three. Unless you go to bed unusually early, I can't imagine you've had much sleep.'

I did the calculation in my head. 'Three hours ten minutes, I think. Give or take. But I suppose it must have been deep sleep. It was one of those mornings when I just woke up fresh as a daisy. They happen to me sometimes, especially in the summer. I think it must be something to do with the light. That was something I was going to ask you about, actually. I have a theory – a hypothesis – that I'm hoping you might substantiate.'

I smiled. I was letting my mouth run a bit, but I was confident that at least some of what I was coming out with might interest him. It was sciencey. We'd already covered the basic pleasantries: Oxford, the beautiful weather, the equally beautiful parkland that enveloped the Department of Experimental Psychology. But Professor Caborn still seemed slightly wary of me. I thought that talking science might help him to relax, and my insomnia seemed a relatively benign place to begin. I didn't want to jump straight in at the deep end and start talking about Simon's corpse.

'So, my bedroom window faces east,' I went on, 'and my curtains are lousy, so summer is always a big problem. The room starts getting bright from about three in the morning, and by four, you might as well be trying to sleep in a solarium.'

Professor Caborn processed this metaphor, then nodded that I should continue.

'I've been thinking about evolution recently,' I told him, 'mostly on account of your work, and it got me wondering about how our minds have evolved – or haven't evolved – to cope with extended daylight in the summer. I mean, we all came out of Africa, right, not so long ago, so presumably we're not adapted to these big seasonal variations? Now that I think about it, I'm fairly sure I've always suffered with sleeping in the summer, whereas I can be a real dormouse in the winter. Perhaps I should hibernate?'

Professor Caborn didn't give me an answer to any of these questions straight away. Maybe it was just that he was an exceptionally deep thinker, and refused to open his mouth until he had every detail of his reply mapped out. Or maybe I was being rather impatient. In any case, his response seemed to take an unnecessary amount of time. I tapped my nails in sequence on the tabletop. Then, eventually, he said, 'Tell me: how much do you know about circadian rhythms?'

I answered instantly. 'I've heard of them. However, it's probably best if you assume, from this point on, that my knowledge of science is extremely limited. I think I understand how the toaster works, but not the microwave. Imagine that you're talking to an intelligent twelve-year-old.'

'Oh.' Professor Caborn thought for a few more moments. 'Well. Microwaves work by agitating the hydrogen atoms in water molecules. Food contains water, microwaves wobble some of the atoms in that water, and this makes the food hot. As for circadian rhythms, they refer to all the processes in animals and plants that recur on a cycle of approximately twenty-four hours. The normal sleeping-waking cycle is one such process. It is affected by light, in that light is one of the cues that inform our body clock. But because seasonal changes happen very slowly, we have plenty of time to get used to them, so few people are adversely affected. It's possible, of course, that you're unusually photosensitive. Or maybe something else is causing you to wake and then the morning sunlight is preventing you from getting back to sleep. Either way, you should probably get some thicker curtains.'

I nodded intently. I should have put up thicker curtains a couple of years ago, when Beck and I first moved in together. But I'd never seen the flat as anything more than a temporary arrangement, a halfway house on the road to better things. Changing the curtains would have meant conceding that we were there for the long haul. Even now, I wasn't sure I felt ready to do this.

'You know,' Professor Caborn was saying, 'one of my colleagues, one of my *real* colleagues' – he gave a small chuckle, which I supposed was a good thing; it meant he was coming to terms with the rather unorthodox way in which I'd engineered our meeting – 'he once did some research into the effect of light cues on sleeping patterns. Basically, it involved isolating a couple of dozen volunteers for an extended period. They were kept in a completely sealed environment: no clocks, no daylight, no external clues whatsoever regarding the passage of time. His aim was to see if he could force them to adapt to an alternative sleeping-waking cycle, one based on an eighteen-hour day. They were given six hours of total darkness and twelve hours of bright light on a continual loop. It made a certain amount of sense as most people spend about one-third of their time asleep.'

Professor Caborn seemed to drift off for a few moments, lost in thought. In the end, I had to prompt him. 'So, what happened? Did it work?'

'Oh, no, of course not. It was a total disaster. The twenty-four-hour clock is hardwired – that point was strongly reaffirmed. Within a week over half the subjects were experiencing hallucinations. Three of them developed full-blown psychosis. It all got rather messy towards the end. Of course, this was back in the 1970s. It was the era of the Stanford Prison Experiment and the like. Health and safety was an alien concept. Still, on the eighth day my colleague decided enough was enough and pulled the plug.' Professor Caborn sighed heavily, then seemed to snap to, remembering where he was. 'The point, as I'm sure you'll see, is that you can't take too many liberties with sleep. Not without suffering consequences.'

'Hmm.' Interesting as this sideline was, I'd decided it was time to move our conversation forward. 'Professor Caborn. Let me tell you how I came to stumble on your work. It's related to the insomnia in a slightly tangential way. My sleeping problems started about a month ago, when I found my neighbour's body . . .'

So, for the fourth time in as many weeks, I found myself giving a full account of that evening in Simon's flat. Professor Caborn didn't say a word. He just listened with his forehead creased, taking an occasional sip of coffee as I talked and talked. I was now very adept at telling the story. In truth, it felt like I was telling someone else's story, in the same way that Professor Caborn could recount the details of his colleague's sleep

105

experiment. There was a certain amount of tension and drama woven through the narrative, but I still felt curiously insulated from the events I was recollecting.

By the time I'd finished, Professor Caborn's lips were pursed in concentration 'Let me check if I have this correct,' he said after a few moments. 'You found your neighbour dead. It was a strange but otherwise not very emotional experience. That night you couldn't sleep. You happened upon some of my work, and now you're in Oxford because . . . Actually, I'm still not entirely clear on this point. You're here because . . . you're trying to make some sense of this?'

I thought about this for a couple of seconds. The connection between Simon's death and my being in Oxford seemed perfectly obvious in my head, but this didn't mean it was easy to explain to someone else. 'I'm not sure I'm trying to make sense – not exactly. It's more that I found your ideas interesting and felt compelled to follow them up. You see, this isn't really my field. I'm not a scientist.' I jangled my turquoise bracelets, as if providing the necessary evidence to corroborate this claim. 'Usually, I write about books, poetry, the odd bit of light cultural analysis. So this is a departure for me. I suppose I'm trying to examine this odd experience of mine as something that could only happen in a modern, urban context. I mean, for most of human history we must have lived in tight little communities. If your neighbour died – if anyone died – if you found yourself in the presence of a body, it would mean something. It would have some kind of emotional resonance. But what I experienced instead was this, this . . . I don't know what. There's probably not even a name for it.'

'Cognitive dissonance?' Professor Caborn suggested. 'Are you familiar with the term?'

'No, but I understand what the words mean. They seem rather apt.'

'Hmm.' Professor Caborn tapped his teaspoon against the rim of his empty coffee cup, then said, 'Cognitive dissonance is the term psychologists use to describe a state of conflicting thoughts or emotions.'

'Like ambivalence?'

'No, it's stronger than ambivalence. It's more like trying to hold two mutually exclusive beliefs or feelings about the world. So in your case, for example, you hold a deep-rooted belief that life has, or *should* have, a certain value. But then you're confronted with a situation that seems to contradict this. The result is a conflict of two opposing ideas. Cognitive dissonance. And this is likely to be felt more keenly if you usually think of yourself as a very moral or sensitive person.'

'Hmm . . . I'm not sure I'd go that far.'

'Or just a generally good person?'

'Yes, perhaps. More good than bad.' Today, at least, this seemed a plausible conjecture. 'Cognitive dissonance.' I tried the words aloud to hear how they sounded. 'Would you say that's a . . . normal response to finding your neighbour's corpse?'

Professor Caborn considered this for some time. 'No, probably not. I mean, in a sense, cognitive dissonance is *always* an abnormal response – from a subjective standpoint. I shouldn't worry too much about it, though. Concentrate on trying to get a good night's sleep.'

I stared at my finished espresso. This seemed like good advice.

DEATH IN THE AFTERNOON

The journey back from Oxford was pleasant and uneventful. Plenty of coffee, plenty of leg room, no meat men to spoil things. Reviewing everything Professor Caborn had told me, I still didn't know, specifically, what my article was going to be about, but this didn't worry me in the slightest. When I closed my eyes, I could see a hundred possibilities sparkling like diamonds in a mine. It was just a case of selecting a handful and fashioning them into a necklace of astonishing brilliance. I smiled at this image and resolved not to think about work until the evening. Instead, with my eyes still tightly shut, I turned to the window and felt the warmth of the afternoon sun flickering through the trees and hedgerows, a series of golden flashes as bright and bewitching as sheet lightning.

At Paddington, I called Dr Barbara from the first-class lounge, having decided I needed to catch her while things were still fresh in my mind. Voicemail, inevitably. It was office hours and she'd be with a client. But a message would do just as well.

'Dr Barbara. It's Abby. Have you heard of cognitive dissonance?

I expect you have. I've just met an evolutionary psychologist who was telling me about it. He says it's rare but I think I experience it at least two or three times a week. We shall talk about it at our next appointment – which I'm very much looking forward to. Cheerio.'

I thought Dr Barbara would be pleased; it was such a neatly worded and interesting message. And it was so nice to be able to call her and *not* be in the middle of a crisis.

This whole day had been an unqualified triumph from the start, and it was not yet four o'clock! As I left the lounge, I resolved that from now on I would only ever travel first class. Anything less seemed such a waste.

We wouldn't normally have had the ingredients to mix a recognizable cocktail, but I had the foresight to stop at the off licence on the way home. A Google search while browsing the spirits turned up a list of about two hundred recipes to choose from. I made a shortlist of cocktails with names I liked, then whittled this list further by eliminating anything too complicated, too boring or that involved raw eggs, and eventually settled on Death in the Afternoon – a shot of absinthe served straight up with chilled champagne. It had been invented by Hemingway, and while I was not a huge fan of Hemingway's writing, I certainly admired his willingness to push the alcohol envelope. Unfortunately, it transpired that the off licence only had cava, but the result was still pretty much as Wikipedia suggested it should be: the mixture frothed, emulsified, and within a few seconds had turned opalescent.

When Beck arrived home, I was waiting for him in the kitchen like a dutiful housewife. He held the tumbler I thrust into his hand in a long, contemplative silence, before saying, 'Um, what's this?'

'It's Death in the Afternoon,' I explained. 'I'm not going to tell you the ingredients because I want you to guess.'

'No, that's not really what I meant,' he clarified. 'Are we celebrating something?'

I laughed and patted his arm. 'Maybe. I don't know. I got my interview with Professor Caborn. I went to see him in Oxford. So there's my next article.'

'Professor Caborn . . . The monkey guy?'

'That's right. The monkey guy.'

'Oh. That's . . . good, I guess. I thought he was ignoring you. What changed?'

'Nothing changed. I had to get creative.' I gestured with both hands in an expansive flowing motion that began at my shoulders and ended at my hemline. 'I made myself harder to ignore.'

At this point, I launched into an intricate and engaging account of my day. I didn't tell Beck about first class as he could be quite uptight about those little indulgences, but other than that, all the details were there. It felt as if I were telling a story full of interesting and amusing twists, but when I'd come to a standstill, Beck just nodded, a strange look of concentration on his face. He took a small sip from his tumbler – his first – and immediately gagged. 'Jesus Christ! Is that Pernod and champagne?'

'No, it's absinthe and cava. The off licence didn't have champagne. Don't look at me like that; it's a recognized cocktail. Hemingway invented it, hence the name.'

Beck set his drink back down on the table. 'Abby, listen. How are you feeling?' He said it in a slightly ominous way that made me want to laugh.

'I'm fine. I'm more than fine: I'm great.'

'Okay. But this is all . . . I mean, champagne, sudden trips to Oxford – it's all a bit—'

I clamped my hands on his cheeks and kissed him on the lips, as this seemed the most efficient way to shut him up. 'I'm fine,' I repeated. 'It's cava, not champagne. And it wasn't a *sudden* trip to Oxford. I've been trying to set up this meeting for a month. Conventional means failed so I took a punt. And it paid off. Jess has already said she'll buy the article – she's even mentioned the possibility of a column. I feel good and I have every reason to.'

'Yes, but . . .' Beck unconsciously reached for his tumbler, raised it to his lips, wrinkled his nose, and set it back down again. 'I just don't want you to overdo things. It's been a diffi-cult month; you need to take things slowly, at least for the next couple of days. Rest. Try to get a full night's sleep.'

I rolled my eyes indulgently. He was being a little patronizing, but I had no intention of ruining the day with an argument. 'Fine,' I said. 'I'll slow down. I'll make sure I get plenty of sleep. And in return, I want you to relax a bit. Drink your cocktail. Trust me: it's an acquired taste but definitely worth the effort.'

Beck frowned again at his tumbler. He did not look convinced.

The problem, of course, was that it was all very well saying that I'd try to get a full night's sleep, but I couldn't just flick a switch and make it happen. I got up as soon as Beck had drifted off, around midnight. It felt ludicrous to be creeping around in the darkness again, but never mind. It was far too difficult to make him understand. Being awake half the night was only an issue if you chose to make it one. If I slept for three to five hours and it was deep, refreshing sleep, then surely that was enough?

It seemed enough. I would only 'suffer' with my sleeplessness if I spent too much time in bed worrying about not sleeping. It made far more sense to stay up until I was actually tired and had some chance of sleeping through for a decent stretch.

This turned out to be impeccable logic. I worked until 3.30, went to bed as the sun was coming up, woke at 8.32, and set about taking down the curtains. Beck had already left at this point – presumably, he hadn't wanted to wake me – so there was no reason not to get straight to work. My sleeping hygiene needed a complete overhaul, especially now that I'd decided to focus on quality rather than quantity. And Professor Caborn was right: the curtains were the obvious place to start. I'd put up with them for over two years, but now their number was up. I yanked them down and stuffed them into a large refuse sack which I tied with a triple knot. It felt wonderfully liberating, like walking out on a failed relationship with no thought of keeping in touch.

An hour later, I was washed, dressed and on my way to the shops. I had dispatched the curtains to the bottom of our wheelie bin with not a moment of regret. Since they were not fit for purpose, I didn't even think of taking them to a charity shop; it would have been an extremely irresponsible thing to do, like passing on that cursed video tape from *The Ring*.

The replacement drapes I had in my head were so clear and vibrant I felt as if I could already reach out and touch them. They were essentially the curtains from Jane Eyre's childhood: a heavy cascade of velvet, the red of clotted blood and so thick they could have stopped a bullet. But when I got to Shepherd's Bush Market, I found that the soft furnishings store had no such fabric. Furthermore, the vendor was far from helpful in dealing with my request.

'It can't be that difficult,' I told him. 'I want dark red velvet curtains to cover a window one hundred and twelve by one hundred and thirty centimetres. There must be somewhere in London I can get them.'

The vendor snorted. 'Try Knightsbridge.'

He was trying to be rude, of course; but actually, this didn't seem like such a ridiculous suggestion. The best alternative I could come up with was to try all the home stores in Westfield. But it was another glorious summer's day, and the thought of being cooped up in a shopping centre made me want to howl.

So a couple of Tube rides and Google searches later, I found myself in Laura Ashley Home, where I bought the perfect set of deep-pleated velvet blackout curtains in maroon. They cost £229, which seemed reasonable given that I'd never bought curtains before, and assumed that a good pair should last me a lifetime. I arranged to have them delivered by courier after five o'clock – since now I was in central London, I intended to spend the day there. I figured it would be a crime to come to Knightsbridge and not at least *look* in some of the clothes shops.

First, though, I sent a text message to my sister asking if she wanted to meet for lunch. I'd ignored three texts and a voicemail since Monday, but now I thought she'd suffered enough. I wasn't a million miles from her work, and it felt like a day for new beginnings. Plus I didn't feel like lunching alone. After a rapid SMS negotiation, she agreed to meet me at one. Then I headed up the road to Harvey Nichols.

I didn't so much find the dress as the dress found me. It drew my gaze from across the store: cobalt blue, satin, spaghetti straps; a just-above-the-knee hemline that would do wonders for my legs, a neckline that I could certainly get away with, as long as I was wearing the right bra.

As soon as I tried it on, I knew I couldn't bear to put it back – not only in the sense that I'd decided to buy it, but also in the sense that I intended to wear it home. The only hitch was that today I *wasn't* wearing the right bra; I'd have to go strapless, and a bit of extra padding couldn't hurt, either. But it wasn't as if the situation I found myself in was insurmountable, or even particularly difficult. One of the assistants escorted me to the lingerie department, where I found the perfect add-two-cups, multiway push-up to complement the outfit. Ten minutes later, I left Harvey Nichols with my credit limit depleted by another £640 and a plan to earn the money back in no time at all. Already crystallizing in my mind were the templates for two new articles, both very sellable.

1) 'Which Blue is Right for You?' (600 words.)

I knew the two blues that worked best for me: baby blue and cobalt. The former matched my eyes and the latter was very flattering to my skin. But blue was such a versatile colour; there was a shade that suited every conceivable combination of hair colour, eye colour, complexion and occasion. I could think of another dozen hues just off the top of my head: navy, azure, ultramarine, true blue, royal blue, Oxford blue, powder blue, cornflower blue, midnight blue, ice blue, sky blue, Pacific blue. Some of these blues might be difficult to distinguish in a line-up, but the point still stood. Carefully chosen, there was no reason why the little blue dress shouldn't be as central to every woman's wardrobe as its black counterpart. It packed the same flexibility with an adventurous, modern punch.

2) 'Dress-Up Friday.' (At least 800 words.)

This idea was basically a write-up of the fashion experiment I was now performing: eveningwear as daywear. After all, what was the point of limiting yourself? On the right sort of day, a cocktail dress could make an ideal outfit for the park, or even the supermarket. It felt magnificent to be wearing something so electrifying, so arresting, for no particular occasion. I felt I was making the day even brighter, and not just for me. Everyone I passed on the street was benefiting too. I was bringing a vivid splash of colour to what might otherwise have been a very run-of-the-mill Friday lunchtime.

So, 1,400 words, minimum; factor in the tax benefits – since my purchases were now work-related – and I was already making a profit. With a little imagination, I could probably find a way to make the curtains pay for themselves too. 'Contemporary Furnishings Inspired by Literature', or something along those lines. It wouldn't be the biggest earner in the history of journalism, but I felt sure that someone would buy it.

I met my sister in a posh pizzeria not far from Leicester Square. It had a huge, ostentatious wood oven, visible through glass doors, and the pizzas were being fed in by two burly men with snow shovels. I was only a few minutes late – ten at the most – but Francesca was already seated, and already looked impatient, as if I were keeping her from something dreadfully important, which no doubt I was.

I smiled and waved; she did a theatrical double-take, then rolled her eyes skyward. 'Oh, Abby! What on earth are you wearing?'

I kissed her on the cheek, then stepped back and did a little twirl. 'Do you like it?'

'It looks expensive.'

I beamed. 'Francesca, it *was* expensive.'

'I thought you were struggling?'

'No, not so much any more. I'm getting a weekly column – probably.'

'Probably?'

'Almost certainly.'

My sister nodded knowingly. 'Right. So you haven't signed a contract? You haven't actually been paid yet?'

'I have lots of other work lined up too.'

'It's a bit much, don't you think?'

She was back on the dress, her eyes flicking between the sculpted flare of my hips and the misleading promise of my cleavage. I shrugged and gestured at her plain white blouse, her drab grey trousers: even with the temperature nudging twenty-seven degrees, Francesca refused to get her legs out; she thought it would undermine her status in the office. 'I wanted to make absolutely sure we wouldn't be wearing the same outfit,' I told her.

'I think it's safe to say that no one else in London is wearing that outfit at this precise moment,' she retorted. 'You know, you're getting a lot of looks.'

'Good. It's a social experiment. I'm trying to find out if people treat me differently, if my day is improved by wearing evening-wear instead of casual wear. Whether it makes it easier to get a seat on the Tube – that sort of thing.'

'My God! You're not going to wear that on the Tube?'

'Already have. It felt fabulous.'

'Yes, but what if it gets damaged?'

'Damaged how?'

'I don't know – caught in a door or something.'

I giggled. 'Fran, you're so endearingly uptight. You're like one of those women who refuses to take the plastic covering off her new furniture.' She scowled as I patted her hand across the table. 'Relax. Let's get some drinks. I've discovered the most incredible cocktail. Death in the Afternoon: it's absinthe and champagne. I'm buying.'

Francesca's scowl deepened. 'Abby, that's *not* a cocktail. You've made it up. Who in their right mind would drink something like that?'

'Hemingway. Google it.'

'I don't need to Google it. I'm not drinking. Some of us have to work.'

'Oh, don't be such a martyr. I have to work too. In fact, I'm working right now.' I hooked a thumb under one of my spaghetti straps and gave it a satisfying twang. 'It's just that I have a much more interesting job than you.'

'Yes, well, that's rather subjective. I happen to like my job. It's challenging and stimulating, and there's a lot of room to develop—'

'Christ! You sound like you're citing the vacancies page.'

Francesca snarled. 'You don't even know what I do – not really.'

'That's because I fall asleep whenever you try to explain it to me.'

'Abby, what's this all about? Are you still pissed off about last weekend?'

'No, absolutely not. All forgotten.'

'Really? Because it seems like you've invited me to lunch with the sole intention of insulting me.'

'Of course I haven't. Don't be so sensitive.'

'So why *are* we doing this?'

'Does there have to be a reason? I was in the area and felt like having lunch with my sister. What's so odd about that?'

Francesca arched an eyebrow but remained silent.

'Look,' I continued, 'let's start again. We won't talk about work and I won't pressurize you to drink anything even remotely interesting. How does that sound?'

She looked at me for a very long time, as if she wanted to say something else but doubted the wisdom of it. Then she just exhaled and nodded. 'Fine. You can get me another Perrier. And let's order, for God's sake. I have to be back in an hour.'

Within ten minutes, I, too, was wondering why I'd thought this lunch would be such a good idea. I'd forgotten, once again, that Francesca and I could no longer sustain a friendly conversation, no matter what topic we settled on. The tragedy was that she used to be fun, once. The twenty-two-year-old Francesca would not have turned her nose up at absinthe and champagne, as if the very suggestion were some kind of hideous cultural faux pas. It was depressing to think that in the space of eight years she'd morphed into the neutrally clad, Perrier-drinking, humourless career girl who now sat opposite. Frankly, she was putting a real dampener on my day.

Nevertheless, I endeavoured to keep our dialogue – increasingly a monologue – light and breezy. I expounded on my trip to Oxford and my suspicion that I was a chronic sufferer of cognitive dissonance. But she didn't seem to get any of this. Several times she interrupted with the most irrelevant questions – why had I turned up at Professor Caborn's workplace uninvited? Why was I suddenly so interested in monkeys? – as if I hadn't explained all this already! She obviously hadn't been paying proper attention, so I decided I should just abandon this narrative and move on. I told her about the dinner with Daddy, and how I thought Marie would make a marvellous stepmother. She told me, with her eyes, that I was being extremely immature about this whole situation. I countered that she was being far too forgiving, as always, though I supposed this was understandable since her life had been far less affected by our father's multiple failings. We fell, eventually, into a barbed silence. For my part, I'd grown tired of carrying the conversation single-handed; and Francesca seemed determined to remain distant and judgemental – even more so than usual. She kept shooting me these wary, searching looks, casting her eyes in narrowed disapproval over my beautiful blue dress. I figured she was jealous; there must have been a part of her that wished she could wear something that astonishing to work.

I left the restaurant feeling a hot dart of irritation that my midday alcohol could not quite blunt. Still, I had no intention of letting Francesca spoil things. The afternoon was young; I didn't have to be home for the best part of three hours. I decided to get a tattoo.

My logic ran thus: I'd put around £900 on my credit card today; I might as well round up so that I could draw a neat line under my spending. And since I'd indulged myself – overindulged, my sister would say – I really ought to get something for Beck. Not only would it be a nice thing to do, but it would also pre-empt, and hopefully preclude, any complaints on his part.

I already had one tattoo, a small tribal dragon curled discreetly round my right ankle. But my new tattoo would be, in some sense, even more discreet. It would be on my breast – the right-hand side of my left breast, to be precise, since that was where my heart was. Already emblazoned on my mind's eye was the pin-sharp image of what I wanted: a butterfly, not much larger than a fifty-pence piece, its wings cherry red and half unfolded, as if it had just that moment landed, or was in the split-second process of taking flight. Delicate, feminine, romantic and sexy; replete with evocative classical symbolism. It was so perfect I wanted to cry. It would be like buying him a work of art, painted on the most intimate of canvases.

I found a nice tattooist called El on the edge of Covent Garden, showed her my dragon so she'd know I wasn't a novice, and not long after, she was busy sketching the butterfly to my exact specifications.

Being tattooed on the breast, it transpired, was not significantly more painful than being tattooed on the ankle – and anyway, it was the good sort of pain, the one that sends a hot electric thrill pulsing through your flesh. Too soon I was being cleaned, salved and dressed, with strict instructions not to touch it for the next two hours, by which time the small amount of bleeding and swelling should have subsided.

I lay on the sun-drenched grass of Victoria Embankment Gardens for the next hour and a bit, until it was time to go home; and when I got back to my feet, I felt completely intoxicated, as light and free as a feather caught on the gentlest of updraughts.

I sensed something was off-kilter the second I stepped through the door. Beck was home. He came to meet me in the hallway as I stood confused and motionless by the coat hooks.

'You're back extremely early,' I noted.

'I took the afternoon off.' His expression was difficult to read.

'Who died?'

'No one died, Abby. It's nothing like that. Fran called me at work. She was worried about you. *I'm* worried about you.'

I didn't say anything. It was like a conversation in a dream. It made no sense. 'Listen. Why don't you come and sit down for a second?'

'No, I don't think I want to sit down. I think I'm perfectly happy here, thank you.'

'Abby, please.'

I shook my head petulantly.

'Okay, fine,' Beck said. 'We'll do this here.'

'Do what here? I haven't the foggiest idea what you're talking about.'

'Abby, you're manic. It's been building up for days, and now it's getting out of hand. I'm sorry: I should have said something earlier – much earlier – but I was hoping it was just a phase. I thought if I gave you some time, things might settle down of their own accord. They haven't. You need to see a doctor.'

'God! *That's* what this is about? Listen, I don't know what Fran has been telling you, but you know what she's like. She thinks she knows it all when really she doesn't have the vaguest clue what's—'

'She told me she could barely get a word in edgeways.'

I launched a laugh but he talked right over it.

'Where are the curtains?'

'The curtains?'

'The curtains – where are they?' He gestured towards the bedroom as if presenting for the jury Exhibit A.

121

'Beck, the curtains are in the wheelie bin, which is precisely where they belong. New curtains will be arriving in due course.'

'When did we discuss getting new curtains?'

'Oh, for heaven's sake! I didn't know we had to discuss it. It's not like it's a fucking   horse!'

By now, I was having to wipe the tears from my eyes. The whole situation was hysterically funny, if viewed from the proper angle.

'How much have you spent today?' Beck asked.

I put my hand to my chest and took several deep breaths to steady myself. 'Nothing. Not a penny.'

'Abby, the dress.'

'Nothing.'

'Did you pay for it or did you steal it?'

'Neither. It's all on credit. I shall pay for it next month, by which time I—'

He cut me off again. 'And where are your other clothes? The ones I assume you were wearing when you left the flat?'

'Fine! So I binned those too. They were old and tired, and I could hardly be carrying them around with me all day. You see, I've been doing this experiment.' I started to talk louder and faster to forestall his next interruption. 'No, Beck. Be quiet for a second. I have an excellent explanation for all this, which I'm sure Francesca neglected to tell you. The dress was effectively free. You see, there's a lot of money in fashion features right now, and you're forgiven for not knowing that, but—'

'Abby, stop. Please stop. Just listen to yourself. You're going a mile a minute.'

'I've costed it all out in my head, but you're welcome to check my maths if you don't believe me. If I can write around fifteen hundred words at, let's say, three to four hundred pounds per five hundred words, then – fuck it! Forget the maths. I've got something wonderful to show you.' I patted my breasts, wincing slightly, at which point Beck reached out and took my hands in his, so gently it was as if he thought I was made of china. I snapped my wrists back and raised my voice even higher. 'No, stop it! This isn't fair! You're not listening to me!'

'Abby, it's okay. Everything is going to be okay. I'm going to ring Dr Barbara. I want you to speak with her.'

'Leave Dr Barbara out of this! She's not going to take your side!'

My shout had the desired effect. Beck took a step back and held up his palms. 'Okay, okay. You don't have to do anything you're not ready for. But please come and sit down. I'll get you some water and we can talk some more. Calmly.'

I could see this was going nowhere – no choice left but to humour him. I threw my handbag to the floor and sat down right where I was in the middle of the hallway. 'Fine. Terrific. Get me a drink and I'll sit here and think of five reasons you and Francesca don't know what the hell you're talking about.'

'Okay. Good. Do that. Just sit here and I'll get you some water. I love you.'

I fixed my eyes on the carpet between my legs, a beige abomination. After a few moments, Beck nodded a couple of times, then slipped back through to the kitchen.

The instant he was out of sight, I rose silently to my feet. I picked up my handbag, stepped out of the door, and did not look back.

BETRAYAL

I take the stairs three at a time, dash through a screeching gap in the traffic, then cut a zigzagging path down a series of side streets, figuring this is a route unrepeatable in its tortuous complexity. My phone is already ringing in my bag, interminably, but I can't stop to silence it, not yet, not until I've put plenty of distance and corners between myself and the flat. I don't have a hope of blending into the crowd; my beautiful blue dress makes me far too visible. There are a dozen twists and turns before I come to a temporary, panting halt, plunge my hand into my bag, and find the off button without once glancing at the screen.

I light a cigarette and keep walking down the nondescript residential street in which I find myself. Weirdly, I have no real idea where I am, and it strikes me as a fact both startling and poignant. A few minutes of alternating turns and the city has already swallowed me. I'm no longer Abby; I'm Alice, tumbling down the rabbit hole, unable to tell up from down, left from right.

Slowly, though, I scrabble back to the surface. The nicotine clears my head and something like normality reasserts itself. It's a Friday afternoon of dazzling summer sunlight, not long past five o'clock. The sun is pretty much straight ahead, blazing in my eyes, so I guess I'm facing west, and if I take a left and keep walking, I'll get to the train track soon enough. But beyond that, no plan is forthcoming. The only solid notion is that I am not going home tonight. I feel too betrayed.

And at the same time, I feel exhilarated beyond words. Because it's not that Beck and Francesca are wrong – of course they're not wrong! They're bang on the money, but that no longer matters. When you're soaring this high, there are no thoughts of returning to earth. How could there be? Right now, my only concern is that I must be allowed to go on feeling as I'm feeling, consequences be damned.

Because there will be consequences. I know this too. This feeling can't last for ever, and that's part of its astonishing, shimmering beauty. The fallout will come, but it belongs to tomorrow, or the day after tomorrow. It has no bearing on the present, which I'll protect like a lioness guarding her cubs. The now is pure, ecstatic, simply sublime; and this is the real reason I cannot go home. I can't let anyone take this feeling away from me.

With these thoughts bursting like fireworks, I quickly comprehend the course the day must run. I can't go home, and neither can I contact any of my family or friends, who are not to be trusted. The only sensible option is to book into a hotel – somewhere nice. Anything less than five-star is unthinkable right now.

Eventually, I find myself at Turnham Green, where I board

the eastbound District for central London. After switching to
the Piccadilly at Earl's Court, I get off at Hyde Park Corner and
walk up Park Lane until I reach the Dorchester. There's a man
in a top hat and tails who opens the doors with a nod and a
smile as I approach the main entrance, confirming what I already
know: I look like I belong here. I return his smile but don't slow
my stride as I walk through the doors and cross the mirror-
polished marble floor to the reception desk, where another
immaculately pressed gentleman in a dark green blazer and
waistcoat is standing straight-backed and expectant, like a cour-
teous meerkat.

'Good afternoon,' he says. 'Welcome to the Dorchester.'

'Good afternoon.' I place my fingertips on the counter, which
is as cool as ivory and edged with gold leaf. 'I'd like a room.
One night, just for me.'

'Certainly.' He doesn't even blink – but, then, why would he?
It's not just professional poise; I expect things like this happen
all the time at the Dorchester: windswept women in cocktail
dresses, flouncing in from the street and making their demands.
Once you reach a certain level of opulence, nothing seems odd,
or even eccentric. 'What sort of room did you have in mind?'

'One with a view over the park. As high as you have available.
I want to see blue sky and open space.' My voice drips with
entitlement.

'I can offer you a Deluxe King on the eighth floor. It would
certainly meet those requirements.'

'Perfect.'

Five minutes later, I've signed a form, handed over my credit
card details, and am being transported through a wondrous
maze of softly lit corridors and antechambers. The porter reveals

not a jot of curiosity regarding my lack of luggage. We ride a lift twice as large as my bathroom in conspiratorial silence, his eyes averted and his hands clasped neatly behind his back. He holds open every door along the way, addresses me as madam as he gestures for me to pass.

My room is bright and spacious, impeccably furnished with antique furniture and a bed that could sleep a netball team. The broad window overlooks the treetops, beyond which Hyde Park shimmers like a dappled green sea. London is a spectacular city for the privileged few.

I have nothing to unpack, of course, so the first thing I do once I've taken in my environment is run myself a bath. The bathroom is like an astonishing chapel of white marble, with a tub as deep as a grave. There's light pouring through a frosted window, a spotless double sink, a wicker basket stuffed with luxury toiletries. While the water is running, I remove my phone from my handbag and wrap it in one of the spare towels. I then stow this package at the bottom of the wardrobe.

I make coffee, then undress in front of the full-length mirror. From a couple of feet away, the slight rawness of my new tattoo is no longer discernible. It's just perfect – so mesmerizing against the creamy softness of my breasts I want to cry. It's a tragedy that Beck didn't want to see it. This was a moment we were supposed to share. But it's his loss, not mine. I gave him the chance and he didn't want to know.

I steep in scalding water for the next fifteen minutes, with the throbbing ache in my left breast partially and pleasantly reignited. I wash my hair, scrub a day's worth of city grime from my skin and nails. I towel off, dry and brush my hair, reapply make-up and put in fresh contact lenses. It's too hot for clothes,

I decide – even a bathrobe – so I spend the next hour or so naked. I sit at the rosewood desk by the window and write up 'Which Blue?' on eight sheets of hotel notepaper. It's a masterpiece, needless to say – less a fashion feature than a prose poem: lyrical, playful, passionate and incisive. The sort of thing Virginia Woolf might have written had she decided to quit fiction and pawn her talents to *Cosmopolitan*. No need for a second draft; I fold and seal the article in a complimentary envelope and pop this in the side pocket of my handbag.

It's now nearly eight o'clock, but the day is still as hot and bright as a hundred-watt bulb. I'm not even remotely hungry, despite not having eaten since lunchtime. I slip back into my dress and go down to the park for a cigarette, which turns into two cigarettes. Then I head back inside for a drink.

The Dorchester Bar is all velvet upholstery and darkly polished wood, and already humming with life. Soft jazz is playing in the background, pumped in by concealed speakers. I would have liked something livelier, with a beat, but never mind. The atmosphere is elegant and moody, and for now that's enough. A suited waiter meets me in the entranceway and tells me there aren't any tables available, but I'm welcome to sit at the bar if I'd like. This is more than fine by me. I decide, in that split second, that I'd much prefer to sit at the bar, which is a sleekly curved work of art. The wall behind it is a tapestry of backlit spirits.

I order a black coffee with a shot of amaretto in it and tell the barman to charge it to my room. I don't plan on having more than a couple of drinks. Too much alcohol would dull me, and all I really want is to sit and absorb the hot pulse of the room for an hour or so. But, inevitably, this plan goes quickly astray. Before my coffee is cold, a man in an expensive-looking shirt, sleeves rolled up to his elbows, has taken the stool adjacent to mine. I can feel the heat from his eyes, burning into my cheek like the laser-sight on a rifle. I turn, fleetingly, take him in at a glance. Dark eyes, impeccably groomed, handsome in an arrogant, narcissistic sort of way. He looks around thirty-five, forty. He looks as if he probably does something well paid and immoral for a living.

'Not much fun, drinking on your own,' he says.

'How do you know I'm alone?' I shoot back. 'Maybe I'm waiting for someone.'

He shakes his head and smiles a self-satisfied smile. 'You're not waiting for anyone. I've been watching you for the last ten minutes.'

I flick my eyes back to him and shrug. Three sentences in and this conversation already feels dangerous.

'Perhaps you'd like to join me at my table,' he suggests.

'Yes,' I reply. 'Or perhaps I wouldn't.'

For most men, this would be enough, but his smile never wavers. 'You'll at least let me buy you another drink,' he says. 'Something stronger than coffee.' And I've already noticed the way he formulates his questions as statements, as if all this is already a done deal.

I should probably end this right now, but I don't. The truth is, I'm enjoying it: the power play, the mind games, the cat-and-mouse. And where's the harm in that, since I know I'm not going to take it any further?

'What are you drinking?' he asks – smugly, as if he's about to put a down payment on a sports car.

'Champagne.'

He nods blithely. 'Of course. I'll get us a bottle.'

He turns to get the barman's attention. I figure he's going to choose the champagne, and while it would be interesting to see what value he places on me, I won't give him the chance of escaping lightly. I've already made a thorough inspection of the drinks menu, before he sat down, so it only takes me a second to find the right page and jab my finger into it like a poisoned dart. 'The 1996 Dom Pérignon,' I tell him.

At £650 a bottle, it's not the most expensive champagne on the menu – but it is the most expensive champagne that I can pronounce with absolute confidence; any slip in my French accent would ruin the effect.

He turns quickly back, stares for a few seconds as if gauging something, then curls his lip into something between a smile and a sneer. 'Expensive taste,' he notes.

'I know what I like.' I give him a look that makes it clear his masculinity is at stake, and I'm sure, for a second, he's going to fold. But after a pregnant pause, he turns back to the barman and nods. 'A bottle of the 1996 Dom Pérignon. Two glasses.'

'And a shot of pastis,' I add sharply. 'Straight up. Absinthe if you've got it, Pernod if you haven't.'

This time the man gives a short, aspirated laugh; but, of course, he has no reason to be displeased with my demand. It's relatively cheap and will get me drunk quicker. He nods again at the barman.

Two crystal flutes are placed before us. The barman pops the cork and pours, then returns the bottle immediately to a cooler.

My would-be seducer raises his glass. 'Here's to expensive taste.'

I raise my glass and we both drink: he sips; I take a generous mouthful so that my flute is half emptied. Then, maintaining eye contact the entire time, I take the shot of pastis and upend it in my champagne, which emits a serpentine rasp as it turns the pinkish colour of mother-of-pearl. The man almost chokes; the bartender's eyes widen in alarm, just for an instant, before he recovers his perfect professional mask. The jazz continues to reel and twist, and no one says anything for a few delirious seconds. I feel lighter than air, so free of ballast that I'm in danger of leaving the ground. It would be the ideal moment to down the rest of my drink and walk away, end the encounter with a flourish and no damage done. But somehow I can't. Our eyes are locked and I have to see what he'll do next – whether he'll cut his losses, pick up the bottle and retreat, or continue to roll with the punches.

It's the latter, of course. There's nothing more attractive to the stupidly wealthy than an absolute indifference to the value of things. It's like a shot of testosterone in the arm. The man's face moulds to another sardonic smile. 'That's one of the stranger things I've seen in this bar,' he says. 'How is it?'

I take another mouthful, letting the aniseed bubbles titillate my tongue. 'It's like nothing you can imagine,' I tell him.

THE KINDNESS OF STRANGERS

Another bar, another Friday. The circumstances very different.

I'm a little high, but not so much that it's a problem. I just have that extra zing, that bit more energy and imagination. Two double vodka and Cokes have been placed before me as I rifle through my purse, searching for usable currency. I don't have any cash – I know that already – but I realize too late that I don't have my debit card either. 'I must have left it in my other jeans,' I explain to the barman, who absorbs this extraneous information as impassively as a slab of granite. 'Can I put it on my credit card?'

'Yes. Of course.' He thrusts the card reader towards me.

'I don't know my PIN,' I add.

'You don't know your PIN?'

'No. I mean, I hardly ever use this card, except online. I'll have to sign for it.'

The barman groans loudly, a noise that is echoed at least twice in the crowd behind me. It's early evening, it's central London – so of course everywhere is frantic. 'You can't sign for it,' he tells me. 'If you don't know your PIN you can't use that card.'

'That's ridiculous!'

'It's company policy. Prevents fraud.'

'Well, look' – I shove my open purse towards his face – 'I have my driving licence here. See? Same name.'

He shakes his head and grips both vodka glasses, as if I might run off with them. 'No PIN, no drinks.'

'Oh, for God's sake! I could buy a diamond over the internet without needing my PIN. So why do I need it to buy a bloody drink?'

'Excuse me?' I feel a tap on my shoulder and spin round angrily. It's the guy next in line at the bar. He's tall and I'm wearing flats, so the first thing I see is his stubble. It's not designer stubble; it's too-busy-to-shave stubble. He's not much older than me – twenty-four, twenty-five perhaps – but he looks fraught, vaguely exasperated. He's still wearing work clothes – shirt, tie and trousers. The shirt has a couple of creases and has come untucked on one side. He looks as if he has come straight from a very long week.

'Yes, I know!' I snap. 'I'm holding everyone up. But unnecessary interruptions aren't going to help matters.'

'Er, no. Probably not,' he agrees, with a slightly worried grin. 'Actually, I was going to offer to buy your drink for you.'

'Oh.' I fumble for a few moments. The barman tuts loudly. 'Thanks. That's extremely kind of you. Or it would have been kind of you. I assume the offer has expired?'

'The offer still stands.'

'Well . . .' I open my purse again to demonstrate its emptiness. 'I do have a bit of a cash flow situation at the moment.'

'Yes, I heard.' He shrugs. 'It's happened to all of us at one point or another.'

'Thank you. That's a lie, I'm sure, but it's a nice lie.'

The barman coughs and drums his fingers.

'You're sure?' I ask, but a twenty-pound note has already been handed over the bar with no further debate.

'Listen,' I tell him. 'I'd like to pay you back for this. If you give me your address, I'll send you a cheque.'

'Oh, no. Not necessary. Really. It's just a drink. No big deal.'

'Actually, it's two drinks,' I point out. 'I'm with someone. My flatmate,' I add quickly. 'She's had kind of a lousy day. Her boyfriend dumped her, and I promised I'd take her out and get her good and drunk.' I nod towards my purse. 'Except it looks like she's going to be buying for the rest of the evening. Turns out I'm an awful friend.'

'No, not awful. Just slightly incompetent.'

I laugh, and it feels warm and wonderfully unforced. 'Yes, exactly.'

'But your intentions were good.'

'They always are.'

The barman hands him the change, along with the two vodkas and a pint of something, and the crowd starts jostling to fill the space we're vacating.

'Look,' I say once we're clear of the serving area, 'usually I'd ask if you'd like to join us, but it's not a good time, like I said. We're probably going to spend the next two hours talking about what shits men are.'

'Then I'll happily give it a miss.'

'I'd still like your number, though,' I persist. 'Or email – whatever.'

'No, really. It's fine. Completely unnecessary. Take it as a random act of kindness.'

I give him a patient smile. 'Yes, I know it's unnecessary. That's no longer why I'm asking.'

'Oh.' I think he blushes a bit, and at that moment I can't imagine anything sweeter. 'Um, yes, that's different, then. Sorry – I'm bumbling. Let me try again: I'd love to give you my number. Do you have a pen?'

'Er . . .' I reach into my bag. 'Yes. Four pens, in fact. No money, but four pens. Perhaps I should have tried bartering for my drinks?' I flash another smile and hand him a ballpoint and a beer mat, on the back of which he scribbles his details – phone *and* email. I read it as he writes – *stephen.beckett113@gmail.com* – then pop the beer mat in my bag.

'Well, Stephen Beckett,' I say, raising both vodkas, 'thanks again for these. I'm Abby, by the way. You shall be hearing from me soon.'

Then I turn and squeeze back through the crowd.

This memory is one of many that surface all at once, like the bubbles in champagne, like the thousands of bubbles in my blood. Alcohol hasn't dulled me; it has just muddled things, turning racing thoughts into overlapping thoughts, a jumble of tightly knotted contradictions.

We're stumbling back to my room in a blur of corners and corridors. He has his hand on my lower back, pushing more than guiding, his fingers grazing my buttocks; and he keeps calling me Julia, since that's the name I gave him at some point. He told me his too – Matt or Mark or Mike – but I've already shut it out. He probably has a wife and kids tucked away somewhere.

In the lift, he kisses me and shoves me back against one of the mirrored walls, hard enough that I feel a sharp pain shooting up my spine. The pain feels so much better than the kiss. There's a thrill, too, in the fact that he wants me so badly, but I can't begin to comprehend what that means. All I know is that I have no real desire for him, this man whose name I can't even remember. But it doesn't seem to make any difference. I don't care enough to stop this from happening.

When we reach my room, I break away from him to unlock the door, and it gives me the momentary illusion that I'm still in control of this situation. But soon he's pushing me again, backwards to the oversized bed. I feel my calves hit the base and I'm immediately off balance. My legs fold and I topple back, but manage to roll and find my feet again. I quickly undo and remove my dress – not because I want to; only because I don't want *him* to. It's absurd, but the thought of him ripping it with his clumsy, aggressive hands is more than I can bear. I can hear Francesca's voice in my head, telling me that I mustn't damage it. It's much too precious to risk.

He's on me again, the second I've let the dress slip to the floor, his shirt unbuttoned and his shoes kicked halfway across the room. He doesn't attempt to remove my bra; he just shoves it over the top of my breasts, where it cuts into my flesh like a noose. There's more shooting pain, but this time there's nothing pleasurable about it. I let out a yelp which he ignores. His mouth is on my left nipple and there's an awful burning as his thumb presses into the still tender skin around my tattoo. My heart wrenches in my chest. I manage to scrabble backwards and get a raised arm between us.

'No!' It comes out as little more than a hysterical pant, but it's enough to stop him for a moment. 'Don't touch me there.'

He stares for a second, then gives a sharp laugh and grabs for me again.

'Stop!' I manage to get some volume, some authority into my voice. 'You can do whatever you like to me, but do *not* touch me there. It isn't for you.'

He continues to stare, his expression somewhere between anger and disbelief, I pull my bra back into place, making sure my tattoo is safely concealed once more.

'Fuck! You can't be serious?'

'I'm completely serious,' I tell him, slapping his hand away a third time. 'If you touch my breasts again, I swear to God I'll scream.'

He looks me straight in the eye, his lip curled and his face red and blotchy. Then, with a deliberate, mocking slowness, he reaches for me, his fingers splayed. The moment he makes contact, I scream. I scream and I don't hold back. A second later his hand is clamped across my mouth.

'Are you fucking crazy?'

I wrench my head back; his hand slips and I manage to get my teeth into the soft flesh between his thumb and forefinger.

'Fuck!' He slaps me across my left cheek, making my ears ring and my vision reel.

I scream again and again, at the top of my lungs, as loud and uninhibited as a wounded animal. Through eyes flooded with tears, I see him retreating. He scrabbles for his shoes, then runs, slamming the door behind him.

My scream dies the instant he's gone. I collapse into a foetal heap on the bed, sobbing uncontrollably.

HURT

A sharp tapping brings me round. I can taste blood in my mouth, but I've no idea if it's mine or his. Could be both. My cheek feels like it's on fire. The tapping persists, and I curl up even tighter, willing the sound away. Silence. Then muffled voices, the click of the door unlocking. Two of the night porters walk in, look at me, and exchange a glance. I stare back. I'm still in my underwear, so I just stay as I am, in the foetal position. There's nothing else I can do.

'Er, madam?'

I start to giggle, or maybe I'm crying; I'm not sure. Even in a situation like this, they still greet me as *madam*, and one way or another, it strikes me as hysterical. I tuck my knees under my chin and close my eyes, tight. I think if I can keep them closed long enough, all this will disappear.

'Madam?' The porter's voice is a little louder this time. 'Please take this.'

I open my eyes and he's holding out a bathrobe, his expression full of concern. It's such a simple gesture, but it completely undoes me. He places the robe next to me on the bed as I continue to sob. 'Whenever you're ready.' He and his colleague turn their backs with the utmost discretion, as if this is just one more scenario that has been thoroughly covered in training.

Slowly, I force my limbs to uncoil. I rise on legs that feel as if they're made of wood, wrap myself in the robe, then sit back down on the edge of the bed. 'I'm done,' I tell them. My voice is completely hollow in my ears.

The porter who has done all the talking turns and gives me a gentle smile. His colleague has disappeared, but he returns from the bathroom that instant, carrying a flannel that has been soaked in cold water. 'For your cheek,' he explains.

I nod and try to say thank you, but nothing comes out.

'Madam?' The first porter again. 'Do we need to call someone? The police?'

'No. Not the police.' I dab my cheek, and this small, cold contact is enough to tell me that it has already started to swell. I'm going to have a spectacular bruise in a few hours' time.

'Madam.' The porter coughs delicately. 'Several of the guests reported screams. Something has obviously happened here.'

'It's not what you think. It really isn't.' Neither of them says anything, but another glance is exchanged. I try to keep my voice calm and clear. 'There was this guy. Things got out of hand . . .' I can't find the words to explain any further. The first porter nods tactfully. 'I don't need the police,' I repeat. 'Nothing happened. Nothing serious. I just need to sleep.'

The second porter shakes his head, the movement barely discernible. 'I don't think we can leave you alone. Not like this.'

'I'm okay. I'm not hurt.'

I press the flannel harder against my cheek; then, before I

can stop myself, I'm crying again. They're right, of course. I can't just go to sleep and hope everything will be normal again in the morning. And it's not sleep that I want; it's oblivion. I want to close my eyes and for everything to stop.

I get up and retrieve the spare towel that's folded at the bottom of the wardrobe. Neither of the porters says anything as I produce my mobile from the middle of this bundle. What could they possibly say? *I see you've wrapped your phone in a towel.*

'I'm going to call a friend now,' I tell them. 'I'm going to ask her to pick me up. If you don't mind, I'd like to be alone. You can call my room when she arrives.'

The first porter throws a questioning look at the second, who, after a moment, nods. 'We'll notify you as soon as she gets here. Is there anything else you need in the meantime? Anything at all?'

'No. Thank you. You've been very kind. Please, could you close the door on your way out?'

There are eighteen missed calls on my phone, and God knows how many texts and voicemails, but I have to ignore them for now. I can't think about those messages yet, not if I want to function. I hit the cancel button, then check the time. It's one twenty. I call Dr Barbara.

The phone only rings a couple of times before she picks up, and when she speaks she sounds completely alert, though I assume I must have woken her. 'Abby, where are you?'

'I'm at the Dorchester.'

She registers no surprise at this fact. 'I'm coming to get you. I'll be there within half an hour. Do *not* go anywhere. I want you to promise me.'

'I won't go anywhere,' I tell her.

'You promise?'

'I promise.'

'Is anyone with you?'

'No. I'm alone. I have a room.'

There's a brief pause as she digests this information. 'Abby, listen to me. I want you to stay in your room. Do not leave. If you have any thoughts of hurting yourself, you are to phone me immediately. *Immediately*. I'll be with you very soon. Stay put.'

'Okay.'

'Okay.'

She hangs up and I place my phone beside me on the bed. I try to picture her on her way, shoes clicking purposefully, headlights flaring to life, but the images quickly spin out of my control. I see her car crumpled at a junction, blood pouring from her mouth and nose and eyes. That would be my fault too. Half an hour seems an impossible amount of time to wait.

I get up and go to the bathroom. In a mirror that covers most of a wall, I see a girl who might have been painted by Picasso. My left eye has narrowed above a hillock of swollen skin, and my hair is in disarray from having lain foetal for so long. My cheek is the red of severe sunburn, and already taking on a darker, purplish hue. And somehow it's all made worse by the flawless luxury of the surroundings: the snow-white towels, the dazzling light, the endless, astonishing marble. Against this back-drop, I look so messed up it's mesmerizing, and for several minutes all I can do is stare, held captive by the grotesque jigsaw where my face used to be.

I no longer feel drunk. I no longer feel much of anything.

It's as if the alcohol and the mania and the tears and the kisses and the slap have all cancelled each other out, leaving a void as blank and formless as fog. But I know that this is only half of the story. Somewhere, buried deep, there is still the urge to run – the black inversion of my earlier elation. My instinct is to get out, to leave the hotel this very minute and let the night swallow me. The only thing standing between me and the door is the promise I made to Dr Barbara.

The light is too bright in the bathroom, so I return to the bed, get in, and pull the covers over my face. The problem, of course, is that this is not enough; I can't switch off all the lights in my head. I need a distraction, so I get up again and ransack the room for something to read. There's nothing very inspiring: just the hotel directory and the Gideon Bible. I try both, but the directory doesn't last long, and the Bible is too brutal. Eve eats some fruit; God says he's going to punish her by making childbirth excruciating. I get back under the duvet and pray for the phone to ring.

Lacking any alternative – other than the bathrobe – I put my dress back on and head down to the lobby, my steps slow and mechanical. Dr Barbara intercepts me before I'm halfway to the reception desk and enfolds me in a tight hug. My own arms hang lifeless at my sides, as limp as overcooked noodles.

'You're hurt,' she says as she pulls away. 'Someone hit you.'

I open my mouth, close it again, then just shrug and nod.

'It's okay. You don't have to tell me now. Tell me in the car. We need to get you home.'

'I don't think I can go home.' My voice is still a cold monotone. 'Not yet.'

'My home, Abby. I'm taking you back to mine. For now.'

'Thank you.' My eyes prickle. 'I need to return my key.'

'Give it to me.'

I do as instructed, and Dr Barbara strides over to the desk and hands the key to the receptionist, touching him briefly on the arm. In anyone else, it would seem overfriendly, a breach of etiquette; but Dr Barbara does it with such a calm and kind authority that it looks the most natural thing in the world.

'My bill,' I say when she comes back. 'I think I need to check about my bill.'

'Don't worry.' She's already ushering me out. The doorman nods politely as we pass. 'It's taken care of.'

'Thank you. That's . . . I'll pay you back, I promise. As soon as I can.'

'Abby, you're not to worry. There isn't going to be a bill. I explained the situation. The staff were very understanding.'

'Oh.' I don't know what else to say.

Dr Barbara gives me a tight-lipped smile and guides me to where her car is parked, in the drop-off zone. It's a Prius, charcoal grey and shiny as a bullet. She gestures to the passenger door and I get in. The interior is spotless, as if it's just been valeted.

She doesn't start the engine immediately. She flips on the interior light and looks at me again, her eyes lingering on my left cheek. 'Abby, I'd like to call Beck if that's all right? Just to let him know you're okay.'

My stomach drops a little. I close my eyes and nod. It's a phone call that has to be made, but there's no way *I* could make it – not right now. Dr Barbara, it seems, has understood this without having to ask.

The call lasts only a couple of minutes, but even this is close to unbearable. All I can think about is burying something sharp or hot in my flesh.

When it's finally over, Dr Barbara slips her phone into the side compartment and turns back to me. 'Abby, I want you to tell me exactly what has happened today. Bits of it I know already; Beck phoned me soon after you left. He was . . . worried, understandably. But I'd like to hear it in your own words. Can you manage that?'

'Is it okay if I smoke?'

'If you absolutely must.'

'I think I must.'

'Okay then.' She starts the engine and rolls down both of the front windows. There is classical music playing quietly on the stereo, something soft and intricate.

It takes me most of the fifteen-minute journey to explain everything to Dr Barbara. I start from the previous morning, with the journey to Oxford to see Professor Caborn, since that seems the place to begin. It's difficult to find the words, and already I think there must be bits I have forgotten; everything happened so quickly, and every minute was packed with too many thoughts and feelings and actions. Now that I'm coming down – now that alcohol and exhaustion are finally taking their toll – it's all too much for me to process. And yet I struggle through somehow, managing to reconstruct most of the story, even if it comes across as a series of poorly drawn incidents, the gossamer logic that connected them now in tatters. Dr Barbara helps me: she prompts occasionally, or asks for clarification when I stop making any kind of sense. But mostly, she stays quiet, lets me find my own circuitous path.

She stays silent afterwards, too, but when I look across, her brow is deeply creased. There are dark crescents under her eyes; and without make-up, wearing a slightly tatty cardigan and jeans in place of her usual office wear, she looks older than I've ever seen her. It feels as if *I've* aged her – by at least a decade.

'I'm sorry,' I say. 'For making you come out in the middle of the night.'

She doesn't look across, but she gives a shrug and a wry smile. 'A hazard of my job. You're not the first, and you certainly won't be the last.'

'Still. Thank you. I don't know what I would have done.'

She shushes me, reaching over momentarily to rest her fingers on my arm. 'Abby, you did the right thing calling me. You're okay. You don't need to think about anything else right now. We're almost home.'

I've never been to Dr Barbara's flat before, but it's nice. It's in Notting Hill, and seems to take up an entire floor in a huge five-storey house. Nothing like my flat, of course – two bedrooms and a study, a large lounge and separate kitchen. It must be worth a million – possibly millions, plural. But I know that Dr Barbara has been living in central London for over two decades. She probably bought it before property prices went completely fucking crazy. I try to imagine what it would be like to live somewhere like this, but I can't. That is, I can't imagine *myself* living somewhere like this. It's ridiculously implausible, a bright boulevard I'm not allowed into. Not unaccompanied, anyway.

Dr Barbara asks me to keep the noise down when we enter, as Graham is sleeping. This information comes as a shock to me. Not the fact that Graham is asleep; it's around two in the morning – this is when the sane people sleep. The shock is the simpler fact of Graham, his existence.

'I didn't know you were seeing anyone,' I whisper.

'I'm not a nun, Abby,' Dr Barbara replies.

'No, of course not. It's just . . . well, you've never mentioned him.'

Dr Barbara shrugs as she places her keys in a bowl on a sideboard. 'It's relatively recent, and it never came up. The main concern of our sessions is talking about what's happening in your life, not mine.'

'Yes, but still . . .' I trail off. Eight months of intense and intimate conversation has made me assume that I know Dr Barbara pretty well – certainly better than I know most of the people in my life. I know all about her messy divorce fifteen years ago. I know about her early career as a GP. I know that she can read Latin and has twice run the London Marathon. But here is something significant that has slipped me by, and as we creep through to her spacious, stand-alone kitchen, there are other signs of a life I know little about: photos of foreign landscapes and mystery children – nephews and nieces? – morphing into young adults; a bookcase crammed with cookery books; a surprisingly extensive collection of fridge magnets. We've talked about sex and death and drugs and orgasms, about love and guilt and humiliation and shame – and yet it appears, now, that Dr Barbara's is just one more life I've failed to imagine in any real detail.

She gestures for me to sit at a sturdy, circular table. Four chairs, completely free of clutter. 'Can I get you a drink? Coffee?'

'Water. Just water, please.'

'And what about food? Have you eaten?'

The question confuses me. 'When?'

'Recently!'

I look at the wall clock, which, it transpires, has no numbers. Just the hands, like some sort of ongoing spatial awareness test. 'I had half a pizza thirteen hours ago, and two, maybe three canapés at the Dorchester Bar.'

'What can I get you?'

My hesitation is long enough that Dr Barbara decides to stop asking questions and just take charge. She gets two bananas from the fruit bowl and watches me eat both. I'm not hungry, and they don't taste of anything, but at least they don't require much chewing, and Dr Barbara tells me they contain a lot of potassium, which will help settle my stomach when my inevitable hangover kicks in. She sits opposite, nursing a cup of tea in both hands and regarding me in silence for a few moments. I know that the serious conversation is coming, the one where we talk about what happens next. But I have no idea what happens next. I still can't bring myself to think about that yet. Looking even ten seconds ahead causes a queasy lurch in the pit of my stomach, and anything beyond that is like the uncharted territory on an ancient map – the bit where it's quite possible to slip off the edge of the world and never stop falling.

I don't want to think. I just want to sit here in Dr Barbara's immaculate kitchen, with its concealed lighting and fridge magnets and clock with no numbers. I want to sit here and pretend that it's a normal day and I'm a normal friend who has just popped over for a glass of water and a couple of bananas.

Luckily, Dr Barbara is much better at handling this situation. She has had the practice, and accelerates through the professional gears, getting swiftly to the crux of the matter.

There's a diagnostic test that GPs use to assess the mental health of their patients – the PHQ-9 questionnaire. It's a checklist I know so well I can recite it by heart, with more feeling and fluency than any poem. Question One: *Over the past two weeks have you felt little pleasure or interest in doing things you usually enjoy? (Not at all/some days/many days/every day.)* Question Three: *Have you had trouble falling or staying asleep, or sleeping too much?* For each of the nine questions, you score a mark out of three, and this gives a total out of twenty-seven, from which the doctor can objectively quantify how nuts you are, zero being fine, twenty-seven being fetch the straitjacket. This is the only test in which I have ever achieved perfection, twenty-seven out of twenty-seven – and on more than one occasion.

But Dr Barbara doesn't bother with this test today; she goes straight to question nine, or a simplified version of question nine, which is the only question she really needs to ask right now.

'Abby, are you having thoughts of hurting yourself?'

'Yes.'

That's all I need to say. I could elaborate and tell her that's *all* I can think about – the only possibility I can see if I allow myself to look beyond the next ten seconds – but what would be the point? A simple yes will suffice.

Dr Barbara nods, and it's like we're shaking hands to seal a deal. 'With your permission, I'd like to have you admitted to hospital.'

I attempt a hollow laugh, but it turns out that even the hollowest of laughs is beyond me. 'What if I don't give you my permission?'

Dr Barbara sips her tea. 'Well, I think I'd have a job forcing you. I could wake Graham, I suppose, but I'd rather not.' Then she smiles, a smile that's somehow warm and sad at the same time. 'Do you want me to wake up Graham?'

I'm not even aware that I've started crying again, not until I feel the tears trickling down my cheeks. 'I don't want you to wake Graham,' I tell her. 'You have my permission to take me to hospital.'

So that's it. A few minutes later I'm back in Dr Barbara's car and heading west to the twenty-four-hour emergency unit.

That's what happens next.

Hammersmith Hospital is not a reassuring place to be visiting at three o'clock in the morning in a fragile state. It has an imposing Victorian façade of dark red brick and dozens of windows staring like latticed spider eyes. It sits behind wrought-iron gates and is crowned by a starkly lit clock tower. Its closest neighbour, just to the west, is Wormwood Scrubs.

We walk through an elaborate entranceway bordered with cornices and columns, through lobbies and winding corridors, and it all feels like a hideous parody of my experience at the Dorchester, only nine hours ago. Everything is white again, but it's no longer the dazzling white of marble floors and crystal chandeliers: it's the bleached-out white of fluorescent strips and rooms without texture. Rich mahogany is now laminate worktop, and the soft aroma of bath oils and freshly washed cotton has become starch and antiseptic.

Dr Barbara has phoned ahead, and once we arrive it doesn't take long to get me formally assessed. We sit in a consultation room with a small, bespectacled psychiatrist who listens attentively as Dr Barbara runs through my medical history. She tells him I'm having a mixed-state hypomanic episode, which has been ongoing for the past forty-eight hours, possibly much longer. The hypomanic part means that I've gone a little crazy but it could be worse: I've been running amok   impulsive actions, reckless spending, promiscuity – but I'm not delusional; I don't think I'm Joan of Arc or an alien visitor or Christ reincarnated in female form. The mixed-state means that I'm simultaneously displaying signs of depression: weeping, despondency, despair; wanting to kill myself.

I sit and listen to the medicalese version of this while staring numbly at a filing cabinet. I'm still wearing my beautiful blue dress, though Dr Barbara has also lent me one of her cardigans to wear over it. It's slightly too big; the sleeves hang a couple of inches past my wrists. And it's camel-coloured, which is a shocking clash with cobalt blue. All in all, I'm not sure it makes me look any saner. Plus it's still a stupidly hot night, and the windowless consultation room feels tight and stuffy. After a couple of minutes, I remove the cardigan and hand it wordlessly to Dr Barbara, who folds it in her lap.

My talk with the psychiatrist lasts no time at all. He asks me a dozen questions and I reply with monosyllables wherever I can. Sometimes, I'm forced to speak a full sentence, but anything more than that seems an insurmountable effort. I tell him I just want to sleep, and soon enough my wish is granted. I sign my own committal form – the one that says the hospital can keep me until such a time as they deem me ready for release – and then I'm led by a nurse to a single room on an unremarkable ward a couple of floors up. It would be too disruptive to put me anywhere else for the moment.

I'm given a hospital gown and some disposable underwear

to change into, and Dr Barbara sits with me while the nurse asks questions about my recent alcohol consumption – what, when and how much. Once she's satisfied that it's safe, she brings me a tiny beaker containing two diazepam.

'Dr Barbara?'

It's the first time in about an hour that I've spoken without being asked a direct question, and my voice sounds like it's coming from far, far away.

'Yes, Abby?'

'I know I have no right to ask . . .'

'Go ahead and ask.'

'Would you stay with me? Just until I fall asleep. I don't think it will be very long.'

Dr Barbara smiles and places her hand on mine. 'Of course. And I'll be back in the evening. I don't know if you'll be awake by then, but I'll be back.'

'Thank you.'

There's nothing else to say. I take my diazepam, and not long after, I drop into a black, bottomless sleep.

SHARPS

I was awoken around midday, groggy and disorientated. A nurse was tapping me on my shoulder, long after most would have given up. She told me that she'd also been in at eight, with breakfast, but it had proven impossible to rouse me. 'Dead to the world, you were.'

I didn't reply. The comment was pointless. I didn't want to get involved in a pointless conversation.

'Still, lunch soon,' she went on. 'Can't have you missing a second meal.'

'I'm not hungry,' I said. 'I just want to sleep.'

The nurse tutted in a way that suggested what I wanted was no longer relevant. 'Doctors' orders,' she insisted. 'I'm to make sure you eat before we move you.'

I shrugged – or tried to shrug – my heavy shoulders to let her know that I wasn't going to play her ridiculous game. I had no curiosity about what the doctors had planned for the next twenty-four hours. I told her that if they wanted to move me to another ward, they could just as well do it while I slept. I had no intention of getting up.

'You're not going to a different ward,' the nurse countered. 'You're going to a different hospital. St Charles. It's all been arranged. They're expecting you mid-afternoon.'

'I can't walk,' I persisted. 'I'm too tired.'

The nurse smiled benevolently. 'You don't have to walk. One of the porters will be very happy to take you down to the ambulance in a wheelchair. After lunch.'

'I'm too tired to chew,' I told her. It was childish but I didn't care. The thought of food made me sick.

'It's soup,' the nurse said. 'You don't have to chew, either.'

Someone from the psychiatric liaison team came in immediately after lunch. He told me I was being moved to St Charles because it had a specialized mental health unit and would provide a much more suitable environment for my recovery. But I knew this was just a euphemism. What he really meant was that they had locked wards there. That was why it would be more suitable.

At two o'clock, with my blue dress and my handbag and my Harvey Nichols underwear heaped in my lap, I was wheeled down to the ambulance and driven a couple of miles across west London to another imposing Victorian hospital. Same stained brickwork and turrets and daunting iron gates. The only difference was that it was in a nicer part of the city. Instead of a maximum-security prison next door, there was a Carmelite monastery.

The ambulance passed through the open gates and followed

a small road to the back of the hospital complex, where the mental health unit was housed in its own three-storey annexe. In contrast to its almost Gothic surroundings, the mental health unit was as modern and nondescript as a newly built block of flats, the sort of building you'd pass on the street without a second glance. Inside, it was obvious that every element of the décor – from the bright blue carpets to the potted rubber plants – had been chosen to reinforce the impression that this was not a hospital at all. The only thing that gave the game away was the doors. Past reception, they were all magnetically locked and could only be opened with staff key cards.

They took me through to a ward called Nile. The wards were all named after rivers for some reason. There was also Amazon, Danube, Ganges and Thames. I never found out why. Maybe it was another way to make the mental unit seem less institutional. Maybe there was some other hidden significance. All I found out, upon my admission, was that Nile was the psychiatric intensive care ward. It was a closed ward housing the psychotics, the suicidal and those deemed at high risk of absconding. It should have been called Styx.

I asked the nurse who was wheeling me through to my room if I was allowed visitors.

'Usually,' he said. 'As long as they're scheduled. A doctor will talk to you about it later. You'll have a personalized care plan.'

'I don't want any visitors,' I told him. 'I only want to see Dr Barbara. No one else.'

Time passed. I'm not sure how much.

I was back on the lithium and feeling like a zombie, which, on the whole, was an improvement. Undead felt so much better than alive at that point. Actually dead would have felt better still, but no one was prepared to give me this option. A couple of rashly scrawled midnight signatures and my right to death had been irrevocably waived.

The downsides of lithium: headaches, stomach aches, nausea like you wouldn't believe, tremors, perpetual lethargy, the inability to read, dizziness, constipation, weight gain.

The upsides: the inability to think, a memory that's shot to pieces, spending most of the day asleep.

I would have spent *all* day – every day – asleep had it not been for the doctors and nurses, who were constantly bothering me. First there was the incessant feeding. Three times a day, a nurse came to watch me eat, not leaving until every plastic spoonful had disappeared. They had me on a strict two-thousand-calorie, sodium-controlled diet. I also had to drink two litres of water a day. It didn't matter that I was neither hungry nor thirsty. The nurse would stay as long as it took. I assumed that if I refused to eat or drink I'd be fed through a tube, like the girl opposite. Occasionally, I wondered if this wouldn't be an easier option.

When it wasn't food, it was blood. My lithium levels were being monitored almost continually. Mere moments after the first blood test of the day, it seemed I was being shaken awake for the second, the third, the fourth. If I'd had a cannula, it might have been possible for them to draw the blood while I went on sleeping, but, of course, I wasn't allowed a cannula. Cannulas counted as sharps and were not permitted on the ward. Neither were my house keys or nail file. Both had been taken from my handbag upon my arrival. They'd also taken my compact, because of the mirror (a 'potential sharp'), and my cigarette lighter, for more obvious reasons. The compact meant nothing to me – it wasn't as if I was going to worry about applying make-up – but the lighter pained me like a missing limb every time I thought of it. If I wanted to go for a cigarette, I had to be chaperoned down to the garden by a nurse who never took her eyes off me. The garden was surrounded by a twelve-foot-high metal fence, beyond which there were tall trellises that blocked out any view of the outside world. You could hear traffic, and occasionally pedestrians, passing on the side road that abutted the hospital, but you could see nothing.

Smoking was the only activity in which I retained any semblance of interest, and whenever I was being uncooperative, refusing to sit up for blood tests or water, the nurses would bribe me with cigarettes. At night-time, I was put on nicotine patches.

I tried to stop washing, too. Of all the pointless activities that constituted my day, this seemed by far the most pointless. I wasn't going anywhere. I wasn't seeing anyone who wasn't mental, or so used to dealing with the mental that it made no difference. And washing seemed such a monumental and fruitless effort. I'd just get dirty again.

I explained the situation to the nurses, as best I could, but that only seemed to make matters worse. Every other day, one of them would march me down to the shower and wait outside while I went through the same mindless farce. The shower had a lock on the temperature control so you couldn't burn yourself. Nevertheless, I was still on ten-minute checks; if my shower lasted longer than that, the nurse would poke her head around the door to make sure that everything was okay.

My showers never lasted more than ten minutes, and I didn't bother with soap or shampoo. I just stood under the tepid water like a mannequin until the nurse started knocking on the door. I didn't shave my legs either. I wasn't allowed a razor unsupervised, and after a few days, my leg and underarm hair was downy rather than prickly, so had ceased to be a problem.

One day, long after time had stopped meaning anything, I happened to catch sight of my reflection as I was undressing for my shower. The only mirrors on the ward were in the toilets and shower rooms, and because of my continual torpor and shaky vision, I rarely bothered to look in them. But on this day my attention was snared out of pure bewilderment. For several moments, I didn't recognize my own face. My skin was pale and oily. My hair was a dirty blonde mop. My cheeks looked too fat and my eyes too narrow. I thought the fatness was probably because of the lithium and the hours upon hours of lying perfectly still. Unfortunately, there was nothing much I could do about this. There was no chance of hiding and later disposing of my meals, much less the lithium. The nurses watched me far too closely. But I couldn't stand seeing myself like this in the mirror: a pale, greasy blob.

After a few minutes of gruelling thought, the solution I struck upon was this: I would make sure I didn't look in the mirror again.

'How are you feeling?' Dr Barry asked.

'Worse.'

He nodded, as if this were the only possible answer. Which it was. How could anyone hope to get better in a place like this?

'How about the nausea?'

I shrugged.

'On a scale of one to ten; ten being very bad, one being—'

'Ten.'

'Ten?'

I shrugged again. It wasn't really a ten and he knew it. If anything, the nausea was starting to taper off. But I couldn't stand the way he was looming over me with his patronizing eyes and his stupid ten-point scale of wellbeing. Dr Barry was constantly making me quantify things that it made no sense to quantify. I resolved that if he asked me to rate my mood, one to ten, just one more time, I'd tell him zero and be done with it. No more talking for the rest of the day. It was times like this I wished I'd been admitted to the Carmelite monastery instead. At least then I'd have some peace. You could bet those nuns knew when to shut the fuck up.

Although he was up against some stiff competition, Dr Barry was by far the worst doctor I'd ever met. He was about eight feet tall and had a beard that made my skin crawl. His default expression was one of smug complacency, except when he knew you were looking at him, when he'd contort his features into a poor imitation of paternal concern. In all honesty, I had no idea why he was even allowed to practise psychiatry. If he'd taken a photo of me, any moron on the street would have been able to diagnose my mood after a single glance. Yet Dr Barry lacked either the initiative or the imagination to discern anything without first conducting a ten-minute questionnaire. I could only assume that he'd been hired based on his height alone. It was probably useful to have a giant on psychiatric intensive care, whatever his medical incompetence.

I didn't know if Barry was Dr Barry's first or second name,

but I presumed the latter. He wasn't the sort of doctor who would offer up his first name, which lost him a lot of respect in my book. Of course, if it turned out that I was wrong, and Barry really was his first name, I'd have had an even harder time respecting him. But that wasn't the point.

He stared at me for a few moments, his face smug and complacent, and I stared straight back. He didn't have the balls to tell me I was a lying bitch and my nausea couldn't possibly be a ten, not still. If he'd said that, I might have been able to warm to him a little. But instead, he just rubbed his beard, then decided to placate me with more medication. 'I'll have one of the nurses bring an anti-emetic with your lunch,' he said. 'How's your appetite?'

I couldn't remember which way the scale ran for appetite, and I didn't care. 'Six and a half,' I told him. Then I pulled the thin NHS covers over my eyes and waited for him to go away.

'You *are* getting better,' Dr Barbara insisted, and I felt a surge of weary disappointment.

'I'm worse,' I mumbled, hardly bothered if my voice was audible or not. 'Every day I'm worse.'

This truth was so self-evident to me that it was inconceivable no one else had noticed. Yet they talked, instead, of positive signs: the fact that I was sleeping less, that I could now sustain a conversation for more than two minutes if I chose to do so (which I rarely did). They didn't seem to realize or care that this was all just surface.

Inside, I was broken. Every hour I had to spend awake, or even half awake, was an ordeal, from the moment the nurses arrived with breakfast until lights out in the evening. And the worst part was that I knew it would go on and on like this for ever. Every morning I awoke with the hollow notion, seeming to emanate from my stomach, that I had another day to get through. Then I'd wonder how many *more* days there'd be after this one. The figure I came up with was ten thousand. I don't know why. And when I tried to think about all those days and what they might mean, I could only envisage them as an endless line of dominoes, every one a double blank and falling in horrible slow motion. One domino every twenty-four hours.

I decided that this – the sheer hopelessness of my situation – must be why everyone was now insisting that I was getting better, despite so much evidence to the contrary. You couldn't trust doctors to be straight with you when you were beyond help. They didn't want to make their lives difficult by admitting you were a terminal case. Of course, Dr Barbara used to be different, but now she'd finally snapped as well. I'd made her snap. I'd pushed her and pushed her and now she was lying to me too, pretending I was improving so she'd have an excuse to stop coming. I thought for a reckless moment that I should make things easy for her, remove her from my visitors list along with everyone else. Except Dr Barbara was still bringing my cigarettes every couple of days. The idea of this final crutch being withdrawn sent ice down my spine. Smoking was the only thing I had left – the only thing that could possibly help those dominoes to fall faster – and I knew I'd fight to the last to preserve this precious resource. There was no way I'd do anything to force Dr Barbara's hand.

In the meantime, I'd just have to put up with her mendacity, in the same way that I had put up with her bringing in clothes and toiletries, and all the other daily accoutrements that no longer held any relevance to my life. There was an overnight bag stuffed into the bottom of the bedside cupboard which I'd never bothered to unzip. I knew that Beck must have packed it for her, and I couldn't bear to think about that. More to the point, there was no reason I could imagine why I would choose to wear my own clothes rather than the ones the hospital provided. The very idea of choosing which clothes to wear seemed a colossal and futile effort. Why wear one thing instead of another? Much simpler to let the nurses take charge and replace my NHS nightgown whenever they deemed it necessary.

Unfortunately, Dr Barbara had not stopped with the pointless overnight bag. Some time after, there had been a pen and a book of crossword puzzles. Later still, when she knew that my headaches and nausea were starting to subside, she'd brought in an imposing copy of *Gone with the Wind*, which had sat untouched for the past few days. Initially, I went through the motions of opening the book and running my eyes back and forth across the countless rows of text, but it might as well have been printed in Arabic. Even though I'd seen the film, the words evoked nothing for me; they passed through my mind like flour through a sieve. For a long time, I wondered why Dr Barbara had brought me such a long and difficult book, one that had no significance or connection to anything I knew about. She claimed that it had just been sitting on one of her bookshelves and she'd thought I might like it. But this seemed implausible. After a while, I realized a more likely explanation was that she'd chosen it *because* it was long and difficult. It was something to keep me fruitlessly occupied, in the same way that prisoners were made to sew mailbags or break up stones with a pickaxe. If I managed to read a page a day – which seemed a very ambitious goal – then *Gone with the Wind* would keep me busy for the next three years. After that, Dr Barbara would probably bring me *War and Peace* or something. *Anna Karenina* would have been a better choice, but there was no chance she'd bring me that because of the suicide.

'Abby?' Dr Barbara's expression told me that she'd continued to talk, but nothing had registered.

'I'm worse,' I repeated, then returned my gaze to a blank patch of wall. She kept looking at me but I didn't meet her eye. I didn't want to see confirmation of what I already knew. That there was nothing to be done.

'Abby, listen to me. This won't last for ever. I know it doesn't feel that way right now, but you have to trust me. You've spent the last week semi-comatose, but now you're beginning to come round. If it seems like things are getting worse, that's only because you're starting to function again. You're starting to think and feel things.'

'I don't want to feel things,' I told her. 'I don't want to feel anything ever again.'

'I know you don't. But trust me, please. It's just a matter of time. Things can only get better from here.'

After Dr Barbara had left and the lights had gone out, I took my cobalt-blue dress from the bedside cupboard and held it in my lap. I had to do this every so often. It made me feel even worse, but I had to do it all the same. Everything else I saw on the ward was blank or pastel or neutral. The pillows and linen and doctors were white. The curtains and walls were off-white. The nurses were an insipid, washed-out green. But my dress was still astonishing – a flash of colour as vivid and violent as lightning on a moonless night. And when I looked at my dress,

I felt like Eve standing outside the Garden of Eden, able to peer back through the gates at something truly sublime and for ever lost. I couldn't look at my dress for very long.

That night, as I sat cradling my dress like it was a murdered infant, I realized that Dr Barbara was right about at least one thing. The new problem I was facing was that I was no longer semi-comatose. I had become alert enough to comprehend, without any filter or anaesthetic, how awful I felt, and this was why I had reached my lowest ebb. From this a more general insight followed, even though I'd assumed that any new insight was now far beyond me.

The problem was thought itself, the self-awareness that made it possible for me to look at my dress and understand where I had been, where I was now, and where I was going – or not going. It was a uniquely human problem, something no other animal had to put up with, this ability to suffer in multiple tenses – simultaneously to mourn the past, despair of the present and fear the future. The kindest thing would be for one of the doctors to give me a full frontal lobotomy; that was the only thing that could solve this problem for good.

I wasn't going to get a full frontal lobotomy. I'd been born in the wrong decade.

The only way out of this prison was to get better. And since this wasn't going to happen, I'd have to fake it. I'd have to make the doctors believe that I was well and no longer a threat to myself. Then I could take the steps to make sure I'd never come back here.

A LETTER, UNDELIVERED

Hello Abby.

I don't know how else to start this letter. I've been looking at a blank sheet of paper for God knows how long, and this is all I've come up with. But it's probably best to keep things simple. Please assume that my words fall short of what I actually want to say.

I came to see you a couple of days ago, or I tried to. I made it as far as reception. I thought that if I could get someone to call you – if you knew I was already there – then you'd have to change your mind and let me in. Turns out you're not taking calls, either. I should have known. I've left about twenty messages on your mobile.

They sent a doctor out eventually. He was nice. He made me a cup of coffee and let me rant at him for five minutes. Then he repeated what I already knew: he couldn't let me see you, couldn't even take a message, since this is expressly against your wishes. Barbara finally agreed to pass this letter on, but only when she thinks you're 'capable of reading it'. That paints a pretty bleak picture.

Needless to say, the doctor I saw at reception couldn't tell me anything about how you are – patient confidentiality. All he could give me were generalities: that you were in a safe environment and would be receiving the best possible care, etc., etc.

I had a plan, of sorts, when I walked into the hospital. I was going to wait as long as it took, just refuse to leave until someone had communicated with you on my behalf, or at least given me some concrete information. Instead, I found myself leaving within half an hour, having apologized profusely to the doctor and receptionist. All very British. They gave me a number I could call if I needed to speak to anyone again. It's for some sort of mental health support charity. I haven't used it yet.

I'm sorry: a couple of pages in and I'm already sounding bitter and self-pitying. That really isn't my intention. I'm not telling you any of this to make you feel bad. I imagine you feel bad enough already – much worse than I do.

I have this problem that never seems to get any easier. When you're at your lowest, I always think that there must be some magic combination of words that would help you. But I can never find them. They're always just beyond my grasp.

All I can find to say right now is that I'm here for you, whenever you're ready.

There's one other thing too, and again it's something you

might not find particularly easy to hear. But I promised I'd tell you if I managed to get in touch.

Your mum phoned, the day after you went into hospital. I hadn't really figured out what I was going to say to your family at that point – I was hoping I'd get the chance to see you first – but I wasn't going to lie to her, obviously. She's called or texted every day for the past week, and yesterday she came over to the flat. (She was here at ten, so God knows when she left Exeter.)

She's worried: that goes without saying. She's worried and she wants you to call her. Please just think about it.

I love you. I miss you. I don't think there's anything else I can add.

Beck x

FAKING IT

When you want to die, smiling is not easy. I discovered this the next morning when the nurse brought my breakfast.

It was premeditated, of course. After I put my cobalt-blue dress back in the bedside cupboard, I stayed awake for a few hours, planning my first move.

It seemed simple in principle: a slight reconfiguration of the eyes and mouth, just to let her know that I was pleased to see her, that I was grateful for my cereal.

The nurse's sharp recoil told me that I'd got it wrong somehow.

Later, I spent several minutes in front of the bathroom mirror, trying to understand and correct my error. I had the vague recollection that all primates could smile, and it wasn't a skill that had to be learned. Baby primates could smile just a few weeks after birth – even those born blind. So why did it seem so unnatural? My mouth felt tense and tremulous, like over-stretched elastic. But maybe this wouldn't be discernible to an outside observer? My lips at least appeared to be curving in the right direction. The bigger problem was my eyes. I'd read somewhere that you could always tell a genuine smile by looking at the eyes rather than the mouth.

I covered my mouth with a hand and stared straight ahead. Two doll's eyes stared back, as cold and hard as marbles. I didn't know how to rectify this.

Soon the nurse was tapping on the bathroom door.

I gave up.

The problem, I later realized, was that I'd started with far too big a step. I couldn't fake a smile right now – any more than I could recalibrate the hollow monotone of my voice. These things would have to be practised, rebuilt piece by piece. In the meantime, I should think small. I should focus on the small cosmetic changes that I had some hope of effecting.

I started by washing again. Real washing, as opposed to sluicing myself off once every forty-eight hours. Soap, shampoo – the works. A couple of days later, I asked to borrow a disposable razor and spent the next fifteen minutes shaving my legs under the unflinching gaze of one of the nurses. It took fifteen minutes because I had to concentrate on every stroke. All my nerves were shrieking at me, telling me to press down as hard as I could. And that would have been disastrous. It would have set me back weeks. I kept my eyes locked on their task, thinking only of the endgame.

When I'd finished, I had a long nap, then spent the rest of the day reading the first chapter of *Gone with the Wind*. That felt even harder than shaving my legs, but it was an investment worth making. Both the day shift and the night shift saw that I was reading. They could see how engrossed I was.

*

I don't know exactly how long it took me to get off psychiatric intensive care – time was still hazy – but it must have been less than a week. It all seemed much too easy.

I washed. I read. I dressed myself in my own clothes. When Dr Barry asked me how I was, I told him three or four rather than zero. These scores seemed unfeasibly high to my mind, but he never questioned them. Instead, he marked them on my chart, and soon the evidence of my 'recovery' was there for all to see, plotted on a tidy graph.

It was a monstrous sham, but it was a sham that no one felt inclined to question. Even Dr Barbara, whom I'd assumed would see through my pretences in an instant, seemed content to accept the signs at face value. It helped, I suppose, that I didn't have to lie to Dr Barbara directly. She wasn't going to ask me to rate my mood out of ten. She was noting the subtler measures of my improvement: the fact that I'd made a bookmark out of a folded paper towel, and this had started to creep down the vast bulk of *Gone with the Wind*; the fact that my hair was washed and brushed. I didn't have to make anything too explicit with Dr Barbara.

It helped, too, that my face was beginning to give hints of expressive capability. I couldn't yet manage anything approaching a warm smile – let alone a happy smile – but I could do a passable impression of a *brave* smile, something that told the outside world I was at least trying.

Still, it struck me that it took so little; just a few minor changes in demeanour and I was indisputably on the mend. So what, exactly, defined the line between crazy and not crazy? The more I thought about it, the more it seemed that sanity was just a matter of behaviour. Its degrees could be measured by the cleanliness of your hair, the set of your facial features, how you respond to a series of social cues.

For the doctors and nurses, this was what sanity was.

Although there was no substance underlying my sham recovery, I could still appreciate the several ways in which being off psychiatric intensive care was better than being on it. First, there were fewer nurses. I'm not sure what the staff to patient ratio had been on Nile, but I am certain there were more of them than us. Amazon, where I now found myself, was closer to being a regular hospital ward. There might have been six to eight nurses present at any one time – slightly fewer at night.

Of course, the practical result of this lower staffing ratio was less supervision. There still weren't locks on the bathroom doors, but most days I could get through a whole shower without anyone interrupting me. Far better than this, though, was the fact that I could now smoke unsupervised. The move to Amazon had come with all sorts of trusts and privileges that would have been unimaginable on Nile. Previously banned personal effects – house keys, nail files, lighters – were retrieved from the locker room behind the main reception. The keys were superfluous, obviously, but I suppose some psychiatrist somewhere had decided there was an important symbolism implicit in their return – the promise that I was one step closer to my eventual release.

I was more impressed by the symbolism of the lighter, since this meant I was now trusted not to set myself or others on fire. For several hours after its return, the lighter never left my person. The keys I buried at the bottom of my bag. They were another item I did not want to think about.

If Nile was essentially a prison, then Amazon was a halfway house, the sheltered accommodation set up to provide a safe transition back to the outside world. At times, it felt no more terrible than a hall of residence – if you allowed yourself to forget that all its residents were insane.

Amazon Ward was a long L-shaped corridor with a dozen bedrooms leading off it. There was a small kitchen, containing a kettle and a microwave and an always-full fruit bowl, which adjoined a larger dining area with two round tables. Opposite the nurses' station was the dayroom, where there were sofas and magazines and a television that seemed to be permanently tuned to *Homes Under the Hammer*. This, I suppose, was someone's concept of safe viewing – the kind of innocuous daytime programming suited to a group of damaged and fragile women. Except I found *Homes Under the Hammer* anything but innocuous, and I was willing to bet I was not the only one. *Homes Under the Hammer* was a programme in which smug, middle-aged idiots bought and sold property, usually generating a huge profit while simultaneously pricing the rest of the population out of the market. These people all owned homes already. Many of them owned multiple homes, which was why they were able to borrow such vast sums of money from the bank. They used phrases like 'strengthening my portfolio', and were constantly referring to the *ladder*.

I avoided the dayroom whenever I could, but this was not always possible. Because on Amazon, independent movement was not just permitted, it was continually encouraged. If you tried to stay in bed past nine in the morning, it wouldn't be long before a nurse was opening the curtains and ushering you into one of the communal areas. This was the flipside of greater freedom. With it came caveats – rules and responsibilities.

Paradoxically, there had been far fewer rules on Nile. On Nile there was really just one rule: no sharps. With that rule in place, we were pretty much left to ourselves. Apart from meals and medication, there was very little to segment the days, and time slid past like a glacier huge and blank and structureless. And there wasn't any communal space on Nile – not in any meaningful sense. Each separate bed might as well have been a separate universe. Two dozen personal hells, with no connection between them.

But on Amazon no one was allowed to languish. Treatment no longer meant lithium, Thorazine or ECT – or that wasn't *all* it meant. Now there were various therapies to be attended: individual therapy, group therapy, art therapy.

Against all odds, I soon found myself missing Dr Barry. He may have been a prick, but at least when he asked me a question, I knew the difference between a good and bad answer. Unfortunately, it seemed that Dr Barry was permanently confined to psychiatric intensive care, where his massive frame was a constant boon and his lack of interpersonal skills neither here nor there.

In his place, I was assigned a new personal therapist. Her job was to help me develop and implement my personal care plan. All the patients had personal therapists and personal care plans. Except we were no longer referred to as patients. Now we were called service users – as if this were a library or swimming pool.

It felt beyond ridiculous, but I kept telling myself that these games had to be played.

My personal therapist was called Dr Hadley. Hadley was her surname. Her first name was Lisa. She told me I could call her Lisa if I preferred.

I called her Dr Hadley – mostly because I had to keep

reminding myself she was a real doctor. Dr Hadley didn't look like a real doctor. She looked like an actress who had been badly miscast. And this was just the start of the problem.

The more I looked at her, the more I realized that Dr Hadley actually resembled *me* in many ways. She was like a better version of me: a little older – early thirties at a push – a little taller; a warmer complexion; much more accomplished. She was a little slimmer, too – at least at the moment – and her hair was a better shade of blonde: rich and honey-hued, where mine, of late, had taken on the appearance of straw on a cloudy day.

I didn't know how I was going to cope with therapy with Dr Hadley.

The smoking area was pretty much indiscernible from the one on Nile. It occupied a small courtyard, surrounded on three sides by bricks and by trees, trellises and the prison-style fence on the other. But for that fence, it could have been any suburban patio: neatly paved, bordered with low-maintenance shrubs and plants. There was a cheap plastic table and four matching chairs, and it was in one of these chairs, in the late afternoon of my second day on Amazon, that I sat smoking my seventh cigarette and listening to my iPod, which I'd discovered at the bottom of my handbag.

Listening to music was a risk, I knew. It was the kind of thing that might have tipped me back over the edge a few days ago – and bursting into tears in one of the communal areas was not part of my plan; I had resolved to keep any crying minimal and private. But when I finally plucked up the courage to press play, I was relieved to find that the music didn't really affect me one way or the other. It was just one more way to block out the external world, and this was my prime objective that day. I was struggling to adjust to people – to people not simply lying motionless in beds, or, at worst, talking to themselves in corridors, but actually wanting things from me: eye contact, acknowledgement, talk. I didn't want to talk to anyone, and I didn't want other people's conversations buzzing in the background. I just wanted to smoke in peace. Wearing my earphones, I thought, was the perfect deterrent to any social interaction.

But it turned out this was just wishful thinking.

There was nothing very remarkable about the girl who sat down next to me – nothing except her age. She was obviously very young; she couldn't have been older than nineteen or twenty, I thought. She was wearing a dark red vest top with shorts and sandals – it was, after all, still a blazing hot summer; as perfect a summer as you ever get in England. This was something that never failed to surprise me, every time I went outside. I don't know why. I suppose there was a part of me that thought the weather should be paying more attention to the turn my life had taken, not just carrying on regardless.

The girl was small. She had very straight dark brown hair cut just above her shoulders. Her forearms were latticed with scars, some old and pale, some red and recent.

I observed all this in a swift, furtive glance, then fixed my eyes back on the parallel lines of the metal fence. I needed my sunglasses, I realized. Then I could look wherever I wanted. I could look at her arms to my heart's content and she'd never know. But the courtyard was almost permanently in shade from the high walls and trees. I couldn't wear sunglasses without looking like I was wearing them to hide something.

If I'd thought I could get away with it, without appearing

even crazier, I would have worn my sunglasses throughout the day, even in therapy. *Especially* in therapy. That would have solved the eye contact problem for good.

I was mulling over these thoughts when the dark-haired girl reached over and tapped me on the shoulder.

She smiled, then mouthed something.

I shrugged and pointed to my earphones.

She gestured for me to take them out.

What choice did I have?

'What are you listening to?' she asked.

My iPod was on shuffle. I wasn't up to making complicated decisions about what music I wanted to hear. Especially since it didn't matter; it was just a shield.

'I'm listening to "Airwave" by Rank 1,' I told her.

The girl shook her head. 'Don't know it. Any good?'

'It's sublime,' I answered automatically.

'Happy or sad?'

'Excuse me?'

'Is it happy music or sad music?'

I had to think about this for several moments. I wasn't sure if the question even made sense. Could all music be placed into one of these two boxes? Or was that an insane way of thinking about music? It didn't seem insane to me, but that told me nothing.

'It's both,' I decided, eventually. 'Or it's neither; I'm not sure. It's the kind of music that moulds itself to your mood.'

The girl nodded, looking unconvinced. She didn't get it, I could tell. Not that it mattered. I'd be leaving in a moment. My cigarette was almost down to the filter. I took one more drag, then crushed it out.

'I'm Melody,' the girl said.

'Right. How appropriate.'

Melody kept looking at me but didn't say anything.

'It's a very pretty name,' I added.

I had already slipped my iPod back in my pocket. If I didn't introduce myself, I was under no obligation to stay and talk. But then Melody did something that stopped me in my tracks – pretty much the only thing that could have stopped me. She took out her cigarettes and extended the pack towards me. There were two left.

I looked at them for a few moments, then looked back at Melody. She smiled and gave a small shrug.

I decided at that point that Melody was an idiot. I wouldn't have given away my penultimate cigarette for anything less than immediate freedom. Not when their supply was so uncertain. But if she was offering, there was no way I was going to refuse. I allowed my poised leg muscles to relax.

'I'm Abby,' I said.

'Hello, Abby,' she replied. 'You're new here?'

'Sort of. I was on Nile for a couple of weeks.'

'Oh, right. Nile.' Melody gave a small, knowing nod. 'Did you try to kill yourself?' I looked at her. She lit her cigarette, then shrugged without apology. 'I was on Nile for a bit. Took a load of pills – about thirty. But I didn't die, obviously. I puked and passed out. Nile was where I woke up.'

'I don't want to kill myself,' I lied.

Melody nodded effusively. 'No, of course not. Me neither. Not any more. I'm having ECT three times a week. That seems to have sorted me out. What about you?'

'Lithium,' I told her. 'I don't think I'm allowed ECT. It might send me nuts again.'

'You went nuts?'

'Yes. Pretty much.'

'What happened?'

'I stopped sleeping. Put myself in some stupid, risky situations. Went on a shopping spree.'

Melody snorted some smoke out from her nose. 'I've been on plenty of those. Nothing crazy about shopping.'

I shrugged. 'It depends how you go about it. I spent the best part of sixteen hundred pounds in a day – on a hotel room, a dress and a tit tattoo.'

'Jesus.'

There was a little silence as we both smoked.

'Can I see it?'

'See what?'

'The tit tattoo.'

'No. You can't.'

This wasn't modesty. What's the point of modesty on the mental ward, with no locks on the bathroom doors? But, still, I had to think of appearances. There was a CCTV camera in one corner of the courtyard, and a chance, at least, that someone was watching. Sharing a conversation with another service user would be seen as a positive step towards recovery; showing her my tits would not. Nevertheless, Melody looked weirdly hurt at my refusal. 'I have one on my ankle, too,' I told her. 'You can see that instead.'

My right leg was crossed over my left, so I only had to reach down and raise the bottom of my jeans a little. Melody looked for a few seconds, took it in, then said, 'You have a scar as well – on your right hand. Looks like a burn.'

Usually, I would have been impressed. People didn't notice my scar, or didn't recognize it for what it was. But Melody had an eye for things like that, which came as no great surprise. And she knew scar tissue when she saw it.

'Cigarette burn,' I said. With the conversation progressing as it was, I saw no reason not to tell her. What harm could it do? 'I was drunk. My boyfriend and I were having this stupid fight. I can't even remember what it was about now – that's how stupid it was.' I paused and tapped some ash into the ashtray. It wasn't for dramatic effect. I was deciding whether it was worth ending the story, since Melody could guess the rest. She knew what you'd have to do to get a scar like that. 'I put it out in my hand,' I told her. 'Next thing I knew I was in a taxi on my way to A&E.'

'Wow.' Melody nodded appreciatively. She was, as I'd already surmised, in the very small fraction of the population who wouldn't respond to a story like this by asking *why* I'd decided to burn myself. She understood that there were various possible reasons. 'How did it feel?' she asked instead.

'Exquisite, for a second or so. After that, it hurt like hell. The pain was so bad I threw up in the taxi. The worst pain you can imagine.'

I could tell from Melody's face that she *was* imagining it, which probably wasn't healthy for her. But I figured a question that honest deserved an honest answer.

'So.' Melody let a pillar of ash fall and scatter on the breeze. 'Have they given you a diagnosis yet?'

'Yes. Not here, though. I was *diagnosed* a few years back. Type two bipolar. You?'

'Acute unipolar depression, and maybe some sort of personality disorder as well. They're still deciding. You know what doctors're like.'

I shrugged. 'They like to find the right box for us.'

We smoked the rest of our cigarettes without saying much. There wasn't much more to say.

A SECOND LETTER: THE MOST ASTONISHING THING IN THE TATE MODERN

Dear Abby,

So here I am again: another letter that you might never read. But Barbara said I should go ahead and write it anyway. She thinks it might do me some good. I've no idea if that's true, but it's not as if I have a lot of other options right now. And I suppose it's liberating, in a way – writing a letter that will probably end up in the bin in a few hours' time. At least I don't have to worry about saying the wrong thing. I figure I can just tell you exactly what's been going through my mind over the past week, good and bad. And if, by some small chance, you are reading this – if you're well enough to read it – then perhaps this is still the best way to go about things. There's no point writing something dishonest, right?

Last night was a bad one for me. I was up until God knows when thinking about us, trying to work out where and when everything went wrong. Because things have gone wrong. That's the conclusion I've been forced to draw. You won't see me, you won't talk to me. If you don't want me around now, of all times, then what exactly does that say about our relationship? The truth is, I'm not sure how much longer I can go on like this. I don't want to leave you, I really don't, but more and more, it feels like the choice is out of my hands. You've already left.

For a while, I tried telling myself that perhaps this is for the best. Because if I can't be there for you right now, as you seem to think, then what future can we possibly have? Just more of the same: endless ups and downs which neither of us can do a damn thing to prevent. We'd be better off apart. It stands to reason.

Except, of course, it's not that easy. I'm reminded of that old cliché – one of your favourites: you can choose your friends, but you can't choose your family. Well, whoever came up with that should have added that you can't choose who you fall in love with either.

So do you know what I ended up thinking about last night? I was trying to list all the reasons we'd be better off apart, and instead I found myself remembering all the details of our first date. You took me to the Tate Modern and made me grade all the paintings A-E. It was a little terrifying, to be honest, or it was at first – less a getting-to-know-you than a weird cultural initiation test. I remember asking you if we couldn't just go for a quiet drink instead, and you told me no, for two reasons: 1)

Taste in art was much more revealing than taste in alcohol. 2) You were flat broke, so we had to do something free. Shortly after that, we had our first ever argument – over Francis Bacon's Seated Figure. I graded it C and you went apoplectic and started waxing lyrical about how it was one of only three pieces in the gallery that was beyond reproach and deserved an A++ (along with Souza's Crucifixion and Dali's Metamorphosis of Narcissus). But the truth is, I'd pretty much stopped looking at the paintings by then. I only had eyes for you, and I came really close to telling you that a couple of times. But I couldn't, of course, not on a first date. It would have sounded too much like a line.

Well, it wouldn't have been a line. So I can tell you now, three years after the fact in a letter you won't read. You were astonishing that day. The most astonishing thing in the Tate Modern. After just a couple of hours together, I already knew that my life would feel much, much poorer without you in it.

And you have to know that a big part of me still feels that way, three years down the line. It's just that things have got a whole lot more complicated.

Early on, I used to think we could get through anything. Actually, no. If I'm being honest, what I thought was more naïve than that. I thought that I could get you through anything, that it was just a case of unconditional support, of drying your tears and patiently waiting for things to get better. But back then I had no idea how draining it can be, trying to look after someone who, at best, doesn't appreciate the effort. God, that sounds harsh, set out in black and white like that, but I don't think it's a judgement you'd contradict. I remember you telling me once that depression is a completely selfish condition, one that takes away your ability to engage with anything beyond the fog in your own head. You have nothing to give, no energy or emotion that isn't turned inwards. So when you're at your worst, it's not a case of being there to dry your tears. There aren't any tears to dry. There's just this void, this empty shell that can't be reasoned with or comforted.

Then there's the mania, which is every bit as intractable, with the added problem that half the time I don't even know how best to support you. Yes, I've got better at spotting the early warning signs, but at what point am I supposed to intervene? You're feeling brighter, happier, creative, energized – perhaps for the first time in weeks – so why would you want any of that to stop? And why would I? I don't want to be the person who's constantly holding you back, smothering that spark that makes you you. But we both know how quickly things can slide. Energy turns to hyperactivity, thrill-seeking, spiralling hedonism, self-destructiveness – at which point it's far too late to rein you in.

There was a time when I used to be an optimist. I used to think that things were bound to get easier in the future, however distant that future might be. Even when crisis followed crisis, I was always able to convince myself that now, finally, we'd been through the worst. We'd hit rock bottom, but now you were going to get the help you needed, and things would have to improve. I felt that way last year when you burned yourself and had to be hospitalized for forty-eight hours. I felt that way after we'd got through that awful couple of months when you were starting then stopping the lithium. But I don't feel like that any more. At some point in the past few weeks, I've stopped believing that things will get better rather than worse.

So where does that leave us? God, I wish I knew. I've been writing for more than an hour now, it's just gone midnight and I'm still no clearer about anything. There's just this jumble of contradictions that seems to amount to one giant no-win situation.

I still love you, I still miss you. But I'm no longer sure that's going to be enough.

THE MIRROR PEOPLE

When she wasn't in therapy or being electrocuted, Melody was almost a permanent feature of the smoking area, as constant and reliable as the twelve-foot security fence. She had an inexhaustible supply of cigarettes thanks to her mother, who brought in a couple of packs most evenings and weekends. Melody would then give them away as freely as condoms in a GUM clinic. This was one of the reasons that Melody was always worth smoking with; but it was not the only reason.

Talking to Melody, it turned out, was far preferable to talking to the sane – mostly because there was none of the usual bullshit to get through: none of the evasion or pretence; no carefully chosen words or timid circling of the point. And there was no need for the inane trivia of everyday life: What do you do? Where do you live? Conversations with Melody didn't start on the ground floor; they started in the attic, with the stuff your family didn't even know about, because they'd never asked – and wouldn't like the answers.

Melody had already been on Amazon for two weeks when I

arrived, and this, combined with her endless cigarettes and continual need for chat, meant that she knew pretty much everyone on the ward. She was also a terrible gossip, and before long, I had been indirectly acquainted with the backstories of most of the other inmates.

Amazon's oldest and longest-serving resident was Mrs Chang, a fifty-nine-year-old Chinese woman who had been on and off psychiatric wards all her adult life. Mrs Chang had been on Amazon so long that she had her own chair in the dayroom – the one opposite the TV – which no one else would use out of respect. For a while, I assumed it was respect, too, that caused Melody to refer to Mrs Chang only by her surname – what with Mrs Chang being so unimaginably old. Or perhaps Melody simply didn't know Mrs Chang's first name. Both were reasonable guesses, but neither turned out to be correct. I later discovered that Melody did know Mrs Chang's first name, but was unable to divulge it; all she could tell me was that it started with an X and was a real mouthful.

Then there was Jocelyn, a six-foot-tall, two-foot-wide black woman in her early thirties who, Melody said, was *proper* crazy – as if the rest of us were just here for a holiday. Jocelyn had been on Nile for more than a month, and could have been kept there even longer. She'd been transferred not because she was getting any better, but on the grounds that she was completely harmless. Despite her formidable appearance, Jocelyn posed no danger to anyone, least of all herself.

Then there was Paula the paranoid schizophrenic, and Angelina the regular schizophrenic, and obsessive compulsive Claire, and so on and so forth. And I had no doubt that my backstory had likewise done the rounds, since Melody didn't know the meaning of the word discretion – literally. Within a couple of days, I was probably bipolar Abby, or Abigail Burns, or something similar. But at least it was a level playing field. Thanks to Melody, there were no secrets on the ward, and because every woman in here had attained a comparable level of craziness, there was little stigma in having your psychiatric history served up for general consumption. I never felt judged.

With the doctors, of course, the opposite was true. I felt judged every hour of every day – including the hours I spent asleep. This was not paranoia; the quality and quantity of my rest was a subject I had to discuss at great length with Dr Hadley, and she always seemed to know when I'd had a bad night, despite my unflagging assurances that I'd slept like a baby. More and more, I found that therapy with Dr Hadley was turning into a fencing match, full of feints and complicated footwork, sudden thrusts and clumsy parries. The never-ending challenge was to give her the impression that I was being open and cooperative while actually being evasive and guarded. It was a challenge that often proved insurmountable. Dr Hadley kept implying that I was being evasive and guarded.

I finally cracked in art therapy. Most of the other service users were drawing or painting; Mrs Chang was shaping an oblong of modelling clay into what appeared to be a tiny coffin. But I was trying to write. Dr Hadley had suggested, in our previous session, that this might help me, that I might find it easier than talking. This made perfect sense to her; since writing was my job, perhaps trying to write would help me to reconnect with 'the old Abby'.

Where the old Abby would have told Dr Hadley to stop being

so fucking patronizing, the new Abby nodded meekly. After all, getting a reputation for being hostile and resistant to therapy was not going to help matters.

This was how I found myself staring for the best part of an hour at a small stack of blank sheets. I could imagine the sort of thing Dr Hadley wanted from me – a mood journal or a long, emotional essay about my childhood – but when I picked up the pen, it felt like a lead weight in my hand. It turned out that it was much harder to lie in writing than it was verbally. I knew that anything I set down on paper was bound to betray me. But I had to give her something. If I didn't, if I refused even to try, it would be yet another black mark on my record.

It was only when I'd stopped trying to write and started stabbing the pen into my palm that I hit upon an answer. I decided to write a short abstract poem. It would be extremely short and extremely abstract, possibly a haiku, and crammed full of evocative but impenetrable imagery. Then Dr Hadley could spend as many fruitless hours as she wanted trying to decipher it. More likely, she'd just be pleased that I was trying to express myself, and all I'd have to do in our next session would be to nod in all the right places and wax lyrical about how much the writing process had helped.

Unfortunately, by the time I'd settled on this plan there wasn't long enough to implement it. Art therapy was almost over, and my next session with Dr Hadley was right after lunch. Even if I'd been in the mood, there was no time to get creative.

Instead, I wrote from memory, jotting down the following four lines:

The hopes so juicy ripening –
You almost bathed your tongue –
When bliss disclosed a hundred toes –
And fled with every one.

Under which I scrawled an explanatory note:

Dear Dr Hadley,
   This isn't my original composition; it's from a poem by
Emily Dickinson which I memorized in school. It's about a cat
stalking a robin. When I sat down to write, this is what
popped into my head. I don't think I can write anything
original right now. I'll try again tomorrow.
   Abby

After art therapy was over, I slipped the single sheet of paper
under Dr Hadley's door. Then I went outside for a smoke.

Of course, it wasn't *just* about a cat and a robin, as Dr Hadley
was quick to point out. Neither was it a poem that had popped
into my head at random.

'It's quite pertinent to your situation, isn't it?' Dr Hadley
asked. Except she wasn't really asking.

She glanced over the lines again, her eyes like little blue
scalpels. I could tell from her expression that literary analysis
was yet another of her strengths. She probably painted astonishing watercolours too.

'Do you want to tell me about being manic?'

'No, I don't,' I replied. Dr Hadley looked at me and waited. I
shrugged. 'Racing thoughts, rash decisions, impaired judgement—'

'That's not what I mean,' she interrupted. 'I don't want a list of symptoms. I want to know what it feels like. Subjectively. You enjoy it?'

'Yes. In the early stages, anyway, I enjoy it very much.'

'Why do you enjoy it?'

I searched for the note of accusation in her voice, but couldn't find it. She was taking a more straightforward approach than was usual, going for the direct, open question; and she waited patiently for at least a minute while I thought about my reply. The easiest way to explain would be to tell her that it felt like being on speed, but much cleaner: all of the focus, energy and confidence, none of the teeth-grinding or stomach cramps. But it didn't seem sensible to tell Dr Hadley this.

'I enjoy it because it's extraordinary,' I told her. 'It's like existing in a perfect little bubble. Everything feels easy, nothing hurts. If I could live my whole life like that, I would.'

Dr Hadley nodded slowly, then said, 'But it doesn't last, does it? Not for very long. The bubble always bursts.'

I shrugged. 'If it lasted, we wouldn't be having this conversation.'

Dr Hadley smiled wryly, in acknowledgement of this truism. 'And what about afterwards? How do you feel then?'

It was the 'then' that allowed me to answer this. If she'd said 'now', I would have lied. But we weren't talking about now. We were still talking in generalities.

'I feel bereft,' I told her.

She waited, and I could tell she wanted me to go on – was going to wait for as long as it took. So I gave her an analogy. She wanted a 'subjective' response, and this was the only way I could get close.

'Imagine you're walking on a sunny day,' I began. 'Somewhere pretty. A beach, for example. You can feel the sunlight on your face and arms, and the warm sand under your feet. Everything is extremely bright and clear. You can see thousands of individual grains of sand – that's how clear it is.'

I'd been staring out of Dr Hadley's window, which faced out onto a bare brick wall, but at this point I looked at her to make sure the words were all making sense. She nodded for me to continue.

'But then, very slowly, a dark cloud starts to pass in front of the sun. The light and warmth begin to fade, the colour drains from everything, and, bit by bit, the landscape is transformed. Nothing is clear any more. The beach is flat and empty. The sea is just an endless grey sheet. And when you look up at the sky, you see that this isn't a temporary thing. The cloud goes on for ever, stretching right back to the horizon.'

I stopped talking. This was far more than I'd intended to say, and it felt like a huge effort to get the words out. Dr Hadley must have sensed this. After a few moments of silence, she told me that she'd see me again tomorrow. In the meantime, she wanted me to keep writing. My words or someone else's. Whatever I preferred.

It was the shortest session we'd had; the whole thing lasted barely ten minutes. But even at the time, as I rose from my chair and stepped out of the office, it felt as if something odd and significant had happened. For the first time since I'd started seeing her, I'd told Dr Hadley nothing but the truth.

It was the next day that it happened. Not in therapy; outside in the smoking area. With Melody.

I was on my own at first. Paula the paranoid schizophrenic came out for a bit, but we didn't talk, and she sloped off as soon as she'd finished her cigarette. I think most of the other crazies were in the dayroom or exercise class. Except Melody. She was with her mother, who had a half-day off work.

I'd come out here intending to write something else for Dr Hadley, or at least to see if I could. But I never got that far. I was rummaging for a pen in my handbag, when my hand brushed instead a folded envelope. When I took it out, I discovered it was the last article I'd written – 'Which Blue is Right for You?' – frenetically scrawled on eight sheets of embossed Dorchester notepaper.

I spent the next ten, maybe even fifteen minutes reading through it. I took my time, and read it twice. After that, I couldn't do anything much but sit and smoke. It wasn't that the writing was bad; it was the opposite. And yes, it was just a throwaway fashion piece that I'd planned to hock to *Cosmopolitan* – but that wasn't the point either. The prose still glittered. It was warm and witty and engaging. It was the sort of thing I could trim, type up and sell tomorrow – had I felt even the smallest desire to do so. Which I didn't, of course. Instead, I had that desolate beach feeling again, or a weaker echo of it. I didn't feel bereft, exactly – just dull and wistful.

I didn't notice Melody approaching. The first moment I was conscious of her was when she plonked herself in the seat opposite. She flicked a cigarette across the table before lighting one for herself.

'What you reading?'

'It's something I wrote when I was manic. The day before I came here.'

'Can I see?'

I didn't see any reason to refuse. Melody read through the small stack of paper while I smoked in silence.

'You wrote this when you were nuts?'

'Yes.'

'It's good.'

I shrugged. 'A paradox.' Then, because I was fairly sure Melody didn't know this word, I added, 'I write well when I'm manic. Always have. I wrote that naked in the Dorchester.'

'Why?'

'It was a hot day. I'd just got out the bath—'

Melody cut me off with a giggle. 'No, that's not what I meant. Why did you write it? What's it for?'

'Oh. It's my job – was my job.'

'You're a writer?'

'Yes. Freelance.' I gestured across at the article. 'I was planning to sell that to *Cosmopolitan*.'

'Cool. How much would you get for it?'

I shrugged. 'Not a huge amount. Maybe two hundred pounds.'

'Holy shit!' Melody's jaw had dropped, which I'd always assumed was just a figure of speech.

'It's not a lot,' I assured her. 'Not when you convert it into an annual salary. I'm lucky if I sell a couple of features a week. Some weeks, I don't sell any.'

'Yeah, but when you do it's like hitting the jackpot, isn't it? It must be good being so brainy.'

As with everything Melody said, there was no hidden agenda here, no spite or sarcasm. She meant it as a genuine compliment, which left me feeling strangely embarrassed. It occurred to me, then, that this was the first time Melody and I had had a relatively normal conversation about the outside world. We'd clocked up several hours talking about lithium and ECT and self-harm and the other service users, but we'd never got round to discussing the basics. I didn't even know her surname.

'What about you?' I asked. 'What do you do?'

'For work?'

'Yes.'

'Trainee nail technician. The pay's shit, but I like the job. I get to talk to a lot of different people.' Melody held out her left hand so I could inspect her fingernails. They were neat and well filed, but extremely short. 'I chewed the fuck out of them on Nile,' she explained. 'But they used to be beautiful, trust me. You ever get your nails done?'

'Yes, sometimes. I got them done a few weeks ago. My dad was taking me to dinner.'

'That's nice.'

'Not really. It was with his new girlfriend. She's only a few years older than I am.'

Melody nodded sympathetically. 'My dad left me and my mum, too, when I was twelve. I didn't see him very often after that. A few times a year. He's dead now.'

'Oh. I'm sorry.'

Melody shrugged, and for once her face was unreadable. She handed me back my *Cosmopolitan* article, then took two more cigarettes from the pack on the table. It was at this point that she started to tell me about the mirror people. I thought at first that she was trying to change the subject, because it was obvious that neither of us wanted to talk about our fathers, but I suppose, in hindsight, there was a connection of sorts.

'Jocelyn's got this theory,' she began. 'It's really fucking crazy.'

'Of course it is.'

'Do you know what parallel worlds are? They're in *Doctor Who* sometimes.'

'*Doctor Who*?'

'Yeah. Jocelyn's a big *Doctor Who* fan.'

'I've never seen it,' I told her. 'But I know what parallel worlds are. I understand the concept.'

Melody nodded. 'I had to look them up on my phone. Didn't think I'd find anything, but there's actually a shitload about them on Wikipedia.' Melody paused and took a long drag from her cigarette. 'Anyway, Jocelyn thinks we're all living in a parallel world. She thinks she got here by travelling through a portal on the Northern Line. In between Goodge Street and Tottenham Court Road.'

'She thinks we're all living in a parallel world?'

'Yes.'

'Everyone?'

'No, not everyone. Just us. Me, you, all the other nuts on the ward. That's what connects us. We've all fallen through portals.'

'On the Northern Line?'

'No, that's just Jocelyn's personal portal. They're all over the place. In lifts and fire exits – places like that. It's just that Jocelyn happens to know exactly where hers was. She noticed the train wobble as it went through it. She was brought to Nile not long after that.'

'I'm not surprised.'

'It gets weirder,' Melody warned.

'Go on.'

'At the same moment Jocelyn passed through the portal, her double from this world passed through the other way.

That's how it works – kind of like a busy nightclub. One in, one out.'

'Oh . . . Jocelyn has a double.'

'Not just Jocelyn. We all have doubles. Everyone here has a double who's taken over their life back in the original world. And we've all realized what's going on – at least on some level. That's why we're here. Whereas the doubles have no idea. They think they're the originals, so they just get on with our lives as if nothing's happened. You know: go to work, do the shopping, pay the bills. Jocelyn calls them the mirror people. They're identical to us in almost every way.'

'*Almost* every way?'

'Yes, except they're not locked up on mental wards, of course. Oh, and they're the opposite colour, too.'

'Excuse me?'

'Opposite colour. Jocelyn told me her mirror person is white. Sane and white.'

'And mine?'

Melody shrugged. 'Black, I guess. Sane and black – same as mine.'

'Right. And Mrs Chang's?'

'Mexican.'

'Mexican? Because . . . Mexican is the opposite of Chinese?'

'Yes. According to Jocelyn.'

And that's when it happened. I don't think I would have even known, had Melody not pointed it out. It felt so fucking natural.

'Hey,' she said. 'You're smiling. You realize that? No, don't stop! I was starting to think you *couldn't* smile.'

I was too shocked to say anything in reply. Melody reached over the table and placed her hand on mine. It was then that I started to cry, as well. I must have cried for the next two minutes, maybe longer. But I don't think the smile ever left my face.

That night I slept straight through for nine hours, and I awoke thinking about the mirror people. I didn't get up straight away; until one of the nurses came in with breakfast, I lay perfectly still, staring at a single spot on the ceiling where the paint was beginning to flake away. Since I'd been admitted, I'd spent plenty of time staring at ceilings, but this was different. My mind wasn't cold and blank. I didn't even feel sluggish. I felt calm and alert, able to focus on a specific idea and examine it from all angles.

The more I thought about Jocelyn's theory, the less bizarre it seemed. Yes, there were things about it that were absolutely cuckoo – Mrs Chang's Mexican double and so forth – but still, overall the idea was not without its merits. It made a strange sort of sense to me, on an intuitive, metaphorical level. Being in here – going crazy – it did feel like your life had been hijacked in some inexplicable way. It did feel like a parallel universe, separated from the real one by only the flimsiest of partitions.

And there was something else, too: like Jocelyn, I knew the precise location of my portal, the where and when that had caused my life to veer off its regular track. Hers was on the Northern Line, somewhere between Goodge Street and Tottenham Court Road; mine was the doorway to Simon's flat. That was where everything had started: the insomnia, Professor Caborn, the weird and racing thoughts. Admittedly, there might have been other contributing factors – other causes stretching further back in time. Yet it was hard to shake the feeling that if I hadn't entered Simon's flat that evening, if I'd turned and taken the mirror path back to my normal Wednesday night, then none of this would have happened. I wouldn't be where I was now – staring at the peeling paintwork in the local mental health ward.

But yesterday the situation had changed again. I hadn't seen it coming, of course, I'd been so focused on taking my recovery that I failed to notice I was actually getting better, albeit in tiny, plodding increments.

Now it felt as if a hairline crack had appeared in the darkness separating this world from the other; and over the following days, it continued to widen. I was soon noticing further signs of improvement. My sessions with Dr Hadley were no longer something I dreaded. I was reading more and sleeping well. I started to think about the things I might enjoy when I finally got out of this place: a decent cup of coffee, a walk to the shops – small things, but significant, nonetheless.

For a short interlude, everything was getting so much better.

That was before I discovered the truth about Melody.

REVELATIONS

I couldn't stay still that morning. I tried lying with my eyes closed and counting down from a hundred. I tried listening to music as a distraction. I tried reading *Gone with the Wind*. I managed a few pages before my mind drifted away. After that, I just sat up in bed, checking the clock every few minutes.

He was due to arrive at eleven and would stay for up to an hour, depending on how things went. Right now, I wasn't sure I'd manage fifteen minutes. This felt weirdly like a first date – same butterflies, same anxieties about what we'd have to say to each other. I'd even thought about putting on some make-up, before deciding it didn't feel appropriate. There was a part of me, I suppose, that was already preparing a defence. I didn't want to appear too normal, too bright or healthy. I was still recovering, after all, and I thought no make-up and dressing down – tracksuit bottoms and a plain, baggy top – was the best way to convey this.

Was it slightly manipulative, trying to control his perception of me like this? Possibly; but it would be equally manipulative if I made any sort of effort to look nice. It's a strange thing, trying to readjust to normal life, with all its complicated social interactions, and it doesn't get any easier once you start worrying about how best to act natural.

The choice of a first meeting place was likewise something that continued to give me a headache. I'd ruled out the dayroom as I couldn't imagine trying to have a serious conversation in there, with *Homes Under the Hammer* blaring in the background and Mrs Chang hovering like a silent spectre in my peripheral vision. The smoking area was, unfortunately, also out of the question. Wonderful as it would have been to be able to smoke, Melody was certain to be present at some point; she had a ten o'clock with Dr Hadley, and I assumed she'd come straight out after that. Of course, she knew Beck was coming, and she knew I was worried about it, but that didn't mean she'd have the tact to allow us any space for a private conversation. More likely, she'd come over and start talking about ECT or self-mutilation.

That left just a few more options. There was the kitchenette – bright, functional and relatively quiet, with bad instant coffee on tap, but also a high probability of people walking in and out every few minutes. The only other communal space that might work was the non-denominational prayer room – but then we'd have to find a nurse to accompany us off the ward, since one room served the entire mental heath unit. Plus it wasn't impossible that someone might actually want to use it for prayer.

After a lot of consideration, my bedside had seemed the least problematic choice, and it did have the advantage of meeting expectation. When you visited someone in hospital, you expected to be sitting by a sickbed, and this could work in my favour. It was another of those visual cues that would make it clear I was still in a fragile state. Yet, at the same time, it felt like a bit of a charade. I never stayed in bed this late any more. Not that I was exactly *in* bed at the moment. I was kind of half in, half out, fully dressed but with the sheets pulled up to my waist; I was certain it all looked far too artful, like someone posing for a painting: *Convalescing Girl*.

These concerns all disappeared the moment Beck entered the room, to be replaced with a fresh wave of dilemmas that I hadn't even considered. The first was that I had no idea how to greet him. I ended up performing a strange sort of half-wave, even though he was standing just a few feet away. When he bent to kiss my cheek, the angle I was sitting at meant that I had to twist my waist and neck awkwardly, placing an unsteady hand on his shoulder blade to keep my balance. My whole posture felt stiff and apprehensive.

'I brought flowers,' he told me, as he seated himself in the chair by the window, 'but they were confiscated at reception.'

'Yes, they're worried we'll eat them,' I replied, immediately wanting to retract this. It would be better, I decided, not to appear facetious. 'Actually, I think it's a hospital-wide policy,' I told him. 'They get in the way, upset people's allergies. They can bring in bugs, too. I don't think you're allowed flowers even if you're dying.'

'Oh . . . What about plastic ones?'

'I'm not sure about plastic ones.'

There was a small silence. Beck gestured at the book that was still splayed on top of my bedside cabinet. 'How's *Gone with the Wind*?'

I shrugged. 'About the same as the film. The odd difference here and there. Ashley's in the Ku Klux Klan.'

Beck smiled because he assumed I was joking, which of course I wasn't. 'And how are you?'

'I'm getting there,' I replied. 'They have me on lithium, and I've been tolerating it pretty well for a week or so. I still have good days and bad days, but slightly fewer of the latter now. Things are heading in the right direction.'

He nodded slowly. 'Have the doctors given you any idea of when you might be out?'

'My personal therapist thinks it could be as soon as next week. But she's also said that they won't discharge me until I feel ready, and . . . well, I'm not sure.'

I could see that he was turning this statement over in his mind, searching for the implications.

'Actually, I'm a little terrified of coming out,' I blurted. 'I mean, there's a lot of stuff I'll have to deal with. Stuff that—'

'That *we'll* have to deal with,' Beck corrected – and it was such a sweet and generous correction that it made me hate myself for what I had to say next. But I didn't have much choice. He wasn't yet in a position to understand what he was offering.

'Listen,' I began. 'It's not that I don't appreciate everything you've done— No, I'm sorry. That's wrong. That makes it sound like you're doing me a favour, and I know this is so much more. Let me try again.' I closed my eyes and took a breath to steady myself. 'You've been incredible, and it's much more than I deserve.'

'Don't—'

'No, please let me finish. This is hard enough already.' I waited for a few moments until he nodded for me to continue.

'You've been incredible,' I repeated. 'But there are some things I need to come to terms with on my own. My medication, for one.'

'You're going to stay on it?' His voice was measured, but there was still an undertone of alarm there that made me feel oddly vindicated.

'I'm going to try,' I told him. 'The way I've felt over the past few weeks, since I came here, I don't ever want to put myself through that again. But that still doesn't make the decision easy – and yes, I know how hard that is for anyone else to understand. But there are things that I'm going to miss – that I already miss. I can't help it. I feel diminished, and that's something I'm going to have to learn to live with.'

Beck didn't say anything for a long time, and neither did I.

'Do you know what the worst thing is, for me?' he asked eventually.

'I can think of a dozen things,' I said.

'It's being held at arm's length all the time. As soon as you feel hurt or scared or threatened it's like this barrier comes up and nothing's getting through. The last couple of weeks, not even being allowed to see you – well, I wish I could say that came as a shock, but it didn't. It felt pretty typical.'

'There's nothing you could have said or done. I was suicidal. I could barely communicate.'

'God, Abby – you're so bloody dense sometimes! It's not about anything I could have said or done. You didn't have to go through that alone. I could have been there with you. Wouldn't that have made some sort of difference?'

'I still would have been alone,' I told him.

I could see how much the words stung, but I had to be honest at this point. It would be kinder in the long run. Anyway, there was worse to come; and I thought if I didn't tell him now, then I wouldn't tell him at all.

'There's another reason you being here wouldn't have been helpful,' I said. 'For either of us.'

He looked at me but didn't say anything. I think he must have known from my tone that this conversation wasn't going to get any gentler.

'The night I walked out . . .' I began. 'I don't know what Dr Barbara has told you – not much, I'd imagine.'

Beck laughed, humourlessly. 'Patient confidentiality again. She said you were safe and hadn't come to any serious harm – anything else would have to come from you, when you were ready.'

'I'm sorry,' I said. 'I know that can't have been very reassuring.'

'No. It wasn't.'

'I booked myself into the Dorchester. Did she tell you that much?'

'Yes – or she said that's where she picked you up. But that was all.'

'Okay.'

For the next five minutes, Beck didn't say anything. He just sat very still while I gave him a complete account of what had happened that night. He stopped making eye contact when I got to the man in the bar – the man whose name I couldn't even remember – but I don't think that made it any easier to go on. The only small consolation I could find was that he must have been prepared for a worse ending than the one I gave him.

'We went back to my room,' I said. 'We kissed, he touched my breasts – but that was as far as it went. I stopped things before they got any further. Actually, I started screaming the place down. Some of the night staff came in. That was when I called Dr Barbara.'

The silence when I'd finished speaking seemed to hang in the air like a storm cloud.

'That's everything?' Beck asked.

'Yes.' The only detail I'd left out was that he'd hit me, but I didn't think it was fair to bring this up. I didn't deserve to look like a victim in any of this.

Beck looked at me again, his face more or less blank. 'I don't know what I can say.'

'You can say whatever you feel like saying. Shout if you want. You have every right to.'

'Do I?' He let the question hang for a few seconds. 'You see, that's the problem, isn't it? I honestly don't know how much of that was you and how much was . . . I don't know – illness, mania, something separate.'

'Neither do I,' I said.

'Can you even tell me what was going through your head at the time? Can you give me any idea?'

'My head was all over the place. I was really out of control – drunk, confused, hyperactive, but . . . God, this just sounds like I'm making excuses, and I don't know that I can. The truth is, there was a part of me that knew exactly what I was doing. But I still couldn't stop it, or I didn't want to stop it. I don't know which. It was completely irrational and self-destructive. I suppose the closest I can come to explaining is to say that I didn't really care what happened. I didn't have the capacity to care. Except this isn't the full story either, because obviously there was a part of me that did care too.'

I fell silent. As messy as this explanation was, it was the only honest answer I could give, and I think Beck understood this – although I could see that he was still at a loss as to how to respond. So I thought I'd make it easy for him.

'Listen,' I said. 'I need some time alone to get my head straight.

And so do you. When I get out of here – whenever that is – I think it would be better if we spent some time apart.'

He left soon after that, and I immediately went outside for a smoke. Melody was already there, as predicted. She smiled as I walked over, and I smiled back.

'How'd it go?' she asked.

'As well as could be expected.'

'That bad?' The way she delivered this line made me certain that she must have heard it on TV or in a film. But I still found it oddly endearing. The truth is, I was glad she was there to talk to.

'I think it might be over,' I told her.

'Shit.'

'Yes, it is.'

'My boyfriend dumped me, too,' Melody told me, to convey solidarity, I think. 'That's when I started cutting again. We'd been together ages. Seven, no, *eight* months.'

'Beck didn't dump me,' I corrected. 'We've agreed to spend some time apart. It was a mutual decision.'

'Mine was by text,' Melody said. 'Turned out to be fucking awful timing too. It was only like a week before . . . Well, before I came here.'

There was something missing in this account, I knew, but it wasn't the first time Melody had been vague about the circumstances that led to her being admitted here. It always struck me because it was pretty much the *only* area in which Melody was vague. With everything else, she was insanely forthcoming. I knew about the thirty-two paracetamol, of course – almost the first thing she told me – and I knew she'd been cutting from the age of fourteen and on medication by the time she was sixteen; we'd exchanged extensive notes on the various anti-depressants we'd both tried. But there was still this conspicuous gap when it came to the days just before her suicide attempt. The only other topic on which I could remember her ever being cagey was her personal therapy, which was fair enough, really. When I asked her, one time, what she talked about in her sessions with Dr Hadley, she gave me the exact same answer I'd given her: 'Daddy issues mostly.'

The ex-boyfriend, I thought, was another piece of the puzzle, but there had to be more, obviously. Still, I assumed that if she ever wanted to tell me the rest, she would do it in her own time. I wasn't going to press the issue, and she was quick to shift the conversation back to my problems.

'You live together, right? You and the boyfriend?'

I nodded.

'So what's going to happen next?' she asked. 'You know, once you're out of here. You gonna move out?'

'Yes, I suppose so. For a while at least. In all honesty, I haven't really thought that part through. But my options are pretty limited; I can't afford much. I've got this massive credit card debt to pay, and I'm still going to be contributing my half of the rent on the flat. For the next couple of months, anyway.'

Melody shrugged. 'Stay at mine if you want. I'll ask my mum, next time she's in.'

This offer was so unexpected and unthinkingly generous – albeit on her mother's behalf – that I was at a loss for words for several seconds. Then I reacted as anyone would. 'Oh, no, I really couldn't impose like that. I mean, thank you – really, thank you – but—'

'You can pay if it makes you feel better,' Melody interrupted. 'I give Mum sixty quid a week for rent and bills. You can afford that, right? Just sell a few of them magazine articles and you're sorted. You got any more up your sleeve?'

I smiled. 'Perhaps. I'd promised to write this piece for the *Observer*; God knows what's going to happen with that. But, anyway, I still think it might be a bit unfair on your mother, having a complete stranger in the house.'

'Oh, she wouldn't mind. She's good like that. I mean it's not a palace, obviously – it's a council flat in Acton – so you might have to kip on the sofa. Or you can have my room, if I'm not out by then, except . . . well, I think I might be.' Melody smiled, a little shyly. 'Lisa's been talking about me becoming an outpatient. I'd just have to come back here a couple of times a week for therapy.'

I have to admit I was surprised by this, though I'm not sure why. A number of other patients had been released since I'd arrived on Amazon; it wasn't as if the hospital was meant to provide long-term accommodation. I suppose it was just that I took Melody's continual presence here for granted. I saw her so many times a day she was like part of the décor.

'That's great,' I said, after a small hesitation. 'You must be pleased.'

'Yeah, I guess. Pleased, scared – you know what it's like.'

I nodded. Because I *did* know, and I realized then how rare that probably was. It was strange: Melody and I had so little in common in so many ways – it was inconceivable that we would have become friends outside this place – and yet I felt we understood each other on a much deeper level. With Melody, I didn't have to explain or justify concepts that others would have found

irrational, just as she didn't have to explain to me why she liked
to cut herself.

That was the reason, I think, why the idea of staying with
Melody once we were out of here no longer seemed so outlandish;
or not for the next few hours.

That afternoon, I had an extra session booked with Dr Hadley.
We'd agreed it would be sensible, in case I needed to talk after
Beck's visit. However, it also meant that Dr Hadley had been
forced to rearrange her schedule and slot me into the gap between
two other appointments – an hour that would usually have been
free office time. Consequently, she had had a very busy day, and
was uncharacteristically flustered before our session.

She was coming out of her office as I was about to knock
on the door, her cheeks flushed and her lips pursed. 'Oh, Abby.'
She gave a small, tired smile. 'Don't worry, I haven't forgotten.
Can you just give me a couple of minutes? You can wait inside
if you like.'

I went in.

Dr Hadley was a compulsively tidy woman. I'd never seen
her office looking anything but immaculate, and even now, it
wouldn't have been called messy by any normal standards. There
was just a handful of signs that today had been exceptionally
fraught: a pen on the floor, an unwashed coffee cup, a pink
Post-it stuck to the side of her computer screen. But as I sat
down in my usual chair, I found these details made me smile a
little. Being in an NHS hospital, Dr Hadley's office was inevitably
rather plain and institutional, lacking the more personal touches
I was used to from my therapy with Dr Barbara. But in addition,
I'd often thought that this environment reflected something of

her personality. She'd always projected a kind of austere professionalism that was difficult to warm to. So witnessing even this limited disorder felt quite refreshing; it was nice to see her human side.

I reached down to pick up the fallen pen and then placed it back in Dr Hadley's pen pot, and as I did, I glimpsed what was written on the pink Post-it note:

Call CRT re: Melody Black.

It seemed completely innocuous at first – and in every normal sense it was. It wasn't personal or sensitive information. CRT, I knew, was the Community Rehabilitation Team, and from this I guessed it must be something to do with what Melody had told me that morning, about her possibly becoming an outpatient. But it wasn't this content that caused me to smile again. It was Melody's name.

Odd as it may sound, I hadn't known Melody's surname up to this point. Mrs Chang aside, I don't think there was another service user whose surname I *did* know. We only ever used first names, as did the staff when they addressed us. So this was the first time I knew Melody as 'Melody Black', and straight away it was a name I loved. It was so gloomy and lyrical it could have been a line from a Sylvia Plath poem.

There was something more than this, though – some other connection that I couldn't yet put my finger on. I thought, at first, that it was just a strange feeling of aptness, as if the two words now resonating in my consciousness were someone's taut synopsis of all the beauty and darkness of the past seven weeks.

It must have taken mere moments for the full revelation to hit me – and this really was how it felt. It was the Dorchester all over again; I'd been slapped full force across the cheek.

Of course, later I'd spend hours trying to convince myself that I might be wrong, that I was suffering from some kind of massive delusion. But the truth is I knew. In that precise instant, all the pieces of the puzzle – the conversations with Melody about her dad, the peculiar gaps in her backstory, even the fact that she looked weirdly familiar – fell into place. And this left no room for doubt.

Simon's surname had been Black.

Melody was Simon's daughter.

A HUGE FUCKED-UP COINCIDENCE

I ran.

I didn't make any conscious decision, didn't think about how it would look or where I was going. The problem, of course, was that I was on a locked ward; there was nowhere I *could* go. But I only realized this when I was out of Dr Hadley's office and halfway down the corridor, and at that point, biology took over. I darted past a bemused-looking nurse and into the nearest bathroom, where I vomited in the sink.

I wish I could say it was cathartic, but it wasn't. I kept retching long after there was nothing left to come up, and I was still bent over the sink when Dr Hadley started talking to me through the door, which I'd only managed to half close.

'Abby? I'm coming in. Is that okay?'

It wasn't okay, but I couldn't speak to tell her this; when I tried, I felt my stomach starting to heave again.

I've wondered, since, what would have happened if I'd been able to talk to Dr Hadley there and then. I've had plenty of time to wonder that, but the truth is I don't think I would have told her even if I'd been capable of doing so. My immediate impulse was to bury what I'd just found out, to shut it away somewhere dark and remote. As it was, I didn't exactly choose to do this, or not straight away; it just became the default option.

Dr Hadley thought I was having a panic attack – which, I suppose, was true – and assumed this must be something to do with Beck's visit that morning, which, of course, it wasn't. But it was so much easier to go along with this version of events. I didn't even have to lie, as such; I just had to stay silent and allow Dr Hadley to draw her own conclusions.

Eventually, when my stomach had stopped churning, we went out into the corridor, where she asked me if I wanted to come back to her office to talk things over. I shook my head, and I must have still looked a real mess, because she didn't press the matter, however much she thought it might help me. Instead, she fetched a glass of water for me to drink, then told me I needed to get some rest; if I wanted, she could have one of the nurses bring me a sedative to help me sleep. At that moment, there was no kinder offer I could imagine.

When I awoke it was still light. A glance at the wall clock told me that it was late afternoon and I'd slept for only a few hours, but this had nevertheless made an appreciable difference to my state of mind. Yes, I still had a cold, sinking feeling in the pit of my stomach, but this was overlaid with a shallower, synthetic calm which I attributed mostly to the diazepam. For now, at least, my head had stopped spinning, and I had enough focus to think through what had happened earlier, slowly and almost rationally.

At first it seemed the most appalling coincidence – that Melody and I should both wind up here, in the same hospital ward at the exact same time. But the more I thought about it, the less coincidental it felt. A coincidence implied blind chance, something entirely random, and, in a sense, there was nothing random about our being here. You could explain it in terms as mundane as NHS catchment areas. We lived in the same corner of west London, and if you happened to go nuts in this part of the city, St Charles was likely where you ended up.

More than anything, I think my initial disbelief was born from a mixture of self-pity and willing self-delusion. Because, straight away, I wanted to deny what I'd discovered, or at least to persuade myself that I could be wrong. And while this was difficult, it was not impossible. After all, what did I really know? They shared a surname – one of the more common surnames in the English language; maybe not top fifty, but certainly top one hundred. Of course, the thing that kept gnawing at me was the way in which Melody had alluded to her dad's death. In hindsight, I suspected that her phrasing could have implied an event more recent than I'd at first assumed. But since I couldn't remember her exact words, it was impossible to be sure; and this, really, was the point. As long as there was a wisp of doubt hanging over my conclusions, it gave me a reason not to act on them. I told myself I had to be certain before I could make any sensible decisions.

As far as I could see, there were only two paths to getting the information I needed: I could ask Dr Hadley, or I could ask Melody herself. The former, I quickly dismissed. Dr Hadley wouldn't discuss another patient with me, not unless I came out and told her everything, which of course would defeat the purpose. With Melody, there was a chance I could ask the relevant questions without her realizing that anything untoward lay behind them. But the idea of manipulating her like that caused another wave of nausea to surge in my stomach. And anyway, there was a part of me that understood how disingenuous this whole thought process was. It was just a way of avoiding the much bigger issue: if my suspicions were correct, what exactly should I do about it?

My gut told me that I'd have to say something to Melody. I couldn't go on acting as if nothing had happened; I'd never wanted to deceive her. Yet there was a problem here, too: I genuinely wasn't sure, in this instance, that being honest could be equated with being kind. Telling the truth might help me – it would be a way of assuaging my guilt – but I couldn't see how it would help Melody. If there were self-serving aspects to this reasoning, I can honestly say that they were secondary at this point. My main concern was that I didn't want to cause any further harm.

On the face of it, there seemed no obvious route to Melody finding out about my article. It probably goes without saying, but she was not the sort of girl who read the *Observer*. The chances of her ever reading the *Observer* were essentially zero – and I assumed this probability could be extended through the vast majority of her friends and acquaintances. It felt horribly snobbish when I voiced these thoughts to myself, but I knew they were true nonetheless. I also knew that while my article had been referenced elsewhere – on Twitter and in forums – any subsidiary interest would have long since vanished. Now that I was no longer manic, I could see my story for what it was. It was the kind of feature that made a big splash in a small pond, but left no significant ripples in its wake. If I didn't confess to Melody, logic told me she would never find out.

So why did I still have this intense sensation of foreboding? Guilt, again, I thought. Whatever the facts of the situation, guilt would not permit me to shake the dread of discovery, and after running in circles for another half hour, I finally understood that I was going to get nowhere on my own. What I really needed was a second opinion; my own perspective was far too clouded.

If it hadn't been for that morning, there would have been no decision to make; I would have called Beck that instant – or I would have had one of the nurses call him from reception, asking him to come in. He knew most of the pertinent facts already, so I wouldn't have to explain too much, and he was one of the only people I could talk to about something like this without feeling judged. But with the way we'd left things, there were just too many other issues that would get in the way.

Dr Barbara was my second choice, but the temptation here was simply to wait until she next came in, and I didn't know when that would be. She'd been visiting less since it became clear that I was improving; the last time I'd seen her was a couple of days ago, when she'd brought in the letters. I could have phoned her, except I was still avoiding my mobile. All those accusing missed calls and texts – yesterday, I might have coped with them, but today there was no chance. So I knew if I were to call Dr Barbara – if I were to call anyone – it would have to wait at least twenty-four hours.

I was feeling anxious again, and having held out this long, I couldn't tolerate my nicotine craving any more. I knew, of course, that there was every likelihood I'd see Melody if I went outside, but I had to face her at some point. Appealing as the idea might have been, I couldn't hide in bed for the rest of my time here. Still, as I left my room and walked down the corridor, my legs felt as if they were someone else's. Just putting one foot in front of the other seemed a Herculean task.

She was out there, talking to Lara, a schizotypal kleptomaniac who had arrived last week. I didn't think that having someone else present would make the situation any easier, and for several moments I stood frozen in the doorway, almost certain I was about to turn round and go back to bed. But then Melody happened to glance in my direction. She immediately grinned, then placed her free hand on her stomach and performed a passable mime of vomiting. News like that tended to travel quickly in this place.

'You look like shit,' she told me.

'Yes,' I said. 'That's how I feel.'

Melody shrugged and flicked me a cigarette. 'Listen, you gotta hear this. Lara was just telling me about the time she stole a horse . . .'

It was hard to respond to this, but I think I managed a wan smile.

After that, the conversation continued to be entirely inconsequential, but I still found it difficult to keep my composure, to nod in the right places – even to concentrate on what was being said. Something of this must have come across, despite my best efforts, because after Lara had left, Melody immediately asked me if I was okay.

'No, not really,' I told her.

She pouted with concern and rested a hand on my shoulder. 'You see: this is another reason you should stay with me once we're out of here. We can be like a mini support group for each other.'

'Melody . . .'

'What?'

She looked at me expectantly.

'Nothing. I'll think about it. Later.'

'What's to think about?'

'I have to go now. I don't think I'm well enough to be up.'

I didn't wait for a response. I crushed out my second, half-smoked cigarette, then went back inside.

It had been a fairly awful experience, but just standing with Melody for those few moments had clarified one thing: I *had* to speak to Dr Barbara. And if it hadn't been a Sunday, I might have called her as soon as I got back to my room. But I couldn't bear the thought of disrupting her weekend yet again.

So I gave myself one night, which seemed entirely justifiable. In the meantime, I planned to get as much rest as I could, even if this meant getting down on my knees to beg the nurses for some more diazepam. I'd feel better again after I'd slept, and then I'd be in the right frame of mind to call Dr Barbara's office first thing.

This wasn't stalling, I told myself. It was just a very short delay so that I could do things properly. What difference could a few hours make?

I phoned Dr Barbara's office at 9.03, by which time she was already with a patient.

'Is it urgent?' her receptionist asked. But I wasn't sure how to gauge this.

'It's quite urgent,' I replied after a brief hesitation. 'I'd really appreciate it if she could call me back as soon as she's free.'

I figured this would be around ten; even if Dr Barbara had back-to-back appointments, she'd probably find five minutes to call. But having to wait even another hour seemed like a very big ask. I'd been awake since four that morning, and I felt tired and restless all at once. So I did the obvious thing: I went out for a cigarette.

I thought it would be reasonably safe at this time of the morning, as Melody was not an early riser. She'd often fall back asleep after she'd been woken for breakfast, and then complain loudly, to anyone who would listen, after the nurses returned to wake her a second time. The only exception was when she had ECT – and if this were the case, she'd still be safely else-where. As long as I didn't linger outside more than half an hour or so, I was unlikely to see her. I was unlikely to see anyone, I thought. Nevertheless, I still felt nervous as I walked out to the smoking area that morning – but this wasn't anything more than the usual anxiety that had characterized the past twenty-four hours.

Weirdly, some of this anxiety faded when I saw her. I don't know why, but I suppose there was some initial sense of relief. It didn't last long, but for a few moments, I felt a little calmer, as if the worst had now happened.

She knew, of course. That was never in doubt. Her mere presence indicated that something was wrong, and the way she was holding herself told me the rest. She was sitting with her back to the door, shoulders hunched and face lowered, with one hand clasped to her forehead.

She didn't realize I was there; there was no way she could have realized. I could have turned and left, had I wanted to. But there wasn't any point now.

'Melody,' I said, trying to make my voice as gentle as possible.

She jumped slightly when I spoke, then turned, the plastic

leg of her chair scraping the ground with an abrasive screech. Her hair was tousled just above where her hand had rested, and her eyes were red raw. It looked as if she might have been crying for hours.

'Melody,' I said again, but she immediately looked away. She took a cigarette from the pack on the table and fumbled with her lighter, sparking it three or four times before she got a flame.

'I Googled you,' she told me. 'Wanted to see what else you'd written so I could tell my mum.'

'Melody, I didn't know.' I realized how self-contradictory this statement was the second I'd said it. 'What I mean is I only just found out. Yesterday.'

She didn't seem to register this, or if she did, then it didn't mean anything to her.

'You knew,' she said.

'I'm sorry. I'm so sorry. It's just a huge fucked-up coincidence, that's all.'

A few weeks ago, I might have said something more. I might have told her that my article wasn't even about her father, not really. It was about something else: modernity, the anonymity of the city, urban alienation. I might have told her that I was on the verge of going nuts at the time, and couldn't really be held accountable for what I'd said or done. But now I had no intention of trying to justify my actions. All I wanted was for her to stop hurting. And I knew there was nothing I could say to make this happen.

We stayed as we were for an agonizing stretch of time, me standing like a statue, her smoking, with her eyes fixed on the ground.

'I thought you were my friend,' she said eventually.

'I *am* your friend,' I told her.

She let out a small wounded sound, somewhere between a sniff and a whimper.

I tried to speak, but I couldn't. There was still nothing I could say. I kept wishing that she'd just look at me, so that I might be able to communicate with her on some other level. But when she did look at me, I almost wished that she hadn't. There was something in her gaze that immediately frightened me. It wasn't anger; anger I could have dealt with. It was something much worse – something cold and unbending, but otherwise impossible to describe.

She stared at me for a few more empty moments, then raised her half-finished cigarette in her right hand, holding it between her thumb and index finger like a dart. I could see what was about to happen, and I was powerless to stop it.

'Melody, please . . .'

Slowly, almost casually, and never breaking eye contact, she crushed the rest of her cigarette into the centre of her left palm.

Then she started screaming.

OUT

Melody screamed and screamed.

It's a rare thing to be able to say you know the exact quality of someone else's pain, but in this case, of course, I did. I could remember precisely how that moment felt. It was a pain that obliterated every other sensation and thought, as if a dozen white-hot needles were being fed into your nerves. The only difference between my case and Melody's was that I'd been drunk when I crushed the cigarette into my flesh. Melody lacked even this token anaesthetic, so, if anything, her pain must have been worse.

I had my arm around her shoulder in seconds and managed to propel her towards the doorway. She didn't offer up any resistance, but neither did she do anything to help. I'm not sure how far she was even aware of my presence. It was like trying to steer a shopping trolley with a broken wheel.

Inside, two nurses were already converging on us, and I could see that some of the other patients had also come out into the corridor to find out what was happening. Melody's screams had

222

diminished to a series of ragged yelps, but her initial outburst had been loud enough to be heard through the nearest walls and windows. Apparently, I had started yelling too, and as the nurses approached, I managed to convey that Melody had burned her hand and we needed to get it under cold water. I was able to help manoeuvre her to the closest bathroom, but after that some sort of official protocol kicked in and I was ushered out by another nurse.

As we left, I caught a glimpse of Melody still being held at the sink, her whole body shaking. I remember it very clearly because it was the last time I saw her. Later that morning, she was moved back to Nile.

Dr Hadley was adamant that I not be allowed to visit, even after I broke down in her office and started sobbing that I had to go and make things better right that instant.

'I think it would be an extremely bad idea,' she told me again, in a voice that was both gentle and firm.

Some hours later, after I'd calmed down, I could see that she was right. There was still nothing I could say to Melody, nothing that would make any difference. And anyway, what I really wanted was the impossible. I wanted her to tell me that it wasn't my fault – that it was just an awful, awful coincidence. I wanted an absolution.

It's a unique sort of guilt, when you hurt someone you care about and whom you never intended to hurt; and for a while, I thought it was *my* unique guilt, as if no one else could ever have experienced anything remotely similar. It was my mum who set me straight, when I tried to explain this feeling to her several weeks later.

'God, Abby,' she said. 'You'll find that most of the hurt you cause in your life will be unintentional. And almost all of it will be inflicted on the people you care about. It's one of life's unfortunate ironies. It's much easier to hurt the people you're close to.'

I've never thought of my mum as particularly insightful; she's more insightful than my dad, but that goes without saying. Yet in this instance, I could see that she knew a hell of a lot more than I did. The only intelligent addition I could make to our conversation, at this point, was to quote Oscar Wilde.

'Each man kills the thing he loves,' I told my mum.

'Yes, exactly,' she replied. 'Or each woman – just as often.'

That night – the night after Melody burned herself – I realized it was time for me to leave St Charles. This wasn't a knee-jerk reaction to the events of the previous day, and it wasn't a decision I came to lightly.

I was given more diazepam and slept through for eight unbroken hours, waking around five thirty. After that, I lay wide awake until breakfast, as I had on so many other mornings over the past weeks. But this time was different. My head felt surprisingly clear. I was rested and lucid, and able to look at my situation with a new objectivity.

Dr Hadley had already convinced me that there was nothing I could do to help Melody at the moment; what she hadn't said, of course, was that my being here – just a few corridors away – might have the exact opposite effect. But this was something that occurred to me now. I knew that by the time Melody was off Nile, I'd probably be gone, and, in any case, there was no way we'd be put on the same ward again. But still, wouldn't it be better if I were out of the picture entirely? The more I thought about it, the more convinced I became that this was the one thing I could do to make her time here easier.

As far as my own recovery went, I honestly believed that I was as well as I was going to get inside a hospital. Being out in the real world was still a daunting prospect, but I could see that my being here served no further purpose. It was odd, but the moment Melody had crushed that cigarette into her hand, it was almost as if I'd been shaken awake from the last grip of a nightmare. Admittedly, I'd felt awful over the past day, but this was not the same as feeling depressed. I found that I could label all my emotions – guilt, fear, sadness, remorse – as if they were ingredients in a recipe, and there was nothing there that wasn't normal and proportionate given the situation. More importantly, I knew that these feelings would pass. There wasn't the sense of lethargy and hopelessness that characterizes depression. I wanted to get out of here and get my life back on track; and then, in time, there might be some way I could make things right with Melody.

I turned all this over in my head several times, rehearsing my lines of reasoning for what was to come. Then, straight after breakfast, I washed, dressed and went to knock on Dr Hadley's door. I knew she'd be in from around eight thirty, but it was unlikely she'd have anything scheduled that early, so this would be my best chance to say the things I needed to.

She waved me in and gestured that I should sit. The other chair was already angled towards hers, as if waiting for me.

I asked about Melody, of course, but there wasn't much Dr Hadley could tell me – just that she was calmer now, and being taken care of. So after that, I got straight to the point.

'I think I'm ready to leave,' I told her. 'The sooner the better.'

I could see the scepticism written all over her face, but this was as I'd expected.

'You know, Abby,' she said after a few moments, 'before yesterday I'd have agreed with you. You were ready to leave, or near enough. But considering everything that's happened . . . I think it would be prudent to give it a few more days. See how things go.'

'Yesterday clarified a lot of things for me,' I said, 'and staying here isn't going to help me any more; if anything it's going to be detrimental.' Then I ran through most of what I'd been thinking that morning, very methodically, setting out my arguments like lines of toy soldiers. The only thing I left out was my realization that this might be better for Melody too, because I knew this would weaken my case. Dr Hadley would be trying to figure out what was best for me, putting all other issues to one side for the moment, and I didn't want her to think that guilt was my prime motivation here.

'I'm extremely grateful for everything you've done for me,' I concluded, 'but I honestly think it's the right time for me to go. You said yourself that it would be better if I made the final decision.'

Dr Hadley tapped her pen against her cheek a couple of times. 'Yes, I did,' she acknowledged. 'But things were quite a lot simpler then, weren't they?'

I decided to change tack and come at this from Dr Hadley's perspective, because I could see she wanted to be persuaded, but wasn't going to agree to anything until she was certain.

'What do you need from me?' I asked her. 'I mean, if you were to draw up a checklist of things that had to happen before you'd be happy to let me go, what would be on it?'

Dr Hadley smiled faintly, perhaps because of how I'd phrased this. 'First, I'd need to know that you were going somewhere safe and secure, with family or friends to support you. I'd also have to be satisfied that your mood is as stable as you say it is. That would mean at least two more days in here – ideally more – and an independent assessment by one of the other doctors. And you'd have to agree to transitional support for the next few weeks, either as an outpatient or under the supervision of another healthcare professional.'

I nodded. There was nothing here that seemed problematic. 'Thank you,' I said. 'I also have one other thing to ask you. A favour.'

Dr Hadley nodded for me to go on.

'Once I'm out, I have something I'd like you to give Melody for me. Or, in any case, there's something I'm leaving behind for her. You can decide when or whether to pass it on. It's nothing that will upset her, I promise. It's . . . well, it's an apology of sorts – one that I think she'll understand. But as I've said, it's your decision what to do with it. I trust your judgement.'

I was out of Dr Hadley's office a little before nine. Then I went straight back to my room and phoned my mum.

MIRANDA FROST'S CATS

They're called Jasper and Colin, and they live in a two-bedroom cottage on Lindisfarne, a tidal island a couple of miles off the Northumberland coast.

I'd heard of Lindisfarne before I arrived, but I had no idea what a tidal island was. Turns out it's pretty straightforward, and obvious when you think about it. Lindisfarne is a tiny finger of land poking out into the North Sea, which becomes cut off from the mainland twice a day by the rising tides. There are two routes on and off the island: you can drive along the causeway, which has carried road traffic since the 1950s, or you can walk across the sand flats, where a rough path is marked out by tall wooden posts that have been driven into the ground every twenty metres or so. Both routes are submerged for up to twelve hours a day, by over six feet of seawater at the highest tides. There are three little huts on stilts – one at the roadside and two spaced out over the sand flats – which serve as refuge points for stranded walkers and motorists, but the locals tell me that it has been a while since they've seen a car stuck in the sea. A couple of years ago, the council invested in a large electronic sign that flashes the safe crossing times day and night, and apparently there have been far fewer incidents since then.

Still, even without the odd four-by-four stuck in several feet of rising water, there's something pleasingly apocalyptic about watching the road get swallowed by the sea every day. I've been down to the causeway to watch the water rushing in over the road at least once a week since I arrived here, and it really doesn't get boring. I even wrote an article about it. It was called 'Imagining the End of the World'.

A little more than half a year ago, Miranda Frost told me that she lived miles from anywhere, and this was not too much of an exaggeration. Hers is the last house on a lane that rapidly becomes a dirt track and then a footpath leading down to the sea. The nearest building – a barn – is about two hundred yards away, and the nearest streetlight is a further two hundred yards back towards the village. The village, I should add, has no name and doesn't need one because it is the only settlement on Lindisfarne. The island's entire population numbers fewer than two hundred people, plus maybe a couple of thousand sheep.

Of course, there were many more people in the late summer and early autumn – I think the car park outside the village can accommodate several hundred vehicles – but they were always clustered in the square, or at the castle or priory. It was still rare to see more than a handful of hikers passing down this road at any one time. Since November, whole days have gone by when I haven't seen a soul.

Aside from the lack of people, the thing that most struck me when I arrived was the darkness. The darkness and the silence. Both, at times, can be absolute.

It's ironic, but after so many nights in London praying for peace and quiet and darkness, I found that the first few nights here I wouldn't sleep. The truth is I'd had no prior experience of this kind of environment. I've always lived in the city, and I wasn't prepared for how the total absence of sound and light would feel. On nights when there isn't any wind or rain, you can't hear anything beyond your breath and the occasional creak of a cooling floorboard. On nights when there isn't a moon, you can't see even your own body in the darkness. You feel as if you're nothing more than a thought in the void.

That first night, I didn't fall asleep until the sun came up and the birdsong started. The three subsequent nights, I slept with the landing light on.

I've never been good at identifying accents, especially northern accents. Yorkshire, Lancashire, Geordie – they all sound pretty much the same to my ear. After more than three months on this island, I think I'm getting slightly better, but I still couldn't say for certain whether there is a specific local accent, much less describe it. All I know is that everyone I've spoken to is from the north, and every time I open my mouth, I might as well be holding up a sign that reads NOT FROM AROUND HERE.

I speak the Queen's English, and I've always taken this fact for granted. But what I've become aware of, more recently, is that people from outside London and the Home Counties actually regard *this* as an accent. It was brought to my attention in the Crown and Anchor one evening, when I got into a small argument with one of the barmen and confessed that, as someone without an accent, it's quite difficult for me to differentiate between the various regional dialects.

He looked at me with this slightly irritating smile on his lips, then said, 'But you do have an accent, pet.'

I've since discovered that if a man addresses you as 'pet', it means he's from Newcastle.

'Excuse me?' I replied.

'You do have an accent.'

This was so patently absurd that I assumed, for several moments, that he must be winding me up. That or there was something wrong with him.

'No, I don't. Of course I don't. What accent do I have?'

He shrugged. 'A posh one.'

I spent the next ten minutes trying to explain the difference between being 'posh' and having clear enunciation, but I'm sure the distinction was lost on him.

Of course, when I first arrived here, I didn't even have to open my mouth to identify myself as an outsider. The problem was I'd had very limited packing space, and most of the clothes I had packed were inappropriate. I was still going through the phase where I was hyper-conscious of my appearance; I was making an extra effort to take care of myself, and a big part of this was ensuring I looked nice every day – because I knew how easy it was to let things slide. One day you go without make-up, and before you know it, you're wearing last week's jeggings and haven't washed your hair for three days.

So the first time I walked into the village, I was probably a little overdressed. Not London Fashion Week overdressed – just my smart three-quarter-length coat, pumps and some moderately expensive fitted jeans – but still. In a place like this, anything more than a fleece is considered glamorous. And I suppose the fact that I'd painted my nails a sparkly silver the night before did not help.

The man behind the counter in the post office looked me up and down, slowly and without subtlety.

'Hello,' I said. 'I'd like a book of twelve first-class stamps, please.'

It took him a couple of seconds to nod and snap into action. No one here does anything quickly.

'You here fo' jus' the dee?' he asked.

Scottish is one of the few accents I can identify with some confidence. In fact, I can even draw some sort of distinction between the different areas of Scotland: if you sound a bit Scottish you come from Edinburgh and if you sound extremely Scottish you come from Glasgow. But that doesn't mean I'm able to decipher it at pace, and by the time I'd started to translate what was being asked of me, the man had already moved on.

'It's jus' that the tide'll be in soon. You'll no' want to be leaving it too late.'

'Oh. Right.' I obviously looked like a rescue mission waiting to happen. 'No, actually I'm staying for a bit. And I know about the tides.'

The man squinted at me for a while.

'You in film?'

'Excuse me?'

'Film, TV. We get a lot o' film and TV people on the island. Lots o' those historical pictures.'

'Oh. I see. No, I'm not in film.'

'Ah, you're a pilgrim, then?'

This, I think, was intended as a joke.

'No. Clearly not.'

'On the run?'

'Escaped from a psychiatric ward.'

'Ha!'

'Actually, I'm a house- and cat-sitter. Miranda Frost's house and cats. Do you know her?'

'Aye. One o' the few that do. Strange lady. Bit of a recluse.'

'Yes, that's her.'

'You a friend o' Miranda's?'

'No, not exactly. Not at all, actually. We've only met once. For work. It's a little complicated. I'm a journalist – that's the day job when I'm not cat-sitting. I interviewed her.'

It was a lot of information, I knew, but with each additional sentence, the man looked a little more bemused.

'You interviewed her?' he asked eventually.

'Yes.'

'Why?'

'Excuse me?'

'Why would you interview Miranda?'

'Er . . . the usual reason, I suppose.'

He looked at me blankly, still squinting.

'She's a poet,' I pointed out. 'She's one of the most prominent poets in the country, right behind Andrew Motion and Carol Ann Duffy.'

Nothing.

In every future encounter, I ditched the more convoluted backstory and just told anyone who asked that I was Miranda Frost's niece. Except this rarely helped matters, either. It's astonishing, really, but on this minuscule island with its minuscule population, I've met perhaps five people who are aware of Miranda Frost's existence; and only one of them knew she was a poet.

It might have been a quip, but the Scot in the post office was not the first to suggest I could be running away from something. My mum, Dr Barbara, Beck – they all questioned my coming here. I've questioned it myself – or I did in the first couple of weeks. I think it was the legacy of how I left London, the day I got out from St Charles.

I didn't see Beck that day, although it wasn't as if I planned it like that; not exactly. I was released on a Friday morning while he was at work. He wanted to be there – we talked about it on the phone the night before – but in the end I told him I wasn't sure I could handle it. I thought it would be easier if we stuck to what we'd agreed: space and time, for us both.

It wasn't easy. There was an eerie quiet in the flat. Not the same quiet I've experienced here, of course, but a London quiet – the white noise of traffic heard through glass. Nevertheless, after weeks spent on a hospital ward, everything suddenly seemed very still.

I'd left my mother parked right outside the building, telling her I'd only be five minutes. But I think I was in and out of the front door in three. I grabbed a rucksack that had been squashed at the bottom of the wardrobe, filled it with clothes – just clothes, whatever was closest – and then left.

'That's it?' my mum asked after I'd slung the bag onto the back seat.

I shrugged. 'There's not much I need.'

'Oh.'

I could tell she wanted to add something for the next fifteen minutes, but it was only when we were on the motorway and leaving the city that she said, 'Darling, are you absolutely sure you're going about this the right way . . . '

I love my mum, and I'm very grateful to my mum; she dropped everything and came to rescue me when I needed her. However, nothing tells you that your life's gone off track like waking up in a parent's spare bedroom with only a bag of crumpled clothes for company.

Technically, I kept telling myself, I wasn't moving back in with my mother; I couldn't be since I'd never lived in this house before. My mum relocated to Exeter shortly after I left for university, and I'd only ever stayed here as a guest – a couple of Christmases and the odd week in summer. So it wasn't as if I had to suffer the indignity of moving back into my childhood bedroom or anything like that. Still, what with her bringing me a cup of coffee every morning, and opening the curtains and preparing my breakfast, it was difficult not to feel like I'd regressed by a decade.

Then there was the constant issue of how much I was smoking – sometimes voiced, sometimes conveyed in a glance, or just through the knowledge that I was being watched. I knew it was all born of the same concern, the same impulse to take care of me that was so evident in the neatly folded clothes that appeared on my bed every few days, or the lunchtime phone calls from work, just to check how I was. But after a week or so, I was finding it increasingly hard to bear.

It was in this mindset that I embarked on the mammoth job of working through my backlog of emails. There were 804 of them, spread out over 23 pages. The sheer number was enough to make my head reel, and after half an hour of staring at all those neat but incomprehensible rows and columns of text, it was clear this was yet another task I could not face alone. So I enlisted my mum's help. More specifically, for the next hour or so she sat at the screen while I issued instructions from the armchair.

I suppose it's a generational thing, but I'm continually baffled by my mum's inability to apply the common sense she uses in every other walk of life to the realm of IT. The really puzzling thing is that she manages to use a computer every day at work, just like the rest of us. In fact, she works for a marketing consultancy, so she even has to advise other people on online profiles and social media and the like. God help the soon-to-be-bankrupt firm that knows less about social media than my mother.

'Okay,' I told her. 'It's probably simplest if you start by just deleting all the junk.'

'Very well.' My mum waited expectantly. I nodded for her to proceed. She clicked her tongue a couple of times. 'So what needs to go first?'

'Just start with the stuff that's *obviously* junk.'

'Abigail, this is your email, not mine. How am I supposed to know what's junk and what isn't?'

'Because it will be obvious. It will be really obvious.'

My mother sighed with unwarranted exasperation. 'Give me some examples.'

I massaged my temples for a few seconds to let her know how dense she was being.

'Start with all the generic mail from eBay and Tesco and Amazon. Then delete anything from a bank or credit card company that isn't NatWest. Then delete anything about PPI or compensation for an accident at work.'

'You had an accident?'

'No, of course I didn't! Delete anything that says I've won the lottery. Delete anything from a pharmaceuticals company. Delete—'

'Oh, really, Abby! Why would there be mail from a pharmaceuticals company? What on earth have you been buying?'

'Delete anything referring to Viagra or hot singles or penis extensions.'

'You don't have to get crude.'

'Jesus, Mum! It's the internet; crudity's the fuel that keeps it running. Delete anything with a subject heading that's all in capitals. Delete anything that uses more than one exclamation mark . . .'

After an hour, 804 emails had become 77. This was the fallout from the past month and a bit. A fair amount of work stuff, a lot of *where are you*s. Two credit card statements that made my eyes hurt. The emails from Beck and Francesca, and even one from Daddy. That was probably the worst thing I had to deal with: his attempt at sensitivity, read aloud by my mum, was so cringe-inducing that I found myself being almost swallowed as I sank deeper and deeper into the armchair.

'He does try, you know,' my mother said. But she did not sound convincing.

And somewhere in the middle of all this was the email from Miranda. It was dated nine days ago, and the subject was *Cats?* But there was no message beyond that.

'It's completely blank,' my mother told me. 'Nothing. I think she must have hit send by accident.'

'No, she didn't. It's all right. I know what that's about.'

Needless to say, I'd completely forgotten about Miranda Frost's rather odd proposition. But hers was the first email I replied to. And it was by far the easiest.

There was no crossover between the two of us. Due to a combination of train, plane and tide times, she was several hours gone by the time I arrived on the island. After a seven-hour journey from Exeter to Berwick, I took a taxi to her cottage. She had left the front door key under a plant pot and a note on the kitchen table:

Abigail,
    Cats are not like human beings. They are natural grazers and prefer to eat little and often. For this reason, I usually feed Jasper and Colin three small meals a day at 7 a.m., 1 p.m. and 7 p.m. These times are, of course, only suggestions, but you'll find that if you delay the morning meal much later than 7, Colin (the larger of the two) <u>will</u> come to get you. Please do not leave him scratching at the bedroom door. They have wet food — half a pouch each — for every meal, and you should also ensure their biscuits and water are topped up every evening. Do not be alarmed if Jasper disappears for 24 hours every now and then. He likes to hunt. If you find any dead rodents in the garden (he seldom brings them into the house), there is a small shovel next to the compost bin.

Milk, bread and other essentials can be bought in the village, but I have everything else delivered. You'll find contact details for the delivery man enclosed, and since he'll be coming once a week with cat food, I imagine it would be easiest if you simply add anything else you require to the existing order.

I also enclose my mobile number. Call me in an emergency but not otherwise.

Miranda

P.S. Very occasionally, you might get a goggle-eyed tourist poking around the garden or knocking at the door asking to look around. I'm not joking. They treat this whole island like it's a bloody museum. Use your good sense and do <u>not</u> let strangers into my home.

P.P.S. If you go crazy again, there's a doctor in the village. She's retired but she once helped me out with an allergic reaction to a bee sting. I'm sure she'd be able to see you if it was critical (number and address also enclosed).

Tentatively, and from a very safe distance, I found myself warming to Miranda. Yes, she was still a sociopath, and God help her students in the States; being taught by the woman, I could only imagine, would be four months of creeping psychological torture.

Nevertheless, at least she was honest. With Miranda, you didn't have to worry about what she was really thinking. This was one of the reasons I knew I could tell her the truth when it came to my recent stay on the psychiatric ward.

Of course, there's still a certain stigma attached to mental illness, but this isn't something that bothers me all that much any more. I've been periodically crazy since my mid-teens, and any feeling of awkwardness on my part long ago lost its sting. But what you can't prevent is the awkwardness of other people – their embarrassment, their hang-ups. They start tiptoeing – and even healthcare professionals are guilty of this sometimes – as if the smallest comment, a misworded question, might be enough to push you back over the edge. Every so often, you have to remind people that you're not all that different from them: same complicated tangle of blood vessels, thoughts and emotions. You have to remind them that seeing a psychiatrist or taking medication is not the same as having had your former personality surgically removed.

I knew I didn't have to worry about any of this with Miranda Frost. I'd tell her what had happened and she'd have some sort of immediate reaction that I didn't have to spend hours decoding. But I suspected, too, that her reaction would not be a bad one. I have a sixth sense that has grown pretty reliable in these matters. Even if Miranda hadn't had personal experience of mental illness – which I thought she probably had – then I was sure she'd know people who'd had similar breakdowns at one point or another; she'd probably driven a fair few of them to it herself.

My lack of worry was well founded.

I sent her the following message:

To: miranda@mirandafrostpoetry.co.uk
From: abbywilliams1847@hotmail.co.uk
Date: Sat, 13 Jul 2013, 6:40 PM
Subject: RE: Cats?

Miranda

Sorry for the delayed reply. I went crazy and was on a psychiatric ward for a month. I'm better now, and would very much like to take care of your cats – assuming you're still okay with this?

And within a couple of hours, I had her response:

To: abbywilliams1847@hotmail.co.uk
From: miranda@mirandafrostpoetry.co.uk
Date: Sat, 13 Jul 2013, 8:27 PM
Subject: RE: RE: Cats?

Abigail,

It's okay with me. I assume you're well enough to take care of two cats; otherwise you'd still be locked up.

Are you on medication? If you need a chemist, there isn't one in the village. However, Berwick is only a short bus or taxi ride away. It's quite easy to get there and back in a morning. If this is not a problem for you, I'll send more information tomorrow.

Miranda

If only everyone had reacted like that.

My mum and sister spent the next fortnight trying to persuade me that I was not capable of living on my own right now. Even Dr Barbara was against it, and didn't soften her stance until I agreed to have phone appointments twice a week. But Beck's reaction was the most vehement, as I knew it would be.

'Why?' he asked, in one typically circular and frustrating phone conversation – the same one we had over and over until the day I left. 'You hate the north! You get a migraine if you have to travel up to Birmingham for a couple of hours. Are you trying to punish yourself?'

'No, of course not. It's . . . I don't know what it is.'

There was a five-second silence down the line.

'Abby, I've tried – really, I have. I've given you space. I've hardly seen you for two months. But we can't go on like this. *I* can't go on like this. It's not fair.'

'I know. And I'm sorry, but I can't help it. This is just something I need to do.'

'You don't *need* to do it. You're choosing to do it. At least be honest about that.'

I didn't say anything.

'You know, Abby, sometimes you're just completely fucking impossible.'

Then he hung up.

To be fair, I didn't explain things all that well. But then, I didn't really understand myself – not until I got here.

There are different ways of being alone, and being alone is not synonymous with being lonely. That's something I realized quite recently. I've not felt lonely since I arrived here, not in all the hours I've spent by myself. But there are plenty of times when I've felt lonely in London. In London, you can feel painfully lonely on a Tube train, penned in by hundreds and hundreds of people.

Here on Lindisfarne, I've taken to seeking out new ways of being alone. Since the tourist season ended, I've spent consecutive hours sitting on my own in St Mary's Church – outside service times, of course. It's not that I've found God or anything weird like that. But there's something very calming about sitting in such an old and impressive building, with all its statues and stained glass and towering stone columns. I think it must be something to do with the sense of history and shared endeavour that infuses the place. In St Mary's, you can sit in absolute silence and solitude and still feel part of a much larger story.

Then there's the beach past the sand dunes at the north-east corner of the island. It's a good mile from the village, so you only get the odd dog-walker there, and not very often. Most of the time, you can sit at the foot of the dunes and see nothing but sand, sea and sky. It's another place that's nice to visit on the rising tide; the water comes in quite rapidly, making you very aware of the land shrinking minute by minute. In a way, I suppose this visceral feeling of being cut off is what draws a lot of people to Lindisfarne in the first place, and certainly those who have decided to live here. Being geographically isolated for up to six hours is an oddly comforting feeling. It's crazy, but from London, six hours would be more than enough for me to get to a whole other continent. But here, I find myself increasingly appreciative of these long stretches when my entire world is limited to just four square kilometres of sand and rock.

The truth is I've never been on my own before – not for any significant amount of time. In fact, since the age of fifteen, I've never been out of a relationship for more than two weeks.

I've just sort of fallen from one into the next, often with some overlap in the transition – though obviously this is not something I'm particularly proud of. I'm not proud of my record in general.

I have over a decade of relationship experience spread across approximately a dozen sexual partners; I tried to make a more accurate count, but in all honesty, I think I might have forgotten one or two somewhere down the line. But the exact number is less important than the general trend. If you discount Beck – we've been together for over three years, so he skews the statistics – I've spent the last decade getting through boyfriends at the rate of about one every nine months. My conclusion is that I'm not good at relationships. Actually, that's a conclusion I reached some time ago.

Quite early on, not long after I started seeing her, I told Dr Barbara that I was very bad at relationships. More specifically, I told her that I'd never felt like I could rely on any of my boyfriends to make me happy – and I was even more certain that I couldn't make any of them happy, not in the long run.

I remember her exact response: 'Abby, you're absolutely right, but not in the way you think you are. You can't *make* anyone happy, just like no one else can make you happy. Because real happiness doesn't work like that. You have to learn to be happy on your own. Then you can start worrying about being happy with somebody else.'

I didn't really understand what she meant at the time, but now I think I do; and it's a big part of what I was unable to explain to Beck and my mother and my sister when I decided to come here.

I'm learning to live alone, to be happy all by myself, and here there's almost nothing to distract me from that task. There's just me, Miranda Frost's cats and a flat empty horizon.

If anyone were to ask me now why I came to Lindisfarne, I'd tell them this: I'm trying to be better.

It's the most complete answer I can give.

WRITING

I wrote to Melody every week, starting when I was in Exeter with my mum. I addressed the letters to Dr Hadley at St Charles, and included a note saying that she could read what I'd written and decide whether or not to pass them on. I don't know if she did. All I know for certain is I never got a reply. I must have written Melody nearly a dozen letters over the past four months, and in every one I included both my email address and mobile number. But I suppose I never really expected to hear anything back. Just writing the letters helped me, which is probably why I persisted so long. It seemed like enough of an end in itself.

And after a while it wasn't just letters to Melody. At one point, I was writing to several different people most days – letters, not email, and always handwritten. Email is too easy and impersonal, and it can be stressful to write, as well. With letters, there's no pressure to hit send before you're certain you've finished; there's no clock ticking in the corner of the screen. You don't get distracted by Google alerts or multiple tabs or flashing banner adverts. When you handwrite a letter, the whole process is much more sedate.

Once I could articulate myself a little better, I wrote several letters to Beck, telling him what I was doing and trying to explain some of my reasons. After that, I wrote to my mum and Francesca – letters in a similar vein, detailed and conciliatory. I even tried to write to Daddy at one point, but this task was the opposite of sedate, and in the end it defeated me. I sent him a postcard instead. On the front was a dramatic black and white shot of the causeway being flooded, which I thought he might like, and on the reverse I added three sentences: *If you're ever making a car ad, this would be a great location. I'm doing a bit better now. Abigail x*

The last, of course, wasn't even a sentence, but I've decided that when it comes to my dad, less is definitely more. Postcards are probably the safest way to start rebuilding our relationship.

If my shortest correspondence was with my dad, then my longest was with Dr Barbara, to whom I wrote at least one long letter every week, usually the day after one of our telephone appointments. There are always things you forget to say on the phone, or don't say quite right, so the letters were useful for both of us. In a way, they were also a continuation of what I'd started with Dr Hadley – a kind of ongoing exorcism by pen. Sometimes, setting your thoughts and feelings down in ink is much more effective than just speaking them.

Then there was the handful of miscellaneous letters it felt necessary to write in order to draw a line under the events of the summer. The first was to Professor Caborn, explaining and apologizing for my slightly odd behaviour – although this was one letter I decided to bin rather than send. Ultimately, I thought I'd harassed him enough, and it was better to leave things as they stood. My stream of emails, unexpected visit and complete lack of follow-up could just be a weird footnote in the journal of his career – inconsequential and quickly forgotten.

The staff at the Turnhouse were another matter. They had looked after me when I needed it; they had been kind and understanding and had torn up a £600 bill I was in no position to pay. I sent them a short but insistent thank you letter, which I addressed to 'The Night Staff, 7.6.13'. So that's another one that may or may not have arrived at its intended destination; but it was important to try, nonetheless.

There was only one letter that felt like a complete waste of a stamp – and I knew this was likely to be the case even as I was writing it. This was the four-page missive I sent to my credit card company asking them to freeze the interest on my payments. I don't think large corporations like receiving handwritten letters at the best of times, and the three paragraphs I got back were terse. Essentially, they told me to go fuck myself. Not their exact wording – and there was a line in there somewhere about calling a debt adviser – but the end result was still the same. After I'd read through their reply a couple of times, I binned it and then cut my credit card into four pieces with Miranda Frost's kitchen scissors – a symbolic gesture that unfortunately did nothing to settle my debt. Which was one of the things that made me think I'd better start working again.

I'd emailed Jess at the *Observer* a few weeks earlier, trying to explain, as best I could, why I'd ignored the string of messages she'd sent and failed to deliver the promised article on monkeys and urban alienation. She seemed pretty understanding on the whole, but I knew I'd still done some significant damage to my professional credibility. You can't drop off the radar for six weeks – you can't spend a month on a psychiatric ward – without raising certain questions about your future reliability.

Still, she had told me that I could ring her any time, that she'd like to hear about any new projects I was working on. Probably, she was just being polite, but I decided to take her at her word. And anyway, sending her my new proposal did make a certain amount of sense; in a strange way, it was the long-promised follow-up to what I'd written for her back in May.

'Lindisfarne?' she repeated, obviously perplexed.

'Yes, that's right. It would be a series of features about the island, what it's like living on the edge of such a tiny community. City girl finds herself dumped in the middle of nowhere – that would be the angle, I guess.'

'God, I don't know, Abby . . . It sounds like it would be a difficult sell.'

I shrugged at Colin, who had just come in through the cat-flap. 'Why don't I just send you something? If you decide not to use it, that's fine. No hard feelings.'

'No, no – you can't go all that way for nothing.'

It took me a few seconds to grasp what she meant. It seemed I'd been so eager to outline my idea that I'd forgotten to cover the basics.

'Oh, right. No, no problem there. I'm already here – have been for a couple of weeks now.'

There was a silence.

'On Lindisfarne?'

'Yes.'

'Why?'

'I'm looking after Miranda Frost's cats. She lives here, but she's in the States teaching for a semester.'

There was another small silence. 'Okay, *that's* an angle I can work. I mean, it's extremely odd, but that's the point. Send me a thousand words on how this happened and I'll pitch it.'

So that was how 'The Lindisfarne Gossip' came about. The name was Jess's idea: she thought that every time someone did a search for the Lindisfarne Gospels, we'd pop up as the second option on Google's autocomplete, and this would help bring in a certain amount of traffic. The strategy seems to have worked. The column has been a surprise hit over the autumn, and a couple of weeks ago, I finally made the last payment on my credit card.

The name is also a bit misleading, of course: there's not a lot of gossip to report from Lindisfarne. The islanders have some lottery funding to build a new village hall. No one is very happy about second home ownership. Nothing that's going to set pulses racing back on the mainland. Most of what I've written has been human interest, along with a little bit of history and environment. My only directive from Jess was to 'keep it quirky', and so far that hasn't been a problem. This is a place with a lot of quirks, and the islanders seem to be enjoying their moment in the spotlight. Since September, I've had no shortage of people wanting to share their stories.

There was a ninety-year-old man in the Crown who told me that he'd wandered over to Lindisfarne one day while hiking the Northumberland coast. That was a couple of decades ago, and he has been here ever since.

'It was peaceful,' he told me, 'so I decided to stay.'

The following week, I wrote a piece entitled 'Mrs Moses',

about a woman who had a very strange experience on the causeway one night. She'd been racing back to the island after an Elton John concert, trying to get home before the tide came in, but had been badly delayed by snow and freezing fog. When she finally made it to the coast, it was barely an hour until high tide, and she knew it was far too late to make the crossing. Except, when she drove down to where the water's edge should have been, what greeted her instead was the most beautiful and astonishing sight she'd seen in all her fifty-five years on the planet. There, under the light of a half-moon, was a dry road cutting a valley straight through the water.

'The sea must have been a foot high on either side,' she told me. 'It seemed completely impossible – a modern-day miracle.'

So she eased onto the accelerator and drove between the waves.

It was only when her headlights dipped with the dropping seabed that she saw what had happened: on either side of the road, the standing water that pools after the tide recedes had frozen solid; on top of this, a good foot of snow and slush from the road had accumulated to form a thick wall of ice, spanning the whole length of the crossing.

'But weren't you scared?' I asked her. 'What if the ice had given way?'

'No, I knew it wouldn't,' Mrs Moses insisted. 'It might not have been a miracle in the biblical sense, but there was something watching over me that night. Every so often, the universe offers you a gift, and when that happens, you'd be a fool to refuse it.'

This was a nice line to finish on, even though I disagreed with the underlying sentiments. In all honesty, I don't think there's a benevolent 'something' that sees us home safely from Elton John concerts; and I don't think the universe offers us 'gifts'. I think we make choices – good or bad – and live with the consequences. Which isn't to say that there aren't moments like the one Mrs Moses described, when decisions suddenly seem easy and obvious, as if we're being pushed in one direction rather than another. But most of the time, I think we have to engineer these moments ourselves. We have to seek them out, instead of waiting for them to fall into our laps.

All this, I suppose, is another way of explaining what I've been doing with my alone time on the Holy Island of Lindisfarne – time that has now run out. In a couple of days, Miranda is returning and I'll be heading back to the mainland. But as for what comes next – that's one decision I've not yet made.

REFUGE

That morning, I woke up just before seven, as I'd done every morning for the past four months. After I'd fed Jasper and Colin, I went to check the weather forecast, which confirmed what I thought I could see from the bedroom window, though it was too dark to be certain. The satellite images showed that the sky was completely clear, and would remain so for the next twenty-four hours at least. There was hardly any wind, and the temperature was high for December: nine Celsius at lunchtime, dropping to around five by the early evening.

The next task was to check the tides. I knew the approximate times, of course – since I knew when Miranda was due back – but with the new idea that was taking shape in my head, I thought it would be wise to note down the specifics. The next low tide, it turned out, was at 10.22, with high tide six and a bit hours later, at 4.39. That meant I had until early afternoon to cross the sand flats, and I knew from talking to the locals that the whole walk shouldn't take more than two hours, even at a tourist's pace.

Miranda had said she'd be back at the cottage by midday, and the agreement had been that I'd leave in the same taxi she arrived in. All in all, it had seemed the obvious plan. Except, when I woke up that morning, I knew straight away that I didn't want to be waiting around until noon – and I didn't feel like being indoors.

I sent her a text at nine o'clock, on the emergency mobile number I wasn't allowed to use: *Hello Miranda. It's Abby. I've decided to walk back to the mainland. I'll phone for a taxi once I get there. The key will be under the plant pot.*

After that, I boxed up all my spare clothes and walked down to the post office with them. The box was heavy and cumbersome, so I had to stop a few times to catch my breath, and it took at least twenty minutes to walk the half-mile to the village square. But this seemed the simplest solution. I wasn't going to attempt to hike across the sands with a fifteen-kilogram rucksack on my back.

The box of clothes was addressed to my mother, since I'd decided the previous night that I should go back to her house for at least a couple of days. Time to adjust. Right then, the idea of London – of King's Cross and the Tube at rush hour – felt completely out of the question. Besides, in all honesty, I wasn't sure what in London I'd be going back to. The last time I'd written to Beck, nine days earlier, he hadn't replied, and I'd heard nothing from him since. To be fair, most people would have snapped long before he did.

After I'd helped the man in the post office to manoeuvre my box into the back room, I bought twenty Marlboro, a sandwich and two bottles of Diet Coke. Then, for the last time, I walked back to Miranda's cottage.

It was 9.59 when I left, and 10.18 when I reached the narrow, stone-strewn beach separating the road from the sand flats. I was dressed sensibly for the weather and terrain: Eskimo coat, complete with furry hood, sunglasses, thick jeans, thick socks and the boots I'd bought in Berwick three months earlier. These were not boots in the same sense as the six other pairs of boots I had crammed into a wardrobe in London. They were actual hiking boots – strong, sturdy and with a sole that could grip on an incline. When I'd set out, I'd also been wearing woollen gloves and a scarf, but these were now stowed in my mostly empty rucksack. Once I'd started walking, I got warm pretty quickly.

The sand flats were deserted, as I'd expected them to be on a weekday in winter. The only signs of life out there were a scattering of wading birds pecking at the ground and a dozen more circling in the sky. When I looked straight ahead, all I could see was perfectly flat and uniform sand, stretching on and on to the bluish smudge that marked the rising hills of Northumberland. Aside from that smudge, only the receding line of wooden posts broke the emptiness of the landscape.

Although it was low tide, the sand I stepped out onto could not be described as dry. It was like the sand right at the edge of the sea – dark, compacted and sodden. It was quite yielding, too – more in some places than others, for reasons I couldn't work out. Before I'd even walked to the second marker-post, there were a couple of points where my boot squelched an inch or more into the ground.

This was the first indication that the environment wasn't quite as uniform as it appeared to be from the shore, and as I walked on, this fact became increasingly evident. The falling tide had left little pools of water here and there, suggesting there must have been small, localized variations in the lie of the land, otherwise undetectable. Then, on two occasions, I came across channels of running water blocking my path. They weren't very deep or wide, but I still had to deviate from the route set out by the posts so that I could find a sensible place to cross; and when I did, the water flowed almost up to my bootlaces.

On the far bank of the second channel, the sand was covered with tiny white shells, thousands and thousands of them, stretching ahead like an elaborately patterned carpet. I've no idea why they had clustered like that, on this particular area of sand – whether by blind chance or according to some obscure underlying principle – but they seemed to go on and on for ever. They crunched underfoot like broken glass, and for a long time this was the only sound I heard. The wind was barely a whisper, and, behind me, the occasional rush of traffic on the causeway had already faded to nothing.

After an hour or so, I reached the first refuge point, and there, I stopped for a break. Although I'd grown accustomed to walking everywhere on Lindisfarne, the soft ground of the sand flats was more tiring than I was used to, and I thought it would be nice to take the weight off my feet for a short while. I knew I still had plenty of time before my route started to flood, so there was no need to rush on yet. Besides, I wanted to take a better look at the refuge point, which prior to now I'd only seen at a distance, from the causeway.

It was hard to guess when it had been put there. It looked as old as a storybook shipwreck; but, then, anything built out here, among the salt and the sand and the water, would probably start to look like that in a matter of months, if not weeks. The rounded stilts that supported the four corners were identical to the marker-posts – a little more than a hand's span in diameter and darkly water-stained to a height a few inches above my head. In one corner was the ladder, rising about twelve feet to the platform that perched safely above the highest waves at high tide. After a short hesitation, I climbed up.

It wasn't a difficult climb, even with my rucksack. The planks that formed the rungs of the ladder had been spaced about a foot apart, and at the top were iron handrails affixed to the chest-high fence that enclosed the platform. I eased myself through the narrow entrance point, then removed my rucksack and set it down in the opposite corner.

The platform was a perfect square, about eight feet by eight feet, formed by ten wooden boards in varying states of disrepair. There was lichen growing on most of them, and a couple had started to rot and splinter. But the floor still seemed solid enough underfoot. There was very little give in the boards, and I assumed that someone, somewhere must have had the periodic job of ensuring the structure was fit for purpose. In any event, it didn't seem in imminent danger of collapse.

Once I'd satisfied myself of this, I stood at each side of the platform in turn and took in the panorama. It was hard to gauge distances across such an empty and almost featureless landscape, but I thought I must be somewhere very close to the middle of the sand flats. Looking ahead from this height, I could just make out the point where the marker-posts appeared to end; and looking back, I could likewise see the sliver of grey where the road met the beach on the curve of the headland. The mainland was off to the right, perhaps less than a mile away, and on my left was a mulchy saltwater marsh, stretching back to the causeway and the pale sand dunes beyond.

Having taken all this in, and having reassured myself that I didn't have so far left to walk, I sat down next to my rucksack, in the corner opposite the entrance point. I ate my sandwiches and then smoked a cigarette, using the empty food packaging as an ashtray. I didn't want to leave any mess behind.

I'm not sure when I decided to stay, or even if I did decide, as such. I suppose if I did make a decision, it was made through conscious inaction rather than action.

Midday came and went, and I told myself that I'd wait another fifteen minutes, smoke one more cigarette, and then get up. Then, very quickly, it was twelve thirty and I was aware that if I left things much longer, I'd be hard pressed to finish my walk. I could actually see the water pushing in at this point; what had started as a narrow trickle in the middle distance was now a swelling river, running faster and broader with every passing minute. And still I did nothing other than watch.

By one thirty, I could see that the water had reached some of the more distant posts on either side of the refuge. I was on a shrinking peninsula of sand, and the marsh stood between me and the dunes beyond the causeway – the nearest high ground. From this moment on, I was effectively cut off.

Oddly, I didn't mind. In fact, I felt a little lighter now the point of no return had passed, despite the glaring consequences of my lack of action. For the next seven or eight hours, minimum, I was staying put. But realistically, it would be even longer than that. If high tide wasn't for another three hours, then it would be pitch-black by the time the water had receded far enough for me to continue my crossing. The moon was already up, and it wasn't much of a moon: a very slender crescent, barely noticeable in the still-bright sky. It certainly wouldn't provide much illumination after the sun went down. It was going to be a dark, dark night, and in all likelihood, I wouldn't be leaving the refuge point until morning.

I still had good phone reception, so I sent my mother a text saying that I'd changed my plans and wouldn't be back in Exeter for another night. Then I stood facing the mainland for the next hour or so, watching the water creep and creep until it was just a few metres away.

It was at this stage I realized that if didn't want to hold it in for the next seven hours, or go in the corner – which I didn't – I'd better nip down the ladder to urinate on the sand. So I did; except, of course, it was a little more complicated than that. I'd never had to pee outside before, or not in the large portion of my life that I remembered. To say it was a challenge would be an understatement. In the end, I half squatted with my jeans around my ankles and my back braced against one of the support stilts, facing away from the road. This last precaution was prob- ably unnecessary – from the road, you'd have needed a telescope to make an accurate diagnosis of what was going on out here – but still. It's hard not to feel self-conscious when you've just exposed yourself in the middle of a wide-open space. I got through the whole procedure as quickly as I could, and then scrabbled back up the ladder to safety. Then I resumed my position overlooking the oncoming waves, and thought some more about the situation to which I had irrevocably committed myself.

On the face of it, the choice I'd made was just plain crazy – as crazy as anything I'd done over the past six months. Yet that was not at all how it felt. In all honesty, it seemed the obvious and inevitable conclusion to my time on Lindisfarne. It was very peaceful out here, with the sea now swirling below me, and a perfect cloudless sky overhead. Now that I was back on my platform, I didn't feel at all vulnerable, and I certainly wasn't in any imminent danger. The weather forecast had said it would remain dry, and even if the temperature was now dropping, it was meant to stay well above freezing overnight. I had spare clothes in my rucksack, along with the two small bottles of Diet Coke, as yet untouched. All in all, I felt very calm and self-assured, and this sense of wellbeing only increased as the minutes ticked on.

Just before three thirty, the sun slipped below the hills on the mainland, and I replaced my sunglasses with regular glasses. The sky was an astonishing shade of violet, as was the sea, which now stretched out in every direction. Soon, it had covered most of the marsh and was lapping at the roadside.

I smoked another cigarette and watched as the land, sea and sky grew darker and darker, until finally I couldn't distinguish one from the other.

It was dark, but not completely dark. Or perhaps, more accurately, it was so dark that the little light there was seemed almost an abundance. I'd underestimated the difference the moon would make out here. It shone low in the west like the blade of a scimitar, and was reflected in the sea as a long ribbon of silver light. Beyond this, there was a kind of diffuse glow, and then just shifting shadows, a vast mass of black water that rippled through the wider fabric of the night. I couldn't make out the shoreline – I couldn't see anything solid past the nearest marker-posts – but there were isolated lights out there too: the lights from the farm buildings at the edge of the mainland, and, looking in the opposite direction, the streetlights of Lindisfarne village. The latter, I knew, would be on all night, so however dark it got, I'd have at least one anchor to give me a sense of distance and direction.

The temperature must have dropped by three or four degrees since the sun went down, so I put on another layer of clothes, along with my gloves and scarf. While rummaging in my bag, I also found a small packet of biscuits, a muesli bar and some mints – relics from some walk I'd taken the previous month. It wasn't much of a dinner, but it was better than the nothing I'd been expecting. I washed it down with a few mouthfuls of Diet Coke, followed by another cigarette for dessert, and afterwards felt surprisingly satisfied.

By then, the sea was audible again; I could hear the faint hiss of the breaking waves, which told me the tide must have dropped some distance back from the causeway. But I had to wait a while until I could actually see the foaming edge of the water, and it did not stay visible for long. By the time the water had receded almost to the refuge point, the moon was so low it appeared little more than a curved needle of light poking out of the horizon. A few minutes later, it set completely. And then it really was dark.

I let over an hour pass before I went down the ladder again. I used the light from my mobile phone to illuminate the entrance point, removed my gloves so I'd have a surer grip, and then shuffled forward on my bottom until I felt the heel of my boot slip over the edge of the platform. Once I'd located the handrails, I turned and manoeuvred both feet onto the first step, and then the second, before returning my phone to my back pocket. After that, I descended very slowly, into absolute darkness, counting another six steps before I again retrieved my phone. Holding it low in one hand, I could make out the sand, just one rung beneath me and one more.

I urinated in the same spot as before, but this time it was slightly easier, despite the fact I couldn't see a thing. Afterwards, I faced away from the refuge point, held my breath, and took ten large strides out onto the sand. I don't know why, exactly. I suppose I just wanted to test myself, to see how it felt to be out there in the open, with nothing but darkness on every side.

It felt okay, or it did for a while. It was only when I switched my phone display on again that I felt afraid. Because then I could see how isolated I was. When I looked back the way I'd come, I could no longer see the refuge point. I was standing in the centre of a pool of blue-white light, but beyond this, there were only curving black walls, endless and impenetrable.

Of course, I knew there was nothing rational about my fear; all I had to do was follow my footprints and I'd be back where I started in a matter of seconds. But right then, this felt a matter of faith rather than fact. Confronted by a void in every direction, it was just as easy to believe that retraced steps might lead somewhere else entirely, or nowhere at all – that the refuge point might even have ceased to exist the instant I let it slip from my sight.

But after a few moments, these thoughts started to wane, and soon I could see how ridiculous they were. I was even a little irritated at myself, which is perhaps why I didn't head straight back the way I'd come. Instead, I got a cigarette from my coat pocket and smoked it almost down to the filter, until I felt absolutely calm once more. Then I aligned myself with my foot-prints and walked the ten large paces back to the refuge.

When I found myself again at the foot of the ladder, it felt as if something inside me was subtly different, as if I'd achieved something more than a short walk on the sand.

Back on the platform, there was now a small breeze blowing in through the entrance point, so I relocated to the corner diago-nally opposite, where I set about fashioning the best bed I could. Using my rucksack as a pillow, and with a long cardigan as a blanket, I lay down in the darkness and looked up at the sky. There were stars, of course – hundreds of them, scattered like glitter. I'd grown used to seeing stars since I left London, but this was something else. Every inch of the sky seemed crowded with them, ready to burst.

After a while, I realized that my lips felt cold. My face was the only part of me still exposed to the night air. My gloves were back on and I had my Eskimo hood pulled up so far that its furry lining stroked my cheeks when I moved. But now I also pulled my scarf up over my face, leaving only a very thin visor through which I could continue to look at the stars. Later, when the temperature seemed to drop further, I covered my eyes too.

I've no idea how long I lay like that, in this strange cocoon I'd built for myself, but time, as far as I could gauge, passed quickly. Soon, I was aware of the sound of the sea again, the increasing rush of approaching water. I didn't check my watch or get up to smoke or stretch. Oddly, the longer I lay motion-less on that hard wooden floor, the more comfortable, the more at ease, I felt. I'd been aware of little irritations at first – the lack of cushioning at my shoulder blades, the moisture from my breath – but before long, these things were barely perceptible. Or perhaps it was that I chose not to perceive them; I just shifted my attention slightly, and they faded out of consciousness.

Then, for a long time, I felt like I was on the cusp of a dream. Scraps of thought – images from the past six months, mostly – came unbidden, with one flowing seamlessly into the next. But there wasn't any logic I could discern; just lots of disjointed impressions that rose and fell in gradually diminishing waves. The last thing I remember seeing is Marie Martin curtsying to me in that ridiculous restaurant in Soho. And soon after that, I must have fallen asleep.

It took me a few moments to get my bearings when I awoke. Then it all came surging back: I was on an eight-by-eight-foot platform in the middle of the sea, waiting for dawn and the tide; and it occurred to me then that this was probably not the kind of thing I'd ever be able to tell anyone about, and that it was probably better that way.

I removed the scarf from my face and was greeted by a blast of air cold enough to sting my cheeks. The sky above was still flooded with stars. I checked my phone and saw that it was six fifty, which meant it would be getting light within the hour.

I wasn't very comfortable any more: my feet were cold and my neck was stiff and my back bruised, and my stomach felt small and tight. But despite this, when I stood up to stretch I found that I felt remarkably refreshed given the circumstances, as if I'd slept for eight straight hours on a well-sprung mattress rather than just a few on bare wooden boards. And my head felt clear too – completely free of clutter, like it had been cleaned and rebooted overnight.

In tiny increments, the sky brightened. I drank some Diet Coke and took my tablets, and then leaned my elbows on the side of the refuge point as the tide crept out and the sun rose over Lindisfarne.

It was a little after eight thirty. The waves had passed beneath me and the sky was a pale blue. I had just shouldered my ruck-sack, and was preparing to climb back down the ladder, when my phone rang. It was my mother.

'Abby, you're awake.'

'Yes. Stating the obvious but—'

'I thought it would be better to call straight away.'

There was something strange in her voice. The sort of strange that immediately makes your stomach drop. 'Mum, what is it? What's happened?'

'Darling, it's your father . . .'

ANOTHER DEAD BODY

The funeral was organized by Marie and my sister. They asked me, when they started, if I'd like to have an input. Actually, I think what Francesca told me over the phone was that she and Marie 'wanted' me to be involved. It was a lie, of course, but I believe it came from a good place. She didn't want me to feel excluded. Nevertheless, it was almost impossible to imagine how the three of us would work together. Arranging the catering for the reception, selecting music, writing the eulogy – everything seemed fraught with danger. Not that I expected anyone to ask me to write, or even contribute to, the eulogy. Whatever Fran and Marie envisaged my involvement could be, I knew they'd have to draw the line somewhere. But even simple things like flowers and sandwich fillings and venue felt far, far beyond me. The truth is I had no idea what Daddy would have wanted, and in my limited experience, this is the first question people ask when planning a funeral. I didn't have a clue if he'd want flowers; I didn't even know if he'd have wanted to be buried or cremated. These were things I'd never thought about.

266

Unfortunately, Daddy had never thought about them, either – or if he had, he'd kept it to himself. My father had left no instructions in the event of his death. In part, of course, this was because he hadn't been expecting to die, and I don't just mean that in the sense it might apply to any apparently healthy fifty-eight-year-old man who suffered a fatal stroke in his sleep. I mean, also, that I don't think the notion of dying ever really entered my father's head. He had too large an ego to contemplate a world without him in it.

If I had been asked to write a eulogy, that would have been the title.

'You know, he doted on you as a child,' my mother told me in the car, as we drove to London on the morning of the funeral; and it wasn't the first time she'd told me this. She'd told me many times over the past week. I think it was meant to make me feel better in some way. 'You were much closer than he and Fran were, or you and me, for that matter.' She gave a small, wry laugh. 'It actually made me a bit jealous at the time, seeing how close the two of you were.'

I threw my mum a look, but she had her eyes fixed on the motorway. 'Mum, you're talking about a very small portion of my life, and one that I hardly even remember. Daddy may have loved me when I was a child – I'll take your word for it – but I'm not going to pretend that our relationship was anything more than it was.'

'Oh, Abby. You make it sound as if he *stopped* loving you. He didn't – of course he didn't. He stopped loving me. There's a huge difference. It was me he wanted to leave, not you.'

'I was a teenager, Mum. He couldn't leave you without leaving me as well. We came as a package. You can dress it up however you like, but at some point he opted for a future that did not involve either one of us. There were things that were more important to him. His penis, mostly.'

I added this last point because I couldn't stand the grim frown that had crept over my mother's face. I'd expected more of her, to be honest. Ostensibly, she was coming today so that she could 'be there' for me and Fran, but it was becoming clear that she would struggle to do this on my terms. She thought it would be much healthier if I just allowed myself to grieve.

What she didn't understand was that I *was* grieving. It's just that my grief was complicated. Because I realized pretty early on that I wasn't experiencing a new grief; I was grieving afresh for something I'd lost many years earlier. Something that may not ever have existed.

Beck wasn't there when we arrived at the crematorium, but we were quite early; and, all things considered, I felt myself lucky that he was coming at all. Last week's phone call was yet another that I'd got very badly wrong.

'The funeral's on Wednesday,' I'd told him, 'if you want to come.'

There was a short pause down the line. 'Do you want me to come?'

'I think Daddy might have liked that,' I answered. 'I mean, let's be honest, you got on with him better than I did.'

I only realized how awful this sounded after we'd hung up. In my defence, I was very tired at the time. It's not much of a defence, but it's the only one I have.

I texted back immediately.

I do want you there – of course I do. There's nothing I want more. Please come.

Then I spent the next two minutes, until I got a reply, worrying that I'd now gone too far the other way, and written a message so effusive it could only be read as disingenuous.

But it wasn't. I meant every word, and I realized that now more than ever, in those several moments when I looked and didn't find him.

Instead, I saw a handful of Daddy's work friends and a few distant relations. Basically, I could glance around the car park and at once divide the assembled crowd into two partially over-lapping categories: people I didn't really know, and people I didn't really like. And, inevitably, many of these people felt duty-bound to seek me out at the earliest opportunity to offer their condolences. In most cases, I responded with a neutral smile and a 'Thank you' and left it at that. But I'd already decided that I wasn't going to feign feelings I didn't have. When people asked me how I was 'holding up', I told them. If they didn't appreciate the answer, this was their problem, not mine. Still, after the third or fourth such occasion, I was aching for a bit of moral support.

For the most part, I still had no idea how things would pan out when Beck arrived; but I was certain that he, at least, would respect my right to mourn – or not to mourn – as I saw fit.

We found Fran and Marie in the small foyer outside the chapel. It came as no great surprise that Marie could be numbered among the tiny fraction of women on the planet who wear grief well. She looked stunning, as ever – long black dress, black shawl, black veil with pretty black flowers on it. Funeral chic.

Fran had offset her black top with a dark grey skirt, appearing poised, pensive and solemn – although, really, this wasn't much of a departure from her everyday look. Fran had a wardrobe that was particularly conducive to funerals.

As for me, I'd not had a lot to work with at my mum's. In the end, I'd gone for black trousers and a black cardigan with a (borrowed) white blouse. It was sober enough, I thought, but without making me look like a wraith. And I was wearing bright pink underwear – just because it made me feel a little better and wouldn't do any harm. I'd checked myself in the mirror and it didn't show through. In this, at least, I felt I could do as I wished and not offend anyone.

There were many things about today that I'd not been looking forward to, but probably highest on the list was this initial encounter with Marie. I had no idea how I should greet her or what I should say, and these questions were still playing on my mind right up to the point when she and my mother were exchanging an awkward handshake. It was only then that I noticed – something I hadn't noticed when I'd inspected her across the distance of the foyer. She looked surprisingly vulnerable. Maybe it was that she was standing next to Fran, who had never looked vulnerable in her life, or maybe it was the slight tremble I detected when she smiled thinly at my mum. Whatever the case, it caused me to do a last-minute rethink. I abandoned my own handshake and, standing on tiptoes, kissed her on both cheeks.

There followed a short, peculiar silence. She was obviously as surprised as I was, but at least she seemed to understand that my action hadn't been intended as mockery.

'I like your bow,' she said after a moment, gesturing at my headband.

'I like your outfit in general,' I told her. Then: 'I'm sorry for your loss.'

'Likewise.' There might have been a small barb at this point; I'm not certain. But either way, I didn't have a reply. There wasn't really anything else we could say to each other.

Fortunately, it was at this instant that I felt a tap on my shoulder. It was Beck, looking slightly flushed, as if he'd been rushing.

'You okay?' he asked.

'Do you mean today or in general?'

'I mean both.'

'I'm okay,' I told him.

Then he held me until the service began. I didn't think it was something I could read too much into, but this didn't really matter right then. It just felt good to be held, and that was enough.

I buried my face in his chest; and on a day when almost everything felt awkward and unnatural, this did not.

The service was simple, and over quickly. Non-religious, of course. No singing, no praying – although we were invited, at one point, to partake of a short silence so that each of us could remember Daddy in whatever way seemed most appropriate. I thought about a time when I was six or seven and he bought me an ice cream after I grazed my knee. Not a very remarkable memory, but one of the better ones.

I don't know if Francesca wrote the eulogy herself or if it was cobbled together by the officiant, based on what Fran and Marie had told him, but in any case, it was a masterpiece of the genre: a five-minute biography consisting almost entirely of suspicious holes. Fran and I got a mention – his 'two wonderful daughters'! – but our mother was left out of the story entirely, as if my father had had us grown in a lab. Marie was the 'beautiful partner he leaves behind', and although they'd been together for less than a year, we were informed that in this time they'd enjoyed a 'deep, deep happiness'. That might even have been true – who knows? Less than a year was a plausible time-frame for a happy relationship with my father. Nevertheless, if this had been a trial rather than a funeral, there'd have been a very long queue of women waiting to testify for the prosecution.

The sanitized personal history was followed by a much longer inventory of his achievements at work. His colleagues, apparently, would remember him as a natural and charismatic leader, one with 'a ready smile and a wicked sense of humour'. And he was generous, too; there was an anecdote about an occasion when he bought champagne for everyone in the office, and then a brief reference to his being a 'passionate supporter of a number of charities', though these charities were not listed (I was fairly sure that the only person, dead or alive, who would have been able to provide such a list would have been my father's accountant). Towards the end, there was also a joke about his love of expensive cars – 'his other children' – which provoked several guffaws from his work friends.

So that was my father in a nutshell: basically, he was Jesus with a Jaguar.

'Well, what did you expect?' Beck asked me afterwards. 'A catalogue of crimes and misdemeanours?'

'Why not? That's what I want in my eulogy. In fact, I want you to promise me right now: if I should die tomorrow, you are to tell the truth – the full truth. Here's a first line to get you started: "Abby could be a real pain in the arse sometimes . . ." After that, I want you to list every one of my faults. Leave nothing out.'

'Christ! How long do you want this eulogy to last?'

'Okay, fair point. So cap the bad stuff at five minutes. Then you can finish by telling them I was kind to animals and had nice handwriting. It's important to end on a positive note.'

The post-funeral reception was at Fran and Adam's, and although their flat was twice as large as the one I shared – had shared – with Beck, that still meant little room to accommodate the twenty or so people who came back from the crematorium. It was hot and crowded, and entailed yet more uncomfortable conversations with people I barely knew.

So before long, inevitably, I found myself smoking on the balcony; and before long, inevitably, Marie came out to join me. No one else was there because no one else *could* be there. Fran's 'balcony' was typical of a central London new-build: more a ledge with a safety rail. Marie and I both leaned on this rail for some time, facing out over the street and saying nothing.

'I had a friend who was in a psychiatric hospital once,' she told me eventually. 'Anorexia.' As conversation starters went, this was not the best, but there was something in her voice that conveyed more than her words.

'What happened to her?' I asked after a moment or two.

Marie shrugged. 'She nearly died, then she got better. It's still a battle, though. Most days.'

The fact that Marie would know a detail like this last one confirmed my suspicions.

'I'm sorry I was horrible to you. You know, at the restaurant. It was my father I was angry with, not you.'

'I know.'

'I didn't like my father very much.'

She laughed, a small laugh devoid of humour. 'Yes, I know that too.'

'But that doesn't mean I didn't love him.'

I wasn't sure how well this sentiment was expressed, or even if there was a genuine sentiment there, or just wishful thinking.

Marie turned to look at me for a moment, as if gauging something, then reached into her handbag. 'I have something for you. I didn't know if you'd want it, but . . . well, you decide.'

It was the postcard, the one I'd sent from Lindisfarne. 'He kept it.'

'He was pleased that you were feeling better.'

I stared at the card for a while, front and back. My message, my final contact with Daddy, ended with a small *x*. There were worse ways it could have ended.

I stubbed out my cigarette on the railing. No ashtray, of course.

'Marie, I'm going to leave now. I hope you're happy again – in the future.'

She nodded once in acknowledgement, then turned back to the city. 'I hope you're happy too.'

Inside, I found Beck talking to one of the distant relatives. I touched him lightly on the arm. 'Would you mind getting me out of here?' I asked him. 'Perhaps we could go for a coffee?' I cut straight across whatever my second cousin once removed was saying, but this seemed rather trivial at this point. Beck let me steer him towards to the door, and a couple of minutes later, we were out in the fresh air.

Going for a coffee turned out to be more complicated than expected. It was close to lunchtime, and close to Christmas, so everywhere was packed. Standing room only in Starbucks, same in Costa. I thought, for a while, that we could just walk and talk, but it soon became apparent that this wasn't really an option either. The streets were almost as crowded as the coffee shops: a constant tide of people to negotiate, Band Aid blaring from every open door. In the end, we decided to go back to the flat – our flat. It was the only choice, really.

In the taxi, I sent my mum a message saying I'd phone her in half an hour. Then, as an afterthought, I sent another to Fran telling her she'd done a very good job organizing the funeral. It wasn't snipey; it was something I knew she'd like to hear. As a further afterthought, I then sent Fran a second message saying we should meet up soon – go for a drink or something.

I couldn't decide if being back at our building felt strange or not. Probably both; a mild case of cognitive dissonance. Nothing had changed, of course – or very little. We passed a woman I didn't recognize on the stairs. She was moving at a pace, carrying two reusable shopping bags and plugged into her iPod, but she smiled and nodded at Beck as she passed.

'Who's that?' I asked him.

He shrugged. 'New neighbour. Well, not that new any more. They moved in a few months ago.'

'They?'

'She and her husband. They're Polish.'

'What do they do?'

'No idea.'
'Right.'

I'm surprised how easy it is.

We go inside, we drink coffee, we talk. I tell him about the conversation with Marie, but apart from that, it's nothing too heavy. We don't talk about *us*. We talk about work, Lindisfarne, London. And then, at some point, with no discussion beyond a couple of exchanged glances, we go into the bedroom and have reconciliation sex.

Reconciliation sex is a sub-genre I've always enjoyed very much. It feels like wounds being instantly healed, or like a work of art restored so its colours glow afresh. Yet now, despite this, I find myself hoping that I won't have to go through it again, or not too often.

Afterwards, I realize that my phone is ringing once more, back in the other room, past a small trail of discarded funeral clothes.

'I think I'd better get that,' I say.

Of course, I don't want to get it; I want to stay exactly where I am now. But it will probably be my mother, and there's a good chance she'll be worried. The phone rings for at least a minute before I manage to get to it.

'Abby, where are you? You said you'd call me.'

'I'm sorry. I . . . lost track of time.'

I stifle a giggle, which I think my mum mistakes for a sob, because her voice becomes much gentler.

'Darling, where are you?'

'It's okay, Mum. I'm fine. I'm still with Beck. We went home.'

'You went home?'

'Yes.'

There's a small pause down the line. 'Darling, please don't take this the wrong way, but nothing would make me happier right now than to hear you say you're not coming back to Exeter with me.'

And now I do laugh. 'Mum, I'm not coming back.'

After we've said goodbye, I switch off my phone and head back into the bedroom.

'So, what next?' Beck asks.

'Have we got wine?'

'Er, no. Beer in the fridge, but that's about it.'

'Fine. So we'll go to the shops. We'll need two bottles.'

'Two? You know, I still have to work tomorrow.'

I smile and throw him his trousers. 'One bottle's for the neighbours. I think we should go over and introduce ourselves.'

TWO GIRLS IN THE PARK

It's early March, but it already feels like summer. Hot pavement smell, sunglasses everywhere, not a cloud in the sky. The weather forecast said temperatures could tip twenty-one degrees by early afternoon, but that sounded very implausible when I got dressed at eight this morning. Now, the cardigan I was wearing when I left the flat is looped over my shoulder bag, and I'm starting to wonder if I shouldn't have brought the sun cream after all.

When I check my phone, not far from the statue of Achilles, the clock shows it's just coming up to eleven thirty. I've arrived half an hour early, mainly because the alternative was to spend that half-hour fidgeting at home. So now I have plenty of time to spare, and, inevitably, I find myself walking out onto the broad, shady expanse of Park Lane. I don't really make the decision; my feet make the decision, and before I know it, they've taken me all the way to the Dorchester – or to the stretch of pavement opposite the Dorchester, on the other side of the road. Thankfully, they don't take me any further than that. It's not that I don't want to go inside; I do want to – that's the problem. I have this notion that it would be nice to go in and find out if they ever got my letter. And if they didn't, it would be nice to explain to someone in there that the night staff are on a list in my purse entitled 'People who Saved my Life'. As if that's a perfectly normal list to have.

Fortunately, I'm getting better at distinguishing the good ideas from the bad ideas. So I don't cross the road and walk into the foyer and start gushing emotional nonsense that only I can understand. I stay where I am, safely separated from any social awkwardness by eight lanes of traffic.

Dr Barbara tops the list, of course, and she's the only person who knows of the list's existence. I showed it to her a couple of weeks ago, explaining that I'd felt the sudden need to write it on the Tube one morning, and the *Metro* was the only paper I had available. Which is why it's incongruously scribbled on the back of an article about a crime-solving parrot.

I felt pretty certain, when I handed Dr Barbara that sheet of crumpled paper, that she would straight away tell me how silly – how ridiculously melodramatic – I was being. But she didn't. She just looked at it for a few seconds, her expression neutral, and then passed it back with a shrug.

'I think it was worth saving,' she told me.

I nodded and smiled. 'Yes, I think it was.'

I assumed we were talking about my life, not the article about the parrot, but who knows. Either way, the list has stayed in my purse ever since, and I haven't shown it to anyone else. I can't really imagine a sensible context in which that would happen.

We've arranged to meet at the bandstand, but when I get there, I'm still ten minutes early, so there's time enough to feel apprehensive. Not that there's anything in particular I need to worry about, I tell myself. We've exchanged a couple of emails now, and she wouldn't have agreed to see me if she didn't want to.

Still, when the clock creeps past midday, I start to worry afresh and when it gets to ten past, I have myself half convinced that she has changed her mind and isn't going to show. I do a couple of circuits of the bandstand just in case – because it's almost feasible that I could miss her if she happened to turn up on the exact opposite side. It's not as crowded here as in other parts of the park, but it's busy enough. Lots of couples and families, dog-walkers, kids on scooters.

And then I see her. She's about twenty metres away, just coming into the clearing from one of the paths that heads across to the Serpentine, but impossible to miss. She's wearing the dress, which is every bit as astonishing as I remember. I raise my hand, and, after a few seconds, she sees me and smiles broadly. Then she stops and does a little twirl, and for the briefest moment, I experience a sharp pang of something that feels like loss. But it's there and gone in an instant, and after that, there's only a warm rush of relief.

'You look beautiful,' I say.

She shrugs, still smiling. 'I think I'm a bit overdressed for a Sunday lunchtime. I got some right looks on the Tube.'

'It's perfect,' I tell her. 'You know, I'd pretty much assumed it would end up in a charity bin. Dr Hadley didn't seem too keen to pass it on. She thought it might upset you.'

'She gave it to me the week before I got out. By then, I was quite a lot better, obviously. Not totally better, but . . .' She shrugs again, and for a few moments we're silent, neither of us sure how to proceed. Then we hug. I don't think that either of us instigates it; it just happens, and after a few seconds, I'm glad of my sunglasses because I can feel my eyes beginning to prickle.

'I've missed you,' I say.

Melody doesn't reply. Instead she takes her cigarettes from her bag and passes me one. 'You haven't quit, have you?'

I laugh. 'No, I'm giving myself three more years. I read somewhere that as long as you stop by the time you're thirty the long-term effects are tiny. So that's my goal.'

Melody nods. 'Yeah, that sounds sensible.' She takes a deep drag and blows the smoke out through her nose. 'They had me on patches for weeks. It was a bloody nightmare.' She holds up her left palm so that I can see her scar, which is more or less a mirror of my own. 'Haven't hurt myself for ages, though. Not even a tiny cut.'

'That's good,' I tell her. 'That's really good.'

'How about you? How are you doing?'

'Oh, you know. Still finding my feet, but generally better.'

'You said you're back with the boyfriend – the one who dumped you?'

'He didn't dump me, not exactly. But yes, we're back together. Three months and counting.'

'How's that going?'

I think about telling her the same thing I told Dr Barbara: that it feels much more stable this time round. But that would require further explanation. Because for most people, stable isn't a word that conjures up a wealth of positive connotations. It's an in-between sort of word, the word they use in hospitals when progress is uncertain – could be better, could be worse – and the value I'd be placing on the word would be something quite different. So in the end, I opt for a much simpler response.

'We're happy,' I tell her.

Melody smiles again, and for a few moments we just smoke in silence. Then she starts tapping a foot. 'So, what now? You want to go get a drink or something?'

The bar at the corner of the Serpentine is packed – of course it is, on a day like this – so after a while, we decide to go for a walk instead. It feels nicer, anyway, to be out and moving in all that wide green space. We walk the full length of the lake, and then, without discussing it, round the shore and start walking back. Walking with Melody – having somewhere to walk *to* – is a novel experience, but other than that, everything feels comfortingly familiar.

We talk almost non-stop, mainly about St Charles. At some point, I tell her that I still dream about it every other night: the long blank corridors, the smoking area, the security fences. In turn, she tells me that there are mornings when she wakes up and thinks she's still there, expecting one of the nurses to come bustling in at any minute.

'But that's only when I'm half asleep,' she explains. 'Most of the time, St Charles feels like a different world – like Jocelyn's mirror world. It starts to feel like that the second you're out.'

I smile at this; because here, in the bright spring sunshine, Jocelyn's Mirror World sounds like an attraction you'd find at a seaside funfair, and just as innocuous.

'I think I saw one of Jocelyn's portals this morning,' I tell Melody, gesturing vaguely in the direction I guess Park Lane to be.

'Cool.' She sounds impressed. 'What did it look like?'

'Well, actually I didn't see it, as such. It was more that I could

282

feel it, hovering there in front of me. I find that happens some-times. There are these little moments when I can see into the gap that separates this world from Mirror World. Do you under-stand what I mean?'

Melody considers this for a while, before saying, 'Yeah, I think I do. Like, there are lots of times when I sort of imagine doing things that would probably lead back there. So, for instance, if I was to take off my dress right now and get into the lake, that's all it would take: I'd be back in St Charles by teatime. Is that what you mean?'

I smile again. 'Yes, that's pretty much it.'

'Is it nuts to even have thoughts like that?'

'No. I think it's only nuts if you act on them.'

'Hmm.' Melody shrugs. 'So you think normal people have those thoughts, too? Or is it just us – you know, people who've been over to the other side?'

I can't answer this, obviously, not without doing some sort of survey. My hunch is that it's a matter of degree – that everyone gets these weird, intrusive thoughts sometimes, but few have to keep a permanent vigil against them.

'Please don't jump into the lake,' I tell her, and a moment later I feel her slip her hand into mine; this, I think, is her way of telling me she won't.

And we walk on like that, hand in hand, and Melody continues to turn heads every now and then. But aside from the fact that one of us is wearing a cobalt-blue cocktail dress, I don't imagine we look very different to anyone else walking along the lakeside on this sunny afternoon. Just two more girls in the park, pretty unremarkable. Which, I decide, is not such a bad thing to be.

AUTHOR'S NOTE

'You have a choice about what you put into the public domain.' That's what Dr Barbara tells Abby quite early on in this novel, and usually I'd agree with her, or at least share her implicit concerns. I'm basically quite a private person. I'm not on Facebook or Twitter, and, as a rule, I find writing as someone else more fun, more comfortable, and often much easier than writing as myself. But I'm also aware that there are certain subjects in fiction that are almost guaranteed to provoke curiosity regarding the relationship between an author's work and an author's life. Mental illness, I suspect, is one such subject. Put more simply, I can't imagine publishing this book without being asked at some point – more likely many points – to talk about my own experience of mental illness.

So I've decided to talk about it here, as briefly as I can without leaving out any of the relevant details.

Back in January 2009, I went nuts. Not Abby nuts – I wasn't on a psychiatric ward and I didn't want to kill myself – but her story certainly has its roots in my own. If you were to reduce

285

our experiences to a list of symptoms (depression, insomnia, hypomania), then the two of us have a lot in common. And, like Abby, I can mark the precise moment when it started; or, to be more accurate, I can tell you the short-term trigger.

It was New Year's Eve 2008. I stayed up for the best part of three days. I took half a dozen ecstasy pills, and God knows how much speed. Unsurprisingly, this was followed by a pretty awful comedown, and by 5 January I was feeling extremely depressed. It wasn't the first time; I'd been depressed off and on since my late teens, and I think the weeks leading up to New Year hadn't been great either. But what was different this time was that it led, very swiftly, to a long period of hypomania. I went to sleep sad and anxious, and I woke up feeling good almost beyond description. At the same time, my thoughts were moving so fast I could barely keep up with them. It was as if my brain had gone into overdrive and was processing ten times more information, but with no conscious effort on my part.

For the next week, I didn't sleep for more than three or four hours a night, because suddenly that was all the sleep I needed. I kept waking up at two or three in the morning with a head bursting with ideas and so much energy I didn't know what to do with it. Then, at some point, I decided I was going to walk around the coast of Great Britain. Here's a letter I wrote about it on 13 January:

Dear Sir or Madam,

This may be a strange request, but here goes.

For some time now my girlfriend and I have been planning to walk around the coast. Unfortunately, we are quite broke – a situation that I'd imagine is not uncommon in those who entertain dreams of walking around the coast. Consequently, we're looking for corporate sponsorship.

The coast of Great Britain is approximately 5,000 miles long. Based on the assumption that we can walk 25 miles per day every day, I should think the entire walk will take 200 days, or just under 7 months. Where there is no direct coastal path or beach, we will keep as close to the coast as physically possible.

As to how much this will cost, that's harder to estimate. Obviously, we'll be camping a lot of the time, but wherever possible we will stay in B&Bs or hostels. Added to this, there is of course the cost of basic equipment and food supplies for 7 months. I might be underestimating, but I think we can probably do it for around £12–15K – and of course, costs could be significantly lower if we find that people are willing to help out with free meals, beds etc. en route. Any money we secure over and above our basic costs will go to charity.

If we are successful in securing the necessary funds, we hope to set off on Saturday March 21st (the vernal equinox) in order to maximise the amount of daylight available to us. Upon completing the walk, I plan to write a book (provisionally entitled *Walking Round the Coast*).

Just so there are no misapprehensions, I want to make it clear that we are not seasoned walkers (I doubt I've ever walked for more than two hours in one go). And neither of us has ever done or attempted anything like this before. But we are **very** determined. I assure you that should we secure enough funding we will complete the walk.

I don't know if you might see this as good PR or free

advertising or anything like that. Possibly you think this whole idea is completely insane. However, any help you might be able to provide would be sincerely, sincerely appreciated.

Yours faithfully,

    Gavin Extence.

I don't think this letter requires much in the way of explanation, but there are perhaps a few points worth noting.

1) The third sentence is an outright lie: my girlfriend and I hadn't been planning to walk around the coast for some time. I'd sprung the idea on her a few days earlier, but I didn't want my corporate sponsors to know this.

2) I couldn't see any reason why people wouldn't want to pay me £15,000 to stay in B&Bs for seven months, and even if I couldn't raise the money before I set out, I didn't think this would be a problem. I had this overwhelming sense that I could walk into any hotel, B&B or private residence in the country, explain what I was doing, and be certain of a free bed for the night.

3) I was feeling extremely persuasive at the time. I'd already half persuaded my girlfriend to come with me, although, in hindsight, I'm sure a large part of this was her trying to buy some time to rein me in. (Originally, I told her that I was going to set off in three weeks, rather than two months, and even that was beginning to seem an unnecessary delay.) But beyond this, I think that there must also have been something quite infectious about my mood at the time. I was so effusive, so self-confident all of a sudden. I had myself completely convinced that walking around the coast was the sole purpose of my life at this point.

'If I don't walk round the coast,' I told my girlfriend, 'I know it's something I'll always regret.'

This was the first of many odd conversations I had with friends and family, although they didn't seem that odd at the time. I remember, in particular, a talk I had with my mum just after I'd told her what I was planning. She asked me what I was going to do for food; I replied that I was going to eat mainly bananas – because they were cheap, portable, and I'd read an article somewhere that said they were packed full of slow-release energy. I wasn't joking, and I think if my mum had realized this at the time – I mean, really understood the extent to which I thought ten bananas a day was a sensible diet – she'd have dragged me to the doctor without a moment's hesitation.

Instead, most of my family thought I was just being a bit eccentric, and suspected, I'm sure, that this out-of-the-blue coast plan would die a very quick death.

In actual fact, it died quite a slow death. There was a part of me that knew right from the beginning that my brain was not operating in the way it usually did. I knew I was manic – how could I not? But, like Abby, my big fear at this point was that if I told anyone how I felt, they'd want to make it stop, and I had no intention of letting this happen.

So I spent a lot of time suppressing the weirder ideas I was getting, and then, very slowly – it took weeks and weeks – my thoughts started to slow down. My mood dipped, dropped, and then plummeted. I became depressed for a couple of months, then got better, then better than better, then much worse again. This went on for the best part of eighteen months, until, in January 2011, I started keeping a mood diary – as I still felt I needed to collect some 'objective' proof that something was seriously wrong with me. I rated my mood three times a day – morning, afternoon and evening – giving myself marks out of ten. After a month, my average score was something like 3.1. At this point I went to my GP and was put on Prozac which I've been taking pretty much ever since.

Abby has a diagnosis of type two bipolar disorder. I don't have this diagnosis; but I suspect that's because I've never told a doctor what I've now set down in these pages. I've only ever talked about the depression, because this is what felt awful and debilitating.

Of course, the whole thing is complicated by the drugs, too. But I can tell you that I've since had a couple of hypomanic episodes – not as serious as the first, but identical symptoms – that had nothing to do with drugs. I haven't taken anything illegal for a very long time now. I came to the conclusion that I need to be very careful when it comes to anything that's likely to affect my mood. I take my low dose of Prozac every day and this seems to be enough to keep me happy; and if my mood starts to slide too far either way, I know the things I need to do to help myself (exercise, healthy diet, plenty of rest, meditation, extra time spent with my children and cat). My wife looks after me as well; she has become very good at spotting the early warning signs.

In short, I think that I've been very lucky. Whatever my problems, I know they are relatively mild in the wider context of mental illness. There are many thousands of people, like Abby, who have been through highs and lows far more dangerous and damaging than my own.

In the past year, I've only been mildly manic a couple of times, and one of these followed on from rereading the section of this book that deals with Abby's mania (chapters 9–14). It took me several hours and lots of sleep to feel calm again. But it also made me hopeful that I might have written something close to what I intended to write: something truthful.

ACKNOWLEDGEMENTS
(AND FURTHER READING)

Professor Caborn's theory is based on the work of Professor Robin Dunbar, and I am particularly indebted to his book *How Many Friends Does One Person Need? Dunbar's Number and Other Evolutionary Quirks*. It's a wonderful piece of popular science writing, and a great place to start for anyone who wants to know more about evolutionary psychology.

The term 'monkeysphere' is not my own, much as I wish it was. It was coined by the American humorist David Wong in an article on Cracked.com – consistently one of the funniest places on the internet. I stumbled upon this article ('What is the Monkeysphere?') in the very early stages of planning this novel and it made me laugh out loud – at a time when I really, really needed to. For this, and the train of thought it set in motion, I am again deeply indebted.

Huge thanks are also owed to:

Carole and Jamie Morrow of Bamburgh View, Lindisfarne,

who gave up an hour to answer my many questions about life on the island, and also provided the anecdote behind the Mrs Moses story.

Anna, Emily, Emma, Jason, Morag, Naomi, Valeria – and everyone else at Hodder who has lent their talent and hard work to this book.

My sister Kara, who was one of the first people to read it, and whose words afterwards were invaluable.

Kate and Stan – for taking the pressure off and giving me all the time, space and support I needed to write the difficult second novel. Your faith and patience made a tough job much easier.

And finally, to Alix, Amelia, Toby and Tigerlily. For keeping me sane.